THE GUARD HOUSE MURDERS

The Guard House Murders: Profiles in Murder: Book 2
by Don Denevi
Published by Creative Texts Publishers
PO Box 50
Barto, PA 19504
www.creativetexts.com

ISBN: 978-1-64738-002-1

THE GUARD HOUSE MURDERS

CREATIVE TEXTS PUBLISHERS
Barto, Pennsylvania

TABLE OF CONTENTS

"No one, absolutely no one, is who he or she seems to be. All humans, without exception, wear the mask of the actor to hide the true face. If evil exists beneath the face, hidden in the deep unknowable clefts and crevasses of the unconscious mind, it must be engaged and pondered for the world at large. We need more understanding of evil's existence, and potential for murder, in human nature, because the only real danger that exists is man himself."

"If in his abysmal darkness he has acquired a nauseating taste for blood, murder further kindles murder. The natural man, with all his wholeness, is in great danger, and we are pitifully unaware of it. We know nothing of the evil murdering man. Far too little. His poisoned mind must be studied, because we, too, on the borderline of madness, are the origins of all coming evil."

C. G. Jung 1977: 436
"What Is the Source of Evil?"
in "Jung On Evil", selected writings,
Introduced by Murray Stein,
Princeton. University Press, 1995

CHAPTER ONE

-

"So long, friend, Pavuvu..."

Something terrible happened to Peter Toscanini's heart and mind during that October of 1944.

Having fought off near-fatal physical and psychological blows within weeks of each other, the young Navy lieutenant emerged knowing more clearly who he was and the cold steel from which he was made.

Nonetheless, a faint trickle of inexplicable doubt and ambivalence seeped into his self-confidence, stunting his spirit and serenity.

Intensifying Peter's shaken sensibility was having to officially witness the execution by firing squad of the Mad Ghoul earlier that morning. Hovering over him for the remainder of the day was the fading image of the condemned multiple-murdering USMC officer tied to a death post nodding specifically at him with a wide grin as an even dozen M-1 Garand bullets scattered half his brain around the large courtyard of the 1st Division Command Headquarters on Pavuvu.

Now, leaning back comfortably on the vinyl-plastic bucket seat of the forward fuselage of the four-seat compartment behind the panel of the cockpit in a fully-loaded Douglas DC-3 militarized as a C-47 troop carrier, Peter, along with 28 silent and sullen wounded but ambulatory Marine riflemen, awaited liftoff.

Only minutes before, Peter and the entourage of wounded had touched-down from Pavuvu and Banika after an hour's flight aboard two B-25 Mitchells of the 41st Bombardment group on Guadalcanal's fighter strip #2 west of the Lunga River. From there, they were immediately bused to the main Henderson Field Fighter strip which had been improved and expanded into a larger bomber and C-54 runway with hard stands and taxiways. Greeting them with smiles and trays of small pastries and donuts were several Army nurses. All were dressed in flight suits, which looked fabulous to all concerned, including those dazed and drowsy from pain medications.

With their confidence, enthusiasm, even courage suddenly bolstered by hot coffee and sweets, the retinue boarded the aircraft and sat at will upon two long wooden benches that stretched parallel to the entire length of the plane's body. As they opposite-faced each other, the ample in-between aisle space allowed Navy corpsmen to carry onto the C-47 a dozen or so reclining wounded servicemen on stretchers adjacent to one another on the floor of the interior cabin.

Since the Coral Sea night weather over Guadalcanal during the fall was always vapid and often turbulent, the 28-hour 3,359 -mile flight, with two long refueling stopovers, was temporarily delayed.

"Boys," said the pilot, exiting the cockpit and strolling down the aisle, "the air out there is becoming increasingly wild, perhaps even violent, so says the tower's balloonery. We're getting out of here now before the usual crosswinds hit an hour or so after sunset. We've been given clearance by radio from the Henderson Field controller to taxi over to the main runway. Tighten up the best way you can for a thumpy ride as we leave the ground. But once we're flying above the clouds at night with a full moon rising is one of nature's most beautiful gifts. In little more than a day, we'll be touching down on Oahu's Hickam Field for you to disperse toward Hawaii's best, most modern rehabilitation facilities."

Just then, Technical Sergeant Janson MacTaggart, a USAF weather observer, exited the cockpit and casually walked down the aisle eye-checking the passengers' baggage, issuing orders and instructions, making suggestions, and ensuring all were preparing for less than a 30-hour flight. He laughed,

"We're moving, boys. We're on our way. Lay back and enjoy the shut-eye."

Wearily, Peter leaned his head back, settling his body more deeply in the bucket seat, although cheaply manufactured, nonetheless singly contoured with a movable back, a small headrest attached to it.

Suddenly, and without so much as a single word, or glance at Peter, a young Marine, his right shoulder heavily bandaged, and arm in a large protective sling, leaned over the empty bucket seat next to the lieutenant and shoved a small course-clothed travel sack underneath. Traveling in his hospital-issued pajamas, the young soldier removed a thick navy-blue blanket off his free shoulder, sat down in his bucket seat, removed his hospital slippers, curled up with the blanket spread over him, including part of his head, and promptly went to sleep.

Within seconds, Peter heard soft snoring, occasionally low moans as the young man seemed to clutch his left shoulder. Without a cap, he appeared to be less than 20 years old. Brown, curly hair drooped down slightly over his forehead, and almost to his ears.

'That's me,' Peter thought, 'ten years ago. Always ignoring the nuisance of a haircut.' He had no idea, having been so heavily absorbed in thought, and oblivious to the arrival of additional ambulatory wounded, while gazing out the aircraft's window.

Meanwhile, outside, night had fallen, darkening the southeastern skies. With the strange-looking clouds and overcast gone, a bright, perfectly round moon, along with trillions of emerging stars combined in sufficient mass to broaden the shadows cast over the Russell Islands and Guadalcanal.

Peter, blinking at the brightly illuminated world around him, felt he could see the entrance to eternity.

With everyone clutching their arm rests, the C-47 began roaring down the runway, the propellers spinning furiously, the accelerating twin engines deafening.

For Peter, who turned back toward the window and gazed into the night illuminations and shadows, the takeoff was impressive, "She's lifting up her wheels as all birds pull theirs up to tuck them under their bellies. Whoever said it was absolutely right--'On a C-47, leaving the earth suddenly creates in you the feeling you've become a songbird of the sky'".

Peter had been shuttled on C-47s before, but none as prescient as this one, he reflected. 'With my mind impacted by concussion after concussion, and now risking my life by going undercover amid murderers, this trip back to stateside is somehow…perhaps prescient, omniscient, foreknowledgeable, of what I don't know. But, whatever, I may as well relax and enjoy it, because soon enough I'll be back in a den of death, perhaps my own included."

For a very, very long moment, Lieutenant Toscanini allayed himself of thought and emotion. He was empty, blank, devoid of caring, or even feeling dreaded anxiety. "The devil himself whispering," as his grandfather often reminded him. All the earth suddenly seemed motionless, although the plane's twin engines droned rhythmically on.

Quietly, Peter turned to cast a final glance into the full blackness of night, the earth no longer visible, all creation seemingly into exiled eternity. In this world of nothingness, other than the C-47 and its voyagers, Peter whispered, "So long, friend, Pavuvu, island of my fate."

CHAPTER TWO

-

The Nightmare

With the C-47's twin Pratt & Whitney 1,200 horsepower engines continuing to twirl and purr smoothly, Peter, prior to dozing off, smiled as he recalled the ancient Mediterranean proverb, "Night is for story-telling, love-making, and demon-filled dreams."

'Oh, for a welcoming dream,' he thought, 'full, rich, and satisfying. It would fill my emptiness and void that everyday life is denying me just now. I'm filled with so many contending feelings that the most insidious one of them is going to battle through all my perplexities and clutch my throat.'

There was, of course, nothing to see in the night other than countless trillions of brightly illuminated stars.

Soon, somewhere beyond dozing and this side of heavy slumber's cessation of conscious life, a dream slowly emerged, finding vivid focus.

Traveling down a narrow, crushed coral lane in the middle of a wild, sparsely populated island during alternating fierce rain showers and silver moonlight, Peter seemed to be standing on the hood of a speeding jeep painted in typical Army camouflaged colors. Standing legs wide apart and arms over his head, he was shouting for the driver who appeared to be Dr. Stuart Schneidermann, the USN physician-psychiatrist assigned to the 1st Division of the USMC. Condemned to death as the Mad Ghoul, Schneidermann, holding fast the steering wheel, was laughing loudly, as were his three passengers, Ellen, sitting beside him, Pinoe, and Joan, in the back seats.

Down the long lane, lined shoulder to shoulder with USMC lieutenants, and across the road, lined with Army nurses, and bordered on both sides by the remnants of once-flourishing coconut tree groves similar to those that peppered Pavuvu, the jeep careened, its driver and three passengers lurching, tilting, and tipping along the way. Blocking the road less than 100 yards away by lining side-by-side were 1st Division Commander Major General William H. Rupertus; his assistant, Brigadier General Lemuel Shepherd; Chief of Staff Colonel Armor LeRoy Sims, and Captain Oscar "Slim" Del Barbra of Company A, 1st Motor Transportation, Military Police. All were standing at attention, shoulder to shoulder, their arms stiff and formal at their sides, their hands flat on their thighs.

In front of the highly ranked officers was Bob Hope, dressed as a circus clown, clutching a red and white striped baton. Unusual for a dream, Tchaikovsky's "Sleeping Beauty" seemed to be playing in the background.

Peter, screaming "faster", "get out of the way", "the driver's mad", "faster", "past goes the jeep", "faster", "out of the way", "the driver's mad", "out of the way", "the driver's mad" saw the comedian perched atop Bill Lundigan's shoulders, somehow whirling and twirling, simultaneously pumping the long staff. Then, defying gravity, amid bursting, colorful pyrotechnics, he leaped off PFC Lundigan and, continuing to dance in large circles, repeatedly screamed, "Did Crosby send you? Did Crosby send you?"

Then, almost as abruptly as it began, the whole luscious, imaginative scenario, within a split second of a deadly pileup, awakened Peter with a startled alarm.

"What was that all about?" he asked himself.

Fully awake, Lieutenant Toscanini turned again to gaze out the small aircraft window. Slowly, he began to feel the return of the engulfing sensation of integrating within himself the terrible physical trauma he absorbed in the officers' latrine behind the stage and baseball field on Pavuvu, and the emotional shock of rejection by his finance at the Rohwer Relocation Center near the Mississippi River in eastern Arkansas.

'I'll have to compact it all into a whole for lifelong reflection and meditation,' Peter nodded to himself.

With the C-47's engines smoothly droning their monotonous, distinct tones, and the pilot and copilot awaiting the radio signal for liftoff, Peter's attention returned to that day's events. With the hint of a smile, he reflected upon his successful work as a subordinate, but integral, member of the court-martial panel assigned to the legal aspects of the trial and execution of the Mad Ghoul. Known as the GCM, or General Court-Martial, it was the main judicatory in the Pacific Ocean Theater of Operation.

As the junior member of the judicial panel, Peter was required to register and record all statements, testimonies, minutes, depositions, entries, etc. For the final paragraph in the death penalty, he wrote the murders had no mitigating circumstances. They were so craven, cowardly, and premeditated that they could only have been committed by a hardened, irredeemable criminal of the worst possible kind. The Ghoul deserved an immediate execution.

Despite the Mad Ghoul's and Joan Ikeda's body blows, Peter worked tirelessly from sunup to sundown as the youngest member of the GCM, often reaching his cot well past midnight. He wanted the court-martial panel, and everyone else for that matter, to notice that if called upon, he was a tower of strength, an undeniable workhorse. No matter how tough the grind, or the increasing tempo of the work as the execution hour neared, he was determined to carry out each assigned task with maximum finesse, despite the myriads of detail demanded. Everyone, the judges and their legal assistants and orderlies, appreciated the young lieutenant's nonpareil professionalism, personal dignity, and sense of purpose. As for himself, Peter hoped no one noticed the inordinate amount of pleasure he received from successfully accomplishing each assigned charge, thus relieving a bit of his personal pain.

Of all his assignments, the most fulfilling was serving as the official recorder of the entire court-martial proceedings including the testimonies of the witnesses. He wrote the meticulous, precise elements of each murder, the 14-page guilty verdict, and the court's responses to its various reviews and panel member appeals.

In addition to selecting the site for the internment of the condemned man's remains, Peter dealt at length with officials in the Graves Division of the U.S. Army in particular, and U.S. Armed Forces in general. He needed permission from each to allow the body of the Ghoul to be buried adjacent outside the fence of the main USMC cemetery on Guadalcanal between Henderson Field and Kukum near the Lunga River. He designed the headstone, which was less than 4 square inches, wrote its inscription, and supervised packaging of the Ka-Bar murder weapon for shipment to the USMC Headquarters in Quantico, Virginia.

Admittedly, Peter's most difficult challenge was interviewing Dr. Schneidermann each day during his noontime meal as to his reasoning for multiple-murdering. Close to 30 such encounters were held in the presence of two unarmed officers, one from the USMC, the other from the Army, standing less than 10 feet away in the Ghoul's cell. Peter repeatedly asked the same dozen questions, hoping to elicit a series of honest responses which could then be synthesized into a rudimentary explanation.

CHAPTER THREE

-

Execution Time

After a few hours into the flight, a light rain began to gently splatter the troop carrier. Flying below the clouds, the normal October nocturnal overcast that extended from Papua, New Guinea in the south to the Gilbert and Marshall Islands in the north opened and a glimpse of moonlight filtered through. Then, seconds later, the full moon in all its splendor again burst forth, illumining the young lieutenant's smart profile.

Peter turned for a quick glance backwards to a somewhat morose, chair-seated and stretcher-borne wounded. All had received severe wounds during the latter phase of the Battle of Guadalcanal.

Attended by four caring medical personnel, the patients seemed uninterested in idle chatter, or, for that matter, the usual, unappreciative grumbling. Of the four staff members, one was a Navy physician; two, corpsmen; and the fourth, a full-fledged, and rare, Army nurse.

For a full moment, Peter reflected, 'You can tell by their acquiesce and facial expressions how completely committed they are to our boys, all of whom are no more than 23 or 24. God, it's wonderful to see such dedication to do whatever it takes to relieve the pain of each man…Thank you, evacuation, staff, thank you!'

Glancing down at the young PFC, who by now had tossed off his blanket, Peter had to smile; the kid couldn't have been more than 18, tall, on the lean and rangy side, and certainly, by just looking at him, full of fun, joking, and normal, psychologically healthy. There was nothing hard, stiff or serious about him, his face or body. He had a pleasant face, certainly not handsome, but alert, with fine, light piercing eyes. His arms, appearing skinny, were, he concluded, lithe and powerful. 'And I bet his voice is little more than a cool drawl. I like this kid without ever talking to him.'

Sitting quietly, virtually oblivious to a young marine rifleman who was sound asleep in Navy pajamas in the seat, Peter felt sickeningly cold. His consciousness was seared again by the final moments of Schneidermann's execution, the expressive nod now sculpted on his memory until his own death.

Suddenly, the quiescent kid stirred. Then, all at once, he yawned, opened his eyes, stretched, smiled at Peter, and asked in a barely audible whisper,

"Have we just arrived at Hickam? Strange, I don't feel like I have to pee…"

For the first time in more than a week, Peter, who had felt so empty, sad, and gloomy, chuckled,

"Hardly. We haven't even left these depressing, lethargic 50 Russell Islands, where you expect one funeral dirge after another."

The PFC said nothing as he stood up in the aisle of the C-47 and folded the blanket.

"I know you, Lieutenant. In fact, the whole world, if truth be known, knows you. I saw you leave with Mr. Hope for the officers' latrine when the Ghoul tried to kill him. Watched, in fact, as all of you in that first row up and headed off."

"How so?"

"I was in the third row and near the aisle. I sort of knew something was up."

"Very observant."

"Saw it the moment I found my assigned seat. I even said 'hello' as I shoved my sack under the seat, but you were staring out the window and you didn't even look at me. You feeling alright?"

There was a moment's pause as Peter turned back to the window.

"Sorry, seatmate. For awhile now I've been feeling singularly unresponsive to everything, emotion, thought, the Guadalcanal's panoramas, the vast ocean below us."

"No problem with me. I know you, as everyone else does, as Lieutenant Peter Toscanini, USN, Medical Corps, the savior of the greatest comic in the world. My name is Lawrence Angelo, a Texas boy from, and you can see by my stripes how high up I am. Private First Class. So, watch yourself, Hero of the USMC 1st Division, or I'll order you to the brig."

"Yes, sir, PFC Angelo. By the way, how old are you? You may be lean and lanky; so are twelve-year-olds. My guess is that at the most you're 15."

"No, sir, almost 18," PFC Angelo blushed. "For such an unwarranted remark, I'm ordering you to the brig."

"Oh, if you only knew how soon enough, I'll be there. Actually, I was within feet of one this morning. I'll explain when time permits."

"No. Explain now. We probably have 25 hours to go, without stopovers. So, tell me. I'm dying to know."

"Well, it might help me get this crud off my chest. O.K. Here's the story."

"While there was great rejoicing among our 16,000 Marines about the execution of the Mad Ghoul, or Charlie the Choker, at 1000 hours yesterday morning, I was reeling from a depressive ambivalence."

"Imposing the ultimate penalty by court-martial upon an American soldier convicted of nine counts of premeditated murder didn't bother me. I was simultaneously conflicted because I was not only directed to stand as the official US Navy witness, and, incidentally the first execution I had ever observed, but also primarily by the condemned officer's smiling nod. He glanced directly at me a few seconds prior to the discharged volley from the firing squad."

"Hours later that afternoon, while boarding the C-47 Skytrain, R4D troop carrier, idling prior to departure from the main Guadalcanal airfield tarmac, I was still numb, the blood in my somber face drawn, leaving my skin ashen. Somewhat dazed as I wearily walked up the ramp to the aircraft's double-wide doors to present the attendant with my official Corps travel orders, I was aware my forehead was still damp from perspiring most of the day. Handing over the large envelope without comment, my knuckles and teeth clenched, my mind was withering. I yearned to take my seat, hopefully next to a window, and nap."

"Earlier that morning, with the normal late-October wind-driven showers waning, me, the great Lieutenant Peter Albinoni Toscanini, subdued, somewhat apprehensively, arrived in the enclosed, unpaved, muddy courtyard quadrangle behind the General Headquarters of the 1st Division on Banika, the second largest of the Russell Group. Lining up shoulder-to-shoulder with 65 other Marine and Naval officers several feet behind strategically stationed armed Military Police along the path to the post to which the condemned man was to be tied for the execution."

"As silence fell over the large assemblage of designated officials assigned to observe the military court-imposed death-by-shooting penalty remained at ease, not a word was spoken. Lost in thought, everyone awaited motionless, some subdued, others aloof, or trembling with expectation for the execution party to emerge at any moment from the reinforced basement of the headquarters makeshift brig with the Mad Ghoul, open-shirted, hands tied tightly behind his back."

"I was weary from the tumult of the past few weeks, the trial by court-martial, the meticulous, thorough presentations of evidence, the daily burdensome interviews with Stuart Schneidermann, the physician-psychiatrist, assigned to the 1st Division, who was the Ghoul himself. I was especially sickened by the reading of the death sentence itself. I admit, I was nauseated, languid, by the cold, systematic, methodical, efficient killing of a man, that was to take place, cruel, even if it was of a murderous, and inhuman person."

"Yet, as I too, awaited the opening of the basement door and the procession to begin, I reflected with pain and indignation that nine unsuspecting, trusting sentries and nurses had lost their lives, not in combat for their country, but for a yet undefined, inexplicable psychological evilness that is as inbred in mankind as long as history itself, but only recently recognized."

"Death of the Mad Ghoul, or Charlie the Choker, by firing squad was not the result of a military ad hoc committee verdict decreeing the death sentence. The proceedings of a Special Court-Martial against Schneidermann had been brief, but thorough, and uncompromising. Basing the warrant for execution on 'The Manual for Court-Martial, U.S. Army, 1928's Article 92', and the clause '…with malice aforethought (either premeditated or unpremeditated), willfully, deliberately, feloniously, unlawfully kill…', nine charges, one specification per Marine death, were levelled, resulting in a swift, competent verdict. The military court did not allow Schneidermann the privilege of choice in carrying out the sentence, death by the gallows or by a dozen sharpshooters."

Now, as the vibrant orange-red rays of early morning flooded through the C-47's cabin windows over the Coral Sea, Peter sat silently and stiffly in sharp-cut profile in his bucket seat.

Gazing out the small sunlit cabin window of the fully camouflaged "Gooney Bird", Peter recalled the pilot, co-pilot, radio operator, and navigator inspecting the aircraft's two Pratt & Whitney Twin WASP 14-cylinder air-cooled 1,200 hp engines revving their various speeds for takeoff. He also recalled the Henderson Field complex, its varying types of fighter and bomber aircraft atop the rain-puddled tarmac, landing strips, some 3,000 feet long; others 5,000 feet long, and the taxiways.

Impressing him the most were the numerous Gruman F4F-4 Wildcat fighters lined up wing-to-wing, as were dozens of SBD Douglass Dauntless Dive Bombers and P-40 fighters.

With the four-man crew on board and safely tucked inro the cockpit preparing the final stages for departure, and the ground crew of mechanics listening nervously for troubling sounds from the engines, parachutes were distributed to the passengers, including those on stretchers, who promptly placed them under their seats or blankets. With that, and the final engine inspection completed, the pilots, who had double and triple checked the cockpit panels, taxied the C-47 onto the main runway for liftoff.

Unless PFC Lawrence Angelo or anyone else for that matter, asked him directly about the Ghoul's execution, Peter vowed at that moment to never again mention the story of the multiple-murderer of fellow Marines. He was sick to his stomach at the mere mention of his involvement with Pinoe, Ellen, and Dr. Schneidermann. The general court-martial and its multitudinous particulars were bad enough. The specific details and minutiae of systematically putting a human being

to death, regardless of that person's malignant evilness was repugnant-
-certainly necessary, but for him, beyond repulsion.

Peter knew, of course, the Ghoul would be in integral part of his
mind for the rest of his life. But, somehow, unless pressed by higher
authority, he would resist, nay, deny the fragments to legalized military
killing: the construction by four Seabee engineers of a heavy 10ft. x
10ft. wooden backstop; the 8 ft. death post to tie the convicted man; the
unarmed six-man MP detail led by Captain Del Barbra to escort
Schneidermann, hands behind his back fastened to a thick leather belt;
the rejection of two chaplains flown to Banika for the purpose of
spending the final hour with the condemned prior to being led to the
post; the placement of a dozen USMC sharpshooters upon recently-
completed platforms on the 12-foot protective wall surrounding
General Headquarters; observing Captain Del Barbra whisper
something to Schneidermann and having the condemned officer
snicker in disgust; Del Barbra then leading the death party with the
convicted man in the middle at the 'slow-step' up the stairs from the
basement and down the execution path lined by USMC and Army
officers; watching Lieutenant Bobby Ellison following the entourage
serving as official recorder, then followed by three officers, each
carrying a small, black valise, each identical to the other; the 12-
member firing squad already lined up at attention with their M-1's 75
feet from the post; the two chaplains waiting at the post, lips moving in
silent prayer, heads bowed; Captain Del Barbra waving the chaplains
aside as the escort guard bound the condemned man to the post with
heavy leather straps; asking in a loud voice if Schneidermann had a
final statement to make, and the bound man, straps around chest and
shoulders, refusing to respond; the placement of two additional straps
to the knees and ankles; Schneidermann refusing a black hood sewn by

the medical staff to be placed over his head; ordering for the last time the chaplains to "move aside"; then almost immediately, the command by Del Barbra, "Ready...Aim...Fire"; one M-1 loaded with a blank, the other eleven had live rounds, so that the recoil of the blank cartridge would tell the rifleman he was the one who hadn't killed the Ghoul.

Peter flinched in recalling the details of what was standard execution procedures already in use in North Africa, Sicily, Italy, and France for crimes of rape and individual murders. Unfortunately, the young lieutenant didn't close his eyes in time when the Ghoul's body stiffened, blood slashed and pieces of Schneidermann's back sticking to the board panel and post as the Ghoul in a horrible contortion drooped forward limply.

CHAPTER FOUR

-

"Private First Class"

Soon after sunrise the following morning, with the reliable C-47 cruising in gentle motion at 90 mph toward Noumea on New Caledonia of the New Hebrides, Peter struggled to emerge from his brief but uninterrupted sleep.

As he gradually lifted his eyebrows, then yawned and stretched, the young Lieutenant, fully reposed and somewhat refreshed, grinned as he glanced over at PFC Lawrence "Larry" Angelo still curled up in his hospital pajamas under the coarse Navy blanket in sound slumber.

"Damn, the kid has been at it for almost 12 hours now," he reflected.

Early the night before, during the initial stages of the flight stateside over San Cristobal Island, the Indispensable Reef, and, to the east, Espiritu Santo, the occasional rolling and pitching bumpy passage at less than 10,000 feet "…certainly is commensurate with the myriad of emotions regarding Joan and the Ghouls searching relief somewhere in the nooks and crannies of my mind."

Turning and gazing out the troop carrier's window amid the unabated, familiar humming drone of the twin engines, Peter, expecting late autumn's glum equatorial overcast, was pleased to observe a glorious morning idyll. Stretching from the southern Coral Sea to the Hawaiian Islands and beyond, the vastness of the indigo Southwestern Pacific Ocean with calm, effervescent wavelet crests was bathed in morning sunlight. "Coupled with a cloudless, azure sky," he weighed for a moment, "the boundless emptiness of the sea and the cloudless upper atmosphere sky will only meet, it being so clear today, beyond eternity, nay, beyond infinity. No haze, no clouds, nothing. Just light blue air, dark blue water."

As Peter continued consuming the illimitable sky and vastness of the South Pacific sea, his brain relaxed, allowing his refreshed mind to clear a bit. Slowly evaporating were the weeks of weighing, wearying sadness due to his subconscious preoccupation of holding Joan in his arms again, smelling her flesh, feeling her pounding blood, and gently touching the living warmth of her golden skin.

Ellen, Pinoe, and Schneidermann were roasting in the hells of their unrepenting graves, but Joan Ikeda?

Suddenly, a thin, squeaky voice from under a blanket in the seat next to Peter whispered hoarsely,

"Are we about to land in Frisco?"

"Yup. There's the Golden Gate Bridge now," the lieutenant chuckled, showing himself back, allowing PFC Angelo to look through the window.

"Aw, you jest me," Larry accused, mockingly.

After a pause, Peter smiled, "Yes, private-first class, I suppose I am that."

On a south-by-west course, the C-47 was not allowed to fly higher than 12,000 to 13,000 feet. Meanwhile, Larry, wide-awake and full of energy after a long, prolonged sleep, chatted gaily as though he were back home riding down Main Street in his jalopy, PFC Angelo giggled and laughed and babbled gibberish nonstop for minutes on end.

Finally, Peter turned back to gaze at the vista, struggling, meanwhile, to retain his composure. Not that he was irritated or annoyed. It was because "the young kid" reminded him of himself back on South Center Street in Stockton, California. Wholesome, healthy, and well-rested, PFC Angelo was full of himself just then. And Angelo's rejoicing while the rest of the cabin's wounded remained silent and appeared hungry and miserable, triggered remembered events and moments with Joan.

"I see no wounds or bandages, private first-class. Only an arm in a sling. They sending you stateside because you broke the fingernail on your pinky?"

"Hardly," Larry laughed, glancing at his right hand. "I'm being sent to some rest-and-relaxation camp on one of the outer Hawaiian Islands because the new psychiatrist who took over the Ghoul's place when he was caught diagnosed my condition as 'battle exhaustion'. Heck, the whole 1st and 5th Divisions are tired, not just me. I feel a little guilty about it, but it means real milk, real eggs, roasted refrigerated meats, genuine coffee, fresh-baked pies every night..." he responded slowly and sadly. "But actually, I would rather be with my buddies headed somewhere in the Palu Islands."

"What happened specifically? What were you given by the medics?"

"Well, the first time I had been in action four straight days and I was supposed to have exhibited 'anxiety' symptoms from blasts near me, hour after hour, mortal blasts, not shell blasts. I don't recall or know what they wrote down, but they took my history, gave me some pills, someone said they were three to five grains of Sodium Amytal, and put to bed."

After a short pause, the PFC continued, "I didn't run like a lot of guys mentally confused under shellfire. So, they placed me in a tent for two days sedation and three days rehabilitation."

"Did you feel better?"

"Are you stupid, Lieutenant? Hell, yes, I felt better. But they watched me carefully. I joined in the final stages of operations for Cape Gloucester in early February of this 1944 year, and instead of resting and refitting, a week later we had to engage the last Jap remnants on Eniwetok Atoll with the Tactical Group 1, V Amphibious Corps."

"You functioned normally there?"

"Not really. They said I became so confused in the fighting I didn't know what I was doing…that I became shaky and weak. That I froze in my foxholes. That I became so completely demoralized I couldn't do anything except shake and cry. One officer, during the steady shelling of our unit, shouted I was a mental 'retard'. Even though I was injected with a lot of phenobarb, my nerves were bad. Sure, I lost my equipment and M-1. But what was wrong with that? I didn't break under the constant shelling, jeopardize the platoon. But I was tired. So, they evacuated me as an exhaustion case. And, here I am, happy to rest and relax, and sad to be away from my friends."

Peter remained silent, continuing to gaze out upon the immeasurable ocean. As Larry looked at his hands, the Lieutenant pondered the plight of such war victims. Combat stress? Who doesn't feel its effects sooner or later?

Finally, Peter asked,

"How old are you, kid?"

"19. I, eh, well, to tell the truth, almost 18, in another two months."

"Well, the war in the Pacific is almost over, I would say. Maybe another eight or ten months. My hunch is that you'll sit the rest of it out in Hawaii, say, for six months, then be sent home. Where you from?"

"Southern California, a little community nestled in the hills of North Pasadena. But do you really think the war will be over soon, in less than a year?"

"Sure do. Look. We have only a few months to go before it's 1945. Tinian and Guam were just declared secured. All organized Japanese resistance on both those advanced islands is over. Our Marine Corps alone has jumped to almost 33,000 and our enlisted men and women to 442,816! Amazing, don't you think? We've landed on Saipan in the Marianas. We've gotten, this year alone, 1944 Roi-Namur, Kwajalein, all of New Britain, the Marshalls, Guam, Parry Island, Emirau, St. Matthias Islands, and most important of all, Rabual, the largest, most heavily defended Naval base in all the Pacific. And, to top all these islands, we've started straying and bombing the Palaus, Okinawa, and Iwo Jima. We're on Japan's doorstep. Now, there's a whole lot of fighting left to be done, but all-in-all, the war is practically over. That is it; the Japanese surrender and we don't have to invade Japan itself, the mother homeland, trying to take those four or five huge islands will be a huge task. We'll lose at least a million men in that struggle which will add on another three years. If that's the way it was meant to be, none of us will be alive when it's over. My God, I pray to whomever will listen, the war must end before our first boys land on the beaches up there."

With the slight turbulence easing the thinning clouds slowly fluttering away, the Pacific in all its shades and hues clearly visible and enhanced by the magnificent sun, the C-47 began its descent.

The heavy fabric door of the cockpit swung open and co-pilot Jeremy Coldwell; tall, sandy-haired, and brown eyes, walked down the aisle past the forward officers' cabin to the main paratroop jumping area. With his 6'2'' superbly built, somewhat stocky frame, a dozen feet in front of Peter and Larry, he announced,

"Everyone, your attention, please. We've begun bringing the 47 down for an approached landing outside the ancient, historic port city of Novmea on the southern tip of New Caledonia, once known as the Loyalty Island. If you look out the windows to your right, you'll see the jagged, rocky elevations and green valleys. You can even see the high tree-covered slopes of the high mountains rising majestically above the horizon."

Glancing around the cabin at all the passengers, he noted one heavily-bandaged man sobbing with another Marine, arm around the rifleman's shoulder, comforting him. No one in the cabin, respectfully, paid any heed to the sobbing man.

"All of you were snoring loudly around 0100 this morning when we dropped down for a 45 refueling landing. The stopover was so silent and uneventful that not one of you yawned or lifted an eyelid."

"Our landing now, requiring at least six hours, maybe longer, is due to a failure in the instrument panel. Nothing serious, but for us to continue to Hickam, the damage has to be addressed."

"We've radioed the field. For those who prefer to rest, a transient barrack is near the airfield to sit, read, or sleep. For those more ambulatory, we'll have a bus ready for a tour of the historic city and a late breakfast or early lunch at the main hotel. You'll appreciate our ships of the Pacific Fleet massed in the harbor. Especially interesting is the huge airfield where not only the hundreds of A-20 Havoc's, A-24 Dauntless, and B-17 Flying Fortress are all lined up in neat, evenly spaced rows, but also the so or so newly-arrived superfortresses. Remember, this base at Noumea in New Caledonia, less than 460 miles from Henderson is the home of the 60th Air Depot Group supplying all our bases."

With the monotonous drone of the C-47's twin engines softening, interrupted with sharp supportings, for the landing, the co-pilot abruptly turned away and quickly returned to the cockpit. In that moment, with the fabric door open, Peter overheard the navigator remind the pilot, "We're over the airfield now. As you circle for the landing, remember how tricky this one is. You've landed here before, right? You know there's a sheer drop from the end of the runway to the ocean. You have to set your wheels down pretty sharply. Fortunately, we have good flying and landing conditions. It won't be difficult. Just hope the landing gear doesn't get stuck."

With Peter and Larry crouched forward with bated breath, the C-47 within seconds, seemed to glide in its perfectly smooth landing.

"Well, private first-class, we're in Noumea. Let's take the tour of the town and base rather than nap in the transient barracks."

With maintenance running on the field toward the plane, Peter could hear someone in the control tower ordering the aircraft to a special maintenance hangar to repair the instrument panel.

"PFC," Peter commented cheerfully, "You were too busy looking across me through the window to notice that as in any island the C-47 flew over the island and 'landed' in the harbor."

"What?"

"Yeah. Very interesting. Because the crosswinds of all, or at least, most, islands are such you usually don't land on water. We flew around the New Caledonia Islands and came in and landed by way of the harbor instead. That was good since the cliff was in front of us and ahead, blindly. Anyway, we're here. And, I hear from the cockpit the tower telling the pilots how and where to tread to get to the repair shed or the shelter for aircraft."

Gazing out the window again, with the young Marine having pulled the Navy blanket over his head again to fall back to sleep, Peter smiled. The ocean cold sullenness he remembered on New Caledonia was not present that day. From where he sat, Peter sensed the air outside the aircraft was warm and usually calm. He had been there when a hurricane, usually unpredictable, always violent, hit the Fiji Islands to the east, then New Caledonia, and finally petering out over New Zealand. It had been the worst weather experience of his life.

Now, the world was bathed in the beautiful sunlight of the South Pacific Ocean, and with the absence of bad weather and the journey thus far uneventful, Peter was somewhat at peace. He would enjoy the layover, especially observing the enormous quantities of supplies needed to conclude the island assaults in the Pacific prior to the invasion of Japan, and the intense assemblage of "warbirds", perhaps as many as 3,000. Such a concentration of offensive planes, bombs, bullets, and other munitions and equipment had never occurred before.

Now, the C-47 was waddling through the Noumea airfield's intricate system of taxiways toward the maintenance hangar behind a string of bright, shiny new liberators. Parked wingtip to wingtip along the runway were squadron after squadron, group after group.

"No question," said Peter, more to himself than Larry Angelo, "This island the Japanese desperately wanted has become our largest rallying point in the whole Pacific. When I was last here, it had one crummy crushed coral runway. Now, overnight, it's become gaudy, showy, and an armed force no enemy can contend with. And, of course, all the pilots are no more than kids, like this little fart sleeping next to me."

"Hey, I heard that," shouted the PFC, again curled up under his blanket in a prone position.

Peter laughed softly.

"If you're awake and sitting up, I'll want to tell you a few things about this part of the Pacific. We're taxiing toward the repair hangar and buses to take us on a tour."

All about the runways and taxiways were heavily-armed sentries carrying carbines and .45s, their uniforms a hodge-podge of everything from standard dress and gear to helmets, Marine corps fatigues, long-billed flight caps.

"Look, private first-class, to my right. A formation of 14 P-38 fighters revved up, waiting their turn to lift off. Where they're going, they'll be firing and bombing later tonight and returning in the wee hours of tomorrow morning. And, look, behind them, lined up ready to follow, are at least 50 Thunderbirds. All of em', cocky, demanding, pushed little toy airplanes, wouldn't you say? Further back are B-24's, C4-6's, C-54's, B-25's, and PB4 Y-2's. Wow!"

After a few moments, Peter said, "We're here, boy. Buses waiting for us, ambulances waiting for the men on the stretchers."

As everyone disembarked, sorted by name, directed to the proper waiting bus, and instructed where to return, Peter was the first to climb aboard, sitting in the front opposite the driver, overlooking the step-up entrance, PFC Angelo following behind him and taking the seat next to him.

"Well, here we are again, private first-class, waiting. 'Hurry up and wait'; 'Hurry, hurry up and wait, wait.' No matter how you mouth or tone it, you're waiting.'"

Larry smiled and said nothing.

"Well, since we're waiting, let me tell you what our route will be from here to Hickam. As pointed out by the co-pilot, the distance from Henderson to Hickam is 3,632 miles, normally two fuel stopovers. Last night, apparently, it was an emergency to drop down to Espirito Santo in the New Herbrides. From Henderson, 640 miles from Espirito Santo to Noumea, 455 miles. Then, once we get to Hickam, no more stopovers for refueling to Hamilton Field near San Francisco, 2,402 miles away. Hamilton is the home of the 38th Reconnaissance Squadron and 30th Bombardment Group."

"How do you know all that crap?"

"Just a personal challenge to my brain. It's fun. Want to know how many miles from Hickam to Anchorage, the seaport in southern Alaska, another of our important Naval bases?"

"No."

"4,500 miles."

As Peter and Larry remained silent, gazing out the front window, lost in thought, wondering about the delay, one of the other nine ambulatory passengers in the silent bus could be heard uttering,

"Darn!"

Peter understood and smiled. He turned and smiled at the heavily-bandaged Marine. Then, glancing at Larry, he said,

"Since we're still sitting, private first-class, let me tell you some interesting features about Noumea."

"No need."

"Well, unless you'd like to hear about some of the cute things I did as a little boy, I'll tell you about this great, great city. First, it sits at the southeastern portion of New Caledonia Island about 930 miles from New Zealand. The first European to 'discover' the island was Englishman James Cook in 1774, who named it New Caledonia. Caledonia is the Latin word for Scotland. He apparently didn't inquire as to what the natives who were already living on the island called it. In 1849, an American ship named the Cutter was wrecked on New Caledonia, and the survivors were the victims of cannibals they encountered on the island."

"Wow! Never knew that. Valuable knowledge to use in killing Japs."

"Now, there is the topic I shouldn't tell an innocent, naïve kid like you…"

"Aw, please tell me. I'm not that pure."

"OK. But you are not to act, I repeat, you are not to act on what I tell you. Give me your word, your solemn promise on your mother's heart, your grandmother's heart. Do you vow not to follow up on it?"

"Certainly. Do I look like the type of youngster who doesn't keep his word?"

"You sure do. But I'll risk it. I didn't know anything about this place at the time. All I knew is that getting here meant two more weeks on that damn ship with that damn Mae West and two bad meals a day. But away we sailed from San Diego, and, sure enough, two more weeks later we sailed into the harbor of Noumea. And for the first time since leaving stateside, they let us off the ship. They didn't give us liberty-- which meant that we had to be back on the ship."

"You were on a ship? I thought you were a Marine? Why were you on a ship?"

"How do you think the 16,000 Marines of the 1st Division got to Guadalcanal to kick the Japanese off? By bus? By balloon?"

"Oh. Yeah, I suppose we did leave Camp Elliott by boat, didn't we? When my unit came through this port in '43, I didn't get off the ship."

"Why?"

"I slept the whole time our troop ship was in the harbor."

"Well, in my case," Peter continued facetiously, "I didn't care. I got off that ship as fast as I could get. And when I stepped off it, it was the first time my feet had ever touched foreign soil. The first thing I discovered about this place was something that the more experienced sailors already knew about, and that was the local businesses catered to soldiers. And the world's oldest profession was alive and well in Noumea, with doxies just waiting for sailors who'd been on a ship for two months. Now, they wait for dumb Marines.

It was the first time I'd ever seen a whorehouse, and I had no idea what it was when I first saw it. It was built on stilts--the actual house must have been fifty feet in the air--and there were women hanging out the windows calling down to us. One of the guys with me had to explain what it was. None of us could get liberty, though, so nobody took advantage of the place. Especially, me, a good Catholic altar boy.

There was a difference between shore leave and liberty, and when you were the one getting off a boat, it was a huge difference. Shore leave meant you were off the boat, but you were still technically on duty. For us, that basically meant that we weren't allowed to do anything men might like to do after being on a ship for so long. Liberty, on the other hand, meant you were free to do what you wanted, within reason. Of course, if you broke the law, you were going to get hauled in by the Military Police. But as long as you obeyed local laws and kept your nose clean, you could do things like visit any number of whorehouses in Noumea."

Now having told you all this, which my better judgment told me not to, you made a promise, you took a vow, on your mother's heart, the houses of prostitution were not for you. Do I…"

"Lieutenant, in all seriousness, I'd rather sleep. My sex life is off-limits to all women other than the woman I've chosen to love and father our children with…on my mom's heart, I swear it again."

With a deep affection, Peter looked at him and said nothing, a simple smile began to release across his lips.

Just then in the far distance from the outskirts of Noumea along a wide, high-backed crushed coral road adjacent to a fenced-off defensive earthworks surrounding New Caledonia's heavily-used airfield sped what appeared to be a tan military vehicle. Catching Peter's attention almost immediately, the relaxed Lieutenant sat up rigidly as it closed quickly, heading directly to the C-47 and the assembled buses and ambulances.

With horn blowing loudly, and two motorcyclists with 30-caliber machine guns strapped to their backs, roaring and sputtering closely from behind, the vehicle turned out to be a shiny new Buick Headquarters command car, its camouflaged paint highly polished.

From his front seat near the door opposite the bus driver, Peter watched the Noumea AAF Depot Center control Lieutenant stand calmly on the taxiway tarmac in front of the now-empty C-47 as the rushing command car arrowed straight at him. He may or may not have been breathing heavily. But Peter thought to himself, "That Lieutenant is not flinching. If anything, he's taken a step forward, daring the Headquarters' driver to run him over."

With various maintenance repair mechanics exiting the hangar to observe the unfolding scene, and nearby MPs and assorted officers walking forward, the honking, speeding Buick squealed on its brakes, skidding to a halt at virtually arm's length in front of the fearless Lieutenant.

"The Lieutenant hasn't moved a muscle," Peter breathed more to himself than Angelo.

"Huh?" asked the young Marine.

"Instead of dreaming, you ought to watch what's going on out there. Something big is happening, and I know not what."

Although a USN Captain had leaped out of the Buick's back seat, Peter was certain three higher-ranking Navy commanders were sitting in the vehicle, two in the back seat, and one in the front seat, next to the driver.

As the southern Coral Sea noonday sun poured its fierce light and heat on the interesting assemblage, the C-47's twin-engine low hum occasionally retching a cough, Peter turned to Larry and said irritably,

"Private first-class, are you still asleep? Watch, for heaven's sake!"

With the USN Captain shouting at the depot officer, the unsmiling Lieutenant saluted smartly. Despite the low din of the idling, Peter thought he heard the Captain yell,

"We are in an urgent hurry, officer. Where is he? Now! Bus or aircraft? Fetch him! Now!"

Other than this insolence, which didn't appear to faze the depot Lieutenant in the least, the two seemed to speak in low, unemotional, and considerate voices. the Lieutenant simultaneously jotted notes on his black leather clipboard, 8 ½'' x 11'' in size, the official transport passenger list neatly clipped on it, while perusing and checking names off. Then, in less than a moment, the depot Lieutenant turned and pointed to the waiting bus arranged for the Noumea tour. At that, the bus driver, an aging noncommissioned sergeant, instantly straightened up and in a swift spring, hopped down the bus steps toward the two officers hurriedly approaching the bus.

"Oh, oh, oho, oh, oh, private first-class, looks like you're in big trouble! They are coming for you and appear plenty mad!" Peter teased, tongue-in-cheek.

"Huh? Me? Why? Just because I shook a little when those Jap mortar shells bombarded all around me on that Canal Hill?" Larry asked, sitting perfectly erect, petrified.

"I'm a proud split-second man of action. You gotta tell them, Lieutenant."

Just then, the USN major walked up the steps of the bus, stood in the aisle facing the occupants and said loudly,

"Whoever Lieutenant Peter Toscan-na-nin-ni is, come with me, DOUBLE TIME! I repeat, COME WITH ME, DOUBLE TIME!"

With that, he literally pranced from the bus, leaving Peter in a dazed stupor. As he stood up, he had to admit the roar of the private first-class's laughter was deafening.

CHAPTER FIVE

-

A Hawaiian Luau

"Can you tell me what this is all about? And where we're going now?" Peter asked expectantly as he almost stumbled down the bus steps in his haste to follow the captain toward the waiting Buick.

Without as much as a glance response from the Naval captain, and only a slight nod by the depot lieutenant as he scrambled by, Peter decided to remain silent for the duration of whatever was happening to him.

After having the backseat door opened by the driver, Peter climbed in and sat next to a high-ranking USN officer whose rank he could not determine since neither he nor his fellow back-seated passenger acknowledged each other. The captain then entered without a word, sitting next to Peter.

Yet, it was impossible for Lieutenant Peter Toscanini to remain graveyard silent amid four other U.S. military officers. He smiled and said,

"Nothing serious, I presume. After all, I was involved in an execution yesterday morning around this time."

Neither sound, a whimper, sigh, or utterance, nor physical movement, flinch, recoil, or gesture could be observed.

"Ah, that was a personal joke I thought might elicit a slight grin, but no matter," Peter concluded, staring straight ahead as were the others, including the captain who was now seated next to him. As the two motorcyclists revved their engines to a roar, the obviously skilled driver, a uniformed sergeant, abruptly turned the Buick around and in a loud roar returned the way in which it had come. Peter, with a swift glance back, searched the bus window for a sign of PFC Lawrence

"Larry" Angelo, but none could be seen. "My God," he thought to himself, "I hope I see that high-spirited kid again, just this side of being a simple dumbass, reminding me of my stupid self at that age."

As the command car, haughtily and self-importantly, raced back along the crushed coral road, startled natives and military personnel leaping away from the thoroughfare, Peter thought, "My God, the death ride of a sweet guy like me with four gruesome funeral directors."

Then, within minutes, turning off a narrow recently-asphalted lane separating what appeared to be acres of Flying Fortresses, it sped smoothly along the empty land bordered by barbed wire high fence barriers. Peter was uncertain whether the B-17s were in service or, now obsolete, mothballed.

Soon, in an obscure area of an open field, several large hangars appeared, with considerable activity and movement around them. Nearby on what appeared to be an unusually long runway, perhaps with a length of 5,000 feet, parked on a dead-end taxiway near the end hangar were what appeared to be two beautiful shiny new B-25 Mitchell bombers of the AAF 41st Bombardment Group. A swarm of aviation specialist mechanics, engineers, technicians, and varying ground crew, staff and flight officers were obviously priming the heavily-armed aircraft for a mission. Beyond, two dozen P-47 Thunderbolts of the 318th Fighter Group were being loaded with rockets. Behind and in front of the hangars were jeep trailers fitted with racks of floodlights. Even with the command car's window closed, the loud, grinding roar of planes flying overhead permeated the interior. Peter, meanwhile, was enjoying the behind-the-scenes of a neat, modern, well-managed, well-laid out American airbase.

"This driver is certainly good," Peter reflected as the sergeant was now forced to slow down as he darted in and out of increasing vehicular and military pedestrian traffic. At a circular intersection of several marrow lands, a M.P., recognizing the command car, stopped all movement by blowing his shrill whistle repeatedly, waved his arm unmistakably for the Buick down one road in particular toward a series of newly-constructed hangars.

Within moments, the command car made its way arrow-like past a small control post. A short distance away was the first of numerous anti-aircraft gun emplacements, obviously strategically placed to protect the new hangars. Surprising Peter were the large number of soldiers in helmets manning the guns, their muzzles off as if preparing for action despite thousands of miles away from the nearest Japanese threat. The troops appeared somber and focused.

Within the field where the hangars were situated, surrounding the 5,000-foot airstrip and its tentacles of taxiways and parkways, were marks of tank treads with countless heavy arm wheels meshed together.

Pulling up before the last hangar, its massive metal doors pulled down to the ground, the Navy captain immediately opened the command car door and jumped out. Peter sat absolutely still in his seat, observing the scene.

"Are you assigned to handle him? If not, I need to urgently speak to the ranking officer here. I was ordered to secure and transport him to hangar 14WP06."

A young Naval lieutenant with a southern accent walked up with an envelope. Saluting smartly, he responded, "Indeed, I am. In addition, I have a receipt for you having accepted him. The captain abruptly turned and walked back to the command car, opened the rear door and without comment, motioned for Peter to exit. Then, unbuttoning his smart U.S. Navy jacket, he reached into the inner jacket pocket and from an oilskin wallet-pocketbook, pulled out a folded white envelope with Confidential Secret boldly printed on it. Below the heavy black lettering was "Lieutenant Peter Toscanini, USN, Medical Division."

"Identify yourself," the captain ordered. After Peter promptly did do with a wide grin, the naval officer climbed into the command car and, rolling down the Buick window, nodded, "It's been pleasant, whoever you are," as the Buick and sputtering motorcycles sped away.

Dazed by the whole proceedings, i.e., the mystery of his "abduction", the exhaust of the departing command car and motorcycles, the contents in the sealed official envelope he was clutching, the buzz and seemingly chaotic activity occurring all around him, including two on-duty, readied tanks and several armored vehicles in front of and behind the hangar in front of him, Peter simply blinked.

"What the heck? Am I on some stupid movie set?" he wondered.

Glancing blankly, almost wearily, at the smiling appearing Naval officer assistant to a top-level commanding admiral of sorts, Peter again blinked. He said more to himself than the adjutant,

"I'm puzzled as to who, what, where, why, how…"

Meanwhile, crowding the two officers as the noonday New Caledonia sun cast broiling tropical beams of radiant energy on them were hundreds of additional USMC and US Army heavily-armed troops scrambling off nearly-arrived vehicles. All helmeted, the combat-ready riflemen thronged the entire area before the hangar field kitchen operating at full force nearby. The air smelled frightfully of coughing engine exhausts and kitchen cooking and frying smells and odors.

Peter looked at the adjutant beseechingly.

"Come with me, Lieutenant. Everything will be clarified soon enough. My orders are to safeguard you for the duration."

At that, the adjutant led Peter to the hangar's side door guarded by two armed sentries who immediately waved them through.

As the two entered, Peter noticed that at the corner of the building were at least a dozen additional armed troops, eating meals on proper plates, lounging, smoking, talking and chatting softly.

"But, as relaxed as they are, they all have heavy guns within arm's reach," Peter reflected, smiling at them.

In return, they, in strange sidelong glances, simply shrugged in amusement and went back to their lounging.

As the young Naval Lieutenant led the way into Hangar No. 4, completed the year before for use by the Allied Technical Intelligence Unit (ATAIU), under the control of the 5th Air Force and its 81st Air Depot Group, it turned out the hangar was not a hangar after all. Although there was a considerable open area in the center of the large complex, a series of high dark-paneled doors leading to offices of varying sizes surrounded the amphitheater-appearing area. Everywhere, there was activity, officers and staff entering and exiting the windowless box-like units.

"We should be in time for the noontime luau. I realize Lieutenant Toscanini, there is much for you to be explained, but the best way for us to begin is for you to read your confidential memorandum which you can do as we stand in line for our Hawaiian Luau lunch. Every day we have a cafeteria-style snack session. Today, in a few moments actually, our high-ranking official important arrivals will be appearing. Both have indicated they would like to say, 'Hello' before heading back to their bases this afternoon. Their planes are just outside the hangar being primed for departure. You probably saw them when you were delivered. Let's step over there where the line will be forming, and you can digest your orders."

"I have just one question, Lieutenant. No. Two questions. Is all this some kind of a lie? And number 2, what am I doing in all this rear-echelon commotion? And, if you don't mind, Lieutenant, question number 3, who are you?"

With a wide grin, the Lieutenant was about to respond when a door from one of the nearby offices opened and a heavyweight sergeant with a cherry-red face hurried out.

"Does he know yet? You two will lunch at the other edge table yonder, with the VIPs I'll bring over. You're ready with the scout car? Their targeted departure is in three hours, precisely 1500, whether he's on board or not. Remember, it's a 30-minute drive to the berth."

"We'll leave here at 1400. The jeep is ready."

Peter broke into an embarrassed smile as the Naval Lieutenant who had yet to identify himself said,

"Let's eat. We'll fill our plates and take our seats and begin eating. If they're late, we'll have our coffee with them. Hell or high water, we leave in two hours."

The two Lieutenants and sergeant walked across the well-lit interior forum to an inner court where long, polished tables were lined. To one side, near the hangar wall, several four-chair tables had been set up. One table, with its four chairs turned inward and leaning against the table designating it "reserved", had two tall lit candles atop.

The apparent supervisor of the native waiters and attendants motioned for the three men were to stand, since they were the first to arrive at the luau tables.

"Two minutes. Two minutes we finish. You eat."

With that, Peter ripped open the "confidential/secret" envelope and unfolded a single page memorandum. It read:

CONFIDENTIAL
U.S. NAVY DEPARTMENT
WASHINGTON, D.C.

In reply referFeb. 4, 1945
to numberOrder #14LGH, 22A
N/C 17/3441Special #K22-31-114

From:
To: Office-In-Charge
Subject: Lieutenant Peter Toscanini,
    USN Medical Division,
    assigned (temp) to the
    1st Division, USMC

Reference: (a) Article 207(c) Criminal
    Justice Manual
    (b) SecNav Memo of
    December 12, 1944

Enclosure: (a) Rescind all previous
memoranda pertaining to
Toscanini travel/special
assignment, USMC 1st Division

Proceed this date from Noumea, New Caledonia, by PBY, Flying Boat, directly Treasure Island, San Francisco; by provided Marin County Jail bus to San Quentin State Prison Reception-Classification Center; immediately preceding by California Department Corrections

to San Diego County Jail, by its bus to Camp Elliott, USMC, stockade.
Contact information restricted to 2 (two). References to follow
unspecified, unannounced.

As the three waited in line for the buffet sideboard tables to fill with
the final Hawaiian luau foods, Peter read and reread the official
memorandum, replaced it in the official envelope, and pocketed it.

While the Naval Lieutenant and sergeant were in hushed
conversation unrelated to Peter and his presence, Toscanini glanced
around the interior of the hangar.

"So," he thought to himself, "it's a floatplane I'm flying in to the
Treasure Island Harbor berth in San Francisco Bay. San Quentin State
Prison? They've got to be kidding. So many unanswered questions."

Studying the unusual interior of the hangar, Peter realized it was a
canard, a ruse, a stratagem. No wonder the facility's camouflaged
painting on every structure within the radius of Hangar No. 4, the
inordinate number of anti-aircraft artillery units disposed around that
one hangar, the two new runways, SW-NE, nearing completion, the
helmeted troops guarding or roaming freely, the nearby runway and
airstrip aprons with ready-to-fly fighter planes, suggested the hangar
housed a command center as critical as any in the Pacific War Theater
of Operations.

As Peter penetrated the hangar's interior architecture and
engineering, i.e. the unusual U.S. Army 104-foot timber truss igloo, a
form of light nailed timber arch construction with ribbon metal sheet
cladding protected with lead-tin coating, some sort of fuss or
disturbance was occurring behind him. Turning around to see what the
commotion was all about, he was stunned to see General Douglas
MacArthur, Supreme Commander-In-Chief of Allied Forces in the

South West Pacific Area (SWPA), walking slowly with Fleet Admiral
Chester W. Nimitz toward him!

CHAPTER SIX

-

Lunch with MacArthur and Nimitz

Peter stared blankly, then unbelievingly at the two elderly, relaxed officers in deep conversation, eyes cast down as they slowly walked toward him. Having exited an obvious map-conference room, they were trailed by more than a dozen of their adjutants and staff at least 15 feet behind. Whether hungry or not, the entourage was bearing down on him, personally, he thought, not that they, too, might want to line up for luau lunch.

As they neared, both men, one, Chester W. Nimitz, who had been designated Commander in Chief, U.S. Pacific Fleet (COMPACFLT) on December 17, 1941, with the rank of Admiral, was of a special emotional interest to Lieutenant Toscanini.

As Peter observed the two, Nimitz appeared unexpectedly quiet and mild-mannered although it was quite noticeable, he radiated a general air of sincerity as he listened intently to the other officer, General of the Army Douglas MacArthur. More compact and muscular than Nimitz, the general's personality and leadership qualities were nonpareil.

"Darn if this isn't a high moment in my life," Peter reflected in a dream-like state. "Two of the most legendary officers in the U.S. Military, and this Second World War isn't over yet. Just look at those coming to get me, two hard-working, resolute, both with thinning white hair over cherry-red faces. Oh my God, thank you for making them both American, and not Japanese, German, or Italian, or for that matter, Russian."

When Nimitz and MacArthur were within a few yards of Peter, who suddenly felt so self-conscious he felt he was standing at the head of the luau line totally naked, the Commander-in-Chief of the Pacific Fleet turned to the Naval Lieutenant standing next to Peter and asked with a pleasing smile,

"Is this him?"

"Yes, sir, Admiral Nimitz."

As he extended his hand, Peter literally swallowed so hastily he caught his breath as if swallowing, uttering a slight but unusual guttural sound. Urgently searching for something to say, the Lieutenant said hoarsely,

"It's a pleasure to meet you, sir," and, reaching over and extending his hand in a handshake, "…and I suppose, you, too, general."

With both Nimitz and MacArthur chuckling softly, Peter, realizing why there was sudden humor, said,

"Oh general, I didn't mean that in that way. Of course, for any military man or woman to shake your hand in a greeting is a lifetime remembrance. For a moment there, I felt so unduly open that you two were both measuring my manliness, my intelligence, my integrity. Silly, so silly, of me."

"I learned of your bravery in saving Mr. Hope's life from Mr. Hope himself, more than a month ago when he, Jerry Colona, and Frances Langford visited me when they passed through Brisbane where my headquarters are."

"Well, Lieutenant, I appreciate your slight fluster. If I was as young as you, Lieutenant, I would be, too. Let's have at the luau. The kitchen sergeant supervising the luau is ready."

With that, the officers in line began to move toward the tables. Admiral Nimitz and General MacArthur, with respect to their high-ranking official positions, were first in line, with Peter and the Naval Lieutenant following directly behind.

Lieutenant Toscanini was pleasantly surprised by the variety of dishes laid out on long counters attached to a specially-designed removeable wall. The food display of the Hawaiian Luau included bundles of meat wrapped in leaves; a variety of taro dishes, especially Poi; taro pounded into a liquid; kulolo, a taro pudding; baked sautéed chicken marinated in soy sauce of garlic and ginger; grilled shrimp; various cucumber salads; Chinese-style barbecued pork; Hawaiian tamales consisting of various baked, fried, and sautéed fish; Macadamia nut baked cookies; fruit punch; and roasted Hawaiian coffee.

As Nimitz and MacArthur moved along the long counter helping themselves using the long spoons and forks on the platters and in the bowls, Peter turned to the Naval Lieutenant and asked,

"Where do we get our utensils?"

"There are none. Luau means dishes, side plates, and appetizers are finger foods. Small finger bowls and towels are placed on the tables ready for use."

At the end of the Hawaiian luau line, a naval captain pointed Nimitz, MacArthur and Toscanini to a small table close to the hangar's fourth wall, allowing for a bit more privacy.

The three settled themselves around the table in comfortable leather-lined chairs with MPs strategically placed around them but yards away.

"Well, young man," Nimitz began as he tasted an item from each of his assorted choices, "I hoped to meet you on your journey to a new kind of assignment. My boys and I have heard how you are a daring visionary in terms of the deep recesses in the mind, that you yourself have a keen intellect coupled with a burning curiosity. You may well be the Medical Services' most promising mind; brave, cultured, wise. Such adjectives flood your personnel file. What do you say to all that?"

Peter smiled at Nimitz and said simply, "Nonsense."

General MacArthur looked up and said quietly,

"We heard as far away as Brisbane, Australia that you were highly competent handling the multiple-murderer's execution. How was all that? I was especially the one most impressed with your work since, like General Eisenhower in the European Campaign who signed off on all executions, I was required to sign off on the so-called Ghoul's execution. I read every page, every single sentence that a Naval Lieutenant named Peter Toscanini prepared for the death panel. When I heard this morning at our conference that you were out here, I insisted, and the admiral here, immediately concurred that we have lunch with you."

Peter, now in a rare red blush, simply whispered, "I'm so, so indebted for your appraisal."

"Your general thoughts, Lieutenant, please." MacArthur requested in deadly silence and seriousness.

Peter, as it was, barely tasting what he had selected for lunch, was now no longer hungry. Suddenly feeling a chill, and more important, empty, he shoved his plate away and looked up at the two officers now studying him.

"All right, gentlemen. I vowed just yesterday to never again recall or reflect executing a fellow American soldier despite the horrendous nature of his crime. The executions that General Eisenhower has signed off, perhaps more than a hundred now, were for crimes of rape, our women and foreign, and deliberate murder. Nothing compared to Dr. Schneidermann's."

Peter paused, then added,

"I am a plain solider who loves and is ready to die for his country. I can neither speak for or cry out against executions. I have no power to stand before the court and demand reprieve or immediate death. When Schneidermann was lined up and tied to the stake, he turned and looked at me. How will I ever forget that look? He may have wanted me to somehow intercede, to stop the nonsense of a well-planned firing squad doing its work, to allow him to live. That look he gave me shouted, 'You're my friend, aren't you? Stop this! Stop this before it's too late!'"

Neither Nimitz nor MacArthur moved a muscle. Both had stopped eating their finger food, as MacArthur, especially, leaned silently forward across the table.

"I was both nauseous and demoralized. Of course, he deserved execution for the nine deaths, if not more, and the mechanical and cold-blooded method he repeated over and over. Yet, I want to believe his mental illness provoking him into murder frenzies of that nature is beyond worded explanations. I will maintain until my own dying day that no little boy or girl at the age of two, three, or four, or five has ever, ever said, 'Oh, I can hardly way to grow up and be strong enough to kill, and kill again, then kill some more."

Again, a pause as Peter looked down upon the food on his plate in his tray. Then, he began again,

"I just stood there. I didn't move a muscle or nerve. I was stone-cold dead, struggling to remain composed. I could no longer look at him. I know his last thought was one of intense disappointment and pain. How do I talk about the grief, the emotional…"

Peter stopped. There was moisture in his eyes. "Of course, he had to die. I, too, wanted that. But, then, no matter how I cut it, I return to,

'Yet...', 'but...'. I had worked with him every day for an hour or so. I felt I knew him, his horrible personal story as a youth, his later brilliance as a medical doctor exploring the great depths of the mind."

"What I remember the most, to answer your inquiry, General MacArthur, was the volley of shots that made his head no more."

After a silence during which MacArthur gazed upon Peter while the admiral and lieutenant looked down upon the tabletop, Nimitz glanced at Peter and asked,

"How do you like our new command post? The general flies in from Australia and I fly down from Hickam. We meet regularly here to discuss and plan our next objectives. This morning, however, we focused upon a variety of issues for example, we dealt with issues pending our invasion of Luzon; our second carrier raid on Tokyo, Jimmy Doolittle's in '42 was the first; our first bombing operations on an island we need as a fighter plane base named Iwo Jima; and our first efforts to take Mindanao and Okinawa. We believe the Pacific War will be over in less than a year, if all goes well with a new bomb we're developing out Nevada way. The war in Europe should be over by August. None of what I just shared with you is secret or confidential, but it's best for you to say nothing about any of it."

As MacArthur leaned back and enjoyed a cup of recently brewed Hawaiian-roasted coffee, Admiral Nimitz told Peter of his youngest daughter, Mary, a Dominican nun teaching freshman and sophomore English courses at the Dominican College in San Rafael, a stone's throw from the northern end of the Golden Gate Bridge in the San Francisco Bay Area. Nimitz concluded the 45-minute lunch by saying,

"What we fear the most around here is a Jap light carrier sneaking up and pinpointing on New Caledonia. By hugging the Northern Australian coast until the sub reached the southern Coral Sea, and launching from the sea a number of Zeros, Mitsubishi AGMs, B5Ns, and D3As straight to Hangar 4, roaring in at a few hundred feet or less, they could drop their bomb loads straight through our roof. Such bombs could kill us all, to say nothing of disrupting all our Pacific War's communications, from stateside to the Philippine Islands."

"And," added MacArthur, "the Supreme Commander of the Southwest Pacific Area, "don't forget a few enterprising Japanese submarines could surface, as one did off California in early 1942, and fire their deck cannons at this Command Center, if a Japanese Captain ordered his submarine to surface at night, he could hit us within a minute or two and dive, fleeing out the Noumea harbor, into the open sea. At Goleta, near Santa Barbara, the single sub surfaced and shelled oil storage facilities, not hitting any, if I recall."

Nimitz leaned forward and commented,

"The scenarios we mention, Lieutenant, are unlikely. We have an amazing number of operating warning posts and search planes in the air at all times, except nighttime. We constantly remind all our military staffs, there is no such thing as 'safe home waters'.

Nimitz concluded,

"All in all, life on New Caledonia is quite boring. The ocean is beautiful, the waters this far south sparkling and crystal clear, and the weather balmy, all incidental to the fact the Japanese front is more than a thousand miles away."

MacArthur reached over the table, extended his hand, and smiled,

"Lieutenant, it's been a pleasure. You're on your way back home for something special. I know you'll succeed. I'll be following it closely because I may be needing your services in my army. Be safe! And, as I leave you now, I echo what was in a 16mm movie the admiral and our staff watched in here last night. The movie was completed about eight months ago and starred Ronald Reagan. Our country's dearly-loved Irvin Berlin wrote the music. My favorite part was watching, and hearing singer Kate Smith sing an inspiring, spirited rendition of Berlin's anthem to our nation, 'God Bless America'. Every military man in our armed forces, all 12 million of them will watch it sometime this year. I won't sing it to you, Lieutenant. But I will say a few words of that anthem song of devotion to you now:

> God Bless America,
> Land that I Love,
> Stand Beside Her, and Guide Her,
> Though the Night, with the Light from Above,
> From the Mountains
> To the Prairies
> To the Oceans
> White with Foam
> God Bless America
> My home sweet home
> God Bless America."

Peter lowered his head in a moment of silence.

Then Nimitz said quietly, "I echo what the general just said, Lieutenant. We deeply, deeply believe those sacred words, and we say them to you, and all our boys, from heartfelt reverence."

Peter sat frozen; hand clasped on the table next to his uneaten luau finger-food selections. As he looked upon both men gazing upon him, he felt the moment was truly the peak experience of his lifetime, that is until his marriage someday, the births of each of his children.

It was so easy to understand why each leader was adored, nay, idolized.

First, General Douglas MacArthur, probably undoubtedly, the most important military man in the history of the Philippians. He would forever be associated with the heroic effort to defend Bataan. Then, upon his escape to Australia, he organized and coordinated the buildup of our forces until he successfully returned to Manila in October of 1944. That he loved the Filipino people and their culture is beyond question, Peter thought. That he had the reputation of being a natural, indeed, eternal, optimist impressed President Roosevelt so much that he gave the General of the U.S. Army carte blanche on just about anything he wanted or intended to do. The one personal characteristic of the General everyone talked about was how after meeting him for the first time, you felt the two of you had been lifelong friends. Everyone had respect for him, steadily increasing as time and experiences were shared. Not one of his staff revealed a flaw in him. Arguments with him always ended in humor and greater admiration. He never wrote up a subordinate staff member or forced his decision upon him. The man was essentially gentle and kind, resolute, inexorable, persevering, and, above all, brave and courageous.

Shifting his intention to Chester William Nimitz, Peter recalled what everyone knew: Selected by the President and Secretary of the Navy, Frank Knox, as Commander in Chief of the Pacific Fleet, Nimitz was disinclined to accept. He hoped for a seagoing command. To show his good faith to the Pearl Harbor staff who served the previous Commander in Chief of the Pacific Fleet, Admiral Hubbard E. Kimmel, Nimitz showed up at Pearl Harbor and his first Cincpac staff meeting with a lone flag secretary. He encouraged everyone to remain in his official position. That single act of benevolence, good faith, and trust for a demoralized group of Navy administrators endeared him to every official throughout the American armed forces. And, within months, Nimitz's humility made him the most accessible, considerate, and loved of all fleet commanders. His favorite characterization of a person was whether he or she was a person "of cheerful yesterdays and confident tomorrows", a designation a classmate attributed to him in his Naval Academy class yearbook.

Like General MacArthur, Admiral Nimitz had an immense capacity for administrative work. He supposedly possessed an impeccable judgment of men and making prompt military decisions. Sitting across from him at this moment, the equally gentle, kind, good-hearted man had a staff of 636 officers, almost 5,000 ships, and over 16,000 planes under his command.

Simply put, Chester Nimitz was calm in demeanor and courteous in speech. He had thinning white hair framing beautiful blue eyes and a red complexion, especially on his cheeks. Like MacArthur, he restored confidence in the defeated Pacific Fleet. For Peter and others, the characteristic they admired the most was that Nimitz had the courage to take necessary risks in order to defeat Japan.

After a slight nudge from the Naval Lieutenant who had positioned himself at an adjacent table for his luau lunch, Peter stood up, as did Nimitz and MacArthur. Again, the three shook each other's hands with genuine warmth. Noticing a hint of moisture in Peter's eyes, Nimitz, as was his wont in such situations, smiled as he stepped closer, then gently placed his arm on Peter and quietly stroked his back. Acknowledging the gesture as one of the kindest, and most innate of all human expressions, Peter, for an instant, quavered. MacArthur, with pipe now in hand, chuckled.

With everyone in the luau's assemblage rivetted to the unfolding scene, as they had been throughout the trio's luau together, not one had ever actually observed the Fleet Admiral's natural physical expressiveness. Rarely in the annals of American military history had such an emotional scene been observed in the open by so many subordinate officers.

Peter, embarrassed, fought back the tear or two sure to come. He smiled graciously, thanked Nimitz, nodded to MacArthur who was still grinning, his unlit pipe now in his mouth, turned away and followed the Naval Lieutenant out of the luau area to the side door exit and out of Hangar #4.

Outside, without a cloud in the light blue sky of the early spring day, the sunlight was blinding. With its motor idling, and an officer sitting in the driver's seat, a jeep was waiting. After the two lieutenants climbed in, the Jeep was on its way to the Noumea harbor where Peter's aircraft transportation was waiting for departure stateside.

It was past midday and a strong breeze was sweeping dust and debris across the base and its runways, taxiways, aprons, barracks, assorted hangars, and maintenance buildings.

The driver drove fast but carefully along the narrow roads, some of asphalt, most of crushed coral or pounded dirt. To Peter, all scenery was little more than a haze. Since he was so contemplative about the luau lunch with the admiral and general, it was difficult to focus on Noumea's ancient ruins in the city's outer areas, their approaches to the docks and wharves, and the hundreds of commercial businesses, churches, public buildings, houses of prostitution, and medical facilities that stretched for miles to the waters of the Pacific.

Past recently-constructed levees, docks, wharves, ferry and other docking slips, the Jeep, now with a much-lowered speed, wove its way through the dense pedestrian traffic; the only noteworthy event in an otherwise uneventful 45-minute trip. Peter's only concern was that in all likelihood he would never again see or meet Private First-Class Lawrence "Larry" Angelo, who, by now, was touching down in his C-47 on Hickam Field in Hawaii.

The Jeep pulled up in a difficult-to-locate restricted area filled with warehouse activity. A small sign in the front window of a long prefabricated, half-cylinder metal-skinned shelter of the Quonset hut read: U.S. Navy Harbor Communications.

"Now, Lieutenant, I've provided you with my base phone number should there be any issue pertaining to your air transportation to San Francisco and its Treasure Island Naval facility where your Catalina will berth," said Peter's escort, the unnamed Naval Lieutenant. "If there is a problem, just tell whomever that you are a personal friend of General MacArthur and Admiral Nimitz. Say that loud and clear, get it? Also, explain your personal bag was retried from under your seat in the C-47 and placed aboard the PB-Y5. Good luck Lieutenant. I especially enjoyed the camaraderie between you and the top brass. Never witnessed anything like it. Neither of those two highest ranks even cast a look at me."

When he finished, Peter climbed out of the jeep, nodded to the driver, and shook the hand of the Naval Lieutenant. Smiling, he said,

"I don't even know your name. But please know this. I am grateful for all your guidance on this day. I hope we meet again, Naval Lieutenant-of-no-name."

With that, Peter exited, turned and hurried to the entrance of the Quonset. At the front door, he waved as the jeep pulled away.

Within moments of entering and identifying himself to the sergeant behind the counter, Peter was informed that this air passage had been approved by none other than Secretary of the Navy, Frank Knox, in Washington. Apparently, Lieutenant Toscanini's mission was of such a critical nature it had to be labelled "Confidential/Secret" with final instructions issued only by proper Naval authorities upon delivery of the "officer involved" to the Commandant of the Treasure Island Naval Station.

"What kind of a plane am I assigned to? And, who and how many others will I be flying with?" Peter queried nonchalantly.

"A new amphibious flying boat, patrol-bomber known officially as a 'Consolidated PBY-5A'. Unofficially, our soldiers and sailors know them as 'Catalina Flying Boats'. They all say the same thing about her: 'She's slow, but reliable'. Yup, you'll even had a bed on it, being all alone in it. Best darn two-motored scout-bomber ever made."

"Yeah, I heard all that, too. 'Tough, but big and clumsy.'"

The one that the Navy assigned for you is the beauty of the lot of 20 that we have at our disposal in the Pacific waters. She's on schedule for your prompt departure at 1500. You have about 45 minutes to look around. Make certain you're returned to this office by 1445 for escort to the aircraft."

"You'll see to my bag?"

"Already on board from the C-47."

"Just a short walk, then I'll be here at 1445."

Within minutes, Peter was strolling along the Noumea waterfront, amazed by the buzz of activity. On the street level, throngs of uniformed men and women were commingling with New Caledonian natives and Australian civilian crews. Positioned in strategically places were heavily-armed pillboxes constructed to repel Japanese Marine landing parties. Rifle and machine-gun bearing sentries roamed at will.

Soon, the Lieutenant found himself standing on a busy wharf gazing upon ships and tenders loading and unloading war materials and equipment. Beyond, he noticed, were the base drydocks, oil and aviation fuel tanks, and a dozen or so cranes of varying heights.

In the harbor of the small bay before him, not a single fishing vessel could be found. Instead, a number of 1,010-foot-long piers, known as "ten-tens", extended from the Navy Yard where the Communications Quonset hut was located. Clustered about them were numerous floatplanes and flying boats being repaired and serviced while berthed. Small boats, crafts, and tugs lingered about. Across the intervening channel to his right, a worn U.S. Navy destroyer was half out of the water, its propeller pointing skyward. Accentuating the vista were the hundreds of repairmen scattered about the quays, moles, and docking facilities amid the ever-present smell of welding smoke. Impressing Peter the most was the absence of debris, not a single oily or greasy paper or cloth. Not a hint of filth or garbage along the shore banks and work yards.

At that moment, the desk sergeant of the Navy's communication hut trotted up waving a clipboard.

"Lieutenant! Lieutenant Toscanini! There are papers for you to sign!"

As he handed the hinged board holding the official documents over for signature, he asked,

"Ready for the big hop to San Francisco? Nonstop, maybe 18 hours. I'm not sure."

"Swell. Let's go. But that spectacle out there sure tingles a military man's blood, you have to admit."

"Me, myself? I never tire of it. The most fun place to work in the whole Pacific. But I have been assigned to escort you down there where that swarm of sailors are all over it."

Glancing where the sergeant was pointing, Peter saw some 15 or 20 men in dungarees and fatigues pouring over the $90,000 land and water airplane's power plant and armament.

"Wow!" exclaimed Peter, "Isn't she a beauty. Always wanted to fly in one. When did she come in? She wasn't there when I walked out this way 45 minutes ago."

"No. It was only a few minutes after you walked by that she motored into that moor to pick you up."

"What a plane, at least from the outside. All aluminum. Look at her shine in the sun!"

"Well, except for the fabric-covered control surfaces and wing panels of the main spar."

"I especially like the 50-calibre machine guns in the middle and the machine guns in turrets."

"Yes, sir. But no Jap planes the direction you're going."

"She have a name? I can see she does, but I can't make it out."

"Yes, sir, she sure does. In fact, she's famous. She was featured on a poster in the states to recruit men into joining the Air Corps to fly 'similar planes'. The poster we don't see out here. I hear its well-received back home because she is silver. But all the boys who didn't make it after they were enticed by it now say when they came to fly the Catalina machines and all they get to do is clean latrines. They feel the poster lied."

"But what's her name?"

"Fly Big-Breasted Virgin! Fly!"

CHAPTER SEVEN

Speeding to Stateside, Still Bound to Joan

With the throng of uniformed flying boat aeronautical engineers, S-J and SD-type radar specialists and clipboard-carrying weapons and systems mechanics scurrying down the docking platform toward the gangplank and wharf, Peter sat on an empty crate and observed the proceedings.

Within moments of the departing skilled servicemen, a second swarm, mostly dungaree-clad maintenance crews arrived carrying hoses, mops, buckets, and brooms, and deliverymen bearing large sacks of mail, cartons of various fruits, and one of green apples, as well as stacks of clean towels, bedding and sheets for the aircraft's galley and bunk compartment, in addition to the medium-sized boxes of small spare parts for the interior bin and receptacle compartments of the waist and nose gunners, pilots, bombardier, navigator, radio and radar men.

"What a commotion to get me stateside," Lieutenant Toscanini marveled to himself.

"Yawning while stretching as he stood up, Peter strolled toward the mooring cables of the Catalina riding high, and resting quietly, in her brief serenity. Having splashed down hours after her nonstop 914-mile flight from the huge Allied support base at the Port of Brisbane in Queensland, Australia, the PB-Y5A amphibious flying boat was tired and a bit dirty, but certainly not worn out.

Smiling in amazement as he gazed up at the 1,200 horsepower Pratt & Whitney twin-row air-cooled radial engines driving three-bladed, constant-speed metal propellers, he mumbled to himself,

"Maybe two years old, serving as one of the two-motored scout bombers capable of carrying on a daily basis 4,000 lbs of bombs, depth charges and torpedoes on her underwings, she hid any war-weariness what-so-ever well. She was streamlined, wing-tipped, chic. With minor repairs completed, fully-inspected, and properly recorded, as well as refueled and reprovisioned, 'Fly, Big-Breasted Virgin, Fly' is ready to fly me to the Pacific west coast."

With a strong breeze from the northeastern South Pacific blowing cooler and cooler in his face, and finding the soft Catalina lines aesthetically pleasing, the burdensome depression Peter carried with him since his journey to the Rohwer Internment began to lift a trifle.

"Lieutenant! Lieutenant Toscanini!" came a shout from the dock platform behind him. His train of thoughtful appreciation interrupted, Peter turned and saw the desk sergeant of the Navy's communication hut clutching his usual clipboard hurrying toward him from the wharf's steps to the gangplank. He was leading a small group of officers in freshly-pressed uniforms all carrying hand luggage and traveling bags, and a line-handling crew with varying sizes of cable wrenches and winches attached to their belts.

"Your flying team. Six of the best Catalina flyers of the Pacific War. those over in the Atlantic are minor league compared to these boys."

"Hope they had a good night's sleep," Peter, suddenly snapped into alertness, responded, grinning broadly.

The pilot and co-pilot, overhearing the remark as they approached, laughed heartily, the pilot, extending his hand to shake Peter's responded,

"Not only did we get to bed early last night, but fell asleep chewing Secretary of the Navy's Knox's admonition to Fleet Admiral Ernest King to have us tucked in by 2000."

"And," interjected the desk sergeant waving his clipboard, "add to that a phone call from Admiral Nimitz a few minutes ago asking if I had the best damn Catalina pilots of World War II assigned to this flight."

Everyone laughed, including the remainder of the crew who joined the assemblage.

"Well, I told him to buzz off, that he was interrupting my work, and if he was nicer than nice, I'd get back to him when I had time as to your states of somnolence."

With everyone at ease, Peter, glancing at the PBY-5A, commented somewhat somberly,

"Every guy in the service I've known has called this aluminum-sheeted stressed-skinned fabric-covered beauty an 'ugly duckling'. Well, that's just not true! Kinda makes me red in the face."

Everyone chuckled.

"Well," smiled the pilot, "we agree. And, especially those boys of ours who are shot down, then riding their dingy Mae Wests, or lifesaving water balloons and one-man air-blown rubber dinghies. A few days and nights on the open ocean, slowly giving up hope of rescue, suddenly seeing a so-called 'ugly duckling', or 'humpy-dumpy' sweeping in to surface on water to pick him up, makes the amphibious flying boat seem like a safe-cushioned golden chariot with her pilots charioteer Gods."

"I bet," echoed Peter. "Can't tell you how much I'm in love with her, too. How high can you go?"

"The ceiling is 15,000 feet, with a range of 2,545 miles."

"What's PBY stand for?"

"'Patrol Bomber', what we do almost every day. The 'Y' stands for Consolidated Airways of Florida, the manufacturer of the ship. By the way, who are you and why are you so important to have a special one-man aircraft deliver you to Treasure Island in San Francisco Bay?"

"Well, Mr. Pilot, and I do hope you had a good night's sleep. Secretary of the Navy told me personally it was because I resemble a new young actor on the Hollywood scene named Gregory Peck. You never heard of him, and, trust me, I'm actually better looking."

As everyone again roared with laughter, Peter added,

"Seriously men, I'm on a special assignment. But I can tell you this, I've been assured, as Knox said, I've got the best crew in the world flying me there."

With that, and smiles all around, the pilot said,

"Time for a moment's formalities. I'm Captain Irving Bobb, the head big show of the sons-of-_____. That's Terry Buttin, my co-pilot. Next to me here is Dwayne Lorenzo, engineer and turret gunner; next to him Sylvester Ryan, assistant and second turret gunner; Joe Rogers, radio operator and waist gunner; Bob Kirby, tail gunner; Lars Jacobsen, belly gunner. Our navigator, Allan Pierce, is jogging down the pier now with the flight charts."

With the introductions completed, the crew, and Peter tagging along, entered the PBY-5A where Peter was provided a brief tour as the others made their way to their posts. With all the work crews completing their work, and slowly easing their departure from the plane, the desk sergeant still clutching his clipboard, shook hands with Peter, and the pilots, and, waving as he exited the aircraft, said, "Good flying, men. See you guys when you return in four days."

As he stepped out, Pilot Captain Irving Bobb announced over the intercom,

"Well, boys, it's a few minutes past our 1500 departure time. Shall we take 'Fly, Big-Breasted Virgin, Fly' up into the pure white Pacific clouds?

Everyone in the PBY-5A stamped his feet and simultaneously shouted,

"HUR-RAH! Let's go! HUR-RAH! All the way, you say? HUR-RAH! All the way!"

Meanwhile, as the airplane slowly taxied from her berth to the open channel for liftoff, Peter comfortably seated behind the navigator a few yards away, observed Lieutenant Allan Pierce, standing and bending over a tiny counter at work. In his heavy flying suit, he was in virtual command of the long flight. Standing next to him and listening intently was co-pilot, Terry Buttin, a 6'2'' tall, nice-looking jovial lieutenant.

Peter watched Buttin nod affirmatively as the navigator pointed to the flight route over the Fiji, Ellice, Phoenix and Palmira and Johnston Islands. At the same time, Buttin provided times, speeds, heights, the possible strengths of wind they would encounter. As the rest of the crew settled into their seats, their amicable, good-natured banter and flippant remarks brought smiles to Lieutenant Toscanini's face.

Captain Bobb made final remarks over the intercom, mainly for Peter's benefit, and all watches synchronized.

None of the crew was hungry, having eaten pre-flight meals of bacon and eggs, but not beans of any variety since they caused intense indigestion issues at high altitudes. They had then taken their Benzedrine pills which would keep them awake and alert. Outside, ground crews and administrative staffs lined the wharf to wave as the PBY-5A began to increase its taxiing in the open channel.

"Gentlemen officers of the USN, with the all-important oil gauges clicking properly, and our ship feeling aerodynamically clean, we'll dash and splash, let's pray we don't stop and plop! We've no time to dabble and paddle. The colorful lights of San Francisco's North Beach call us to saddle. So here we go! Boys, up, up and away!"

With that odd call for liftoff, the lightly laden flying boat, upon negotiating its way to the perimeter, belting its way across the channel at a 10 miles per hour clip to the open ocean. There, in less than 180 seconds of acceleration, the big flying boat, reaching 100 miles an hour, lifted off. Although Peter wasn't interested in praying that much, he did quietly make the sign of the cross on his forehead in hopes the PBY would fly straight and not have an engine explode. Although those on the docks and wharf were miles away, all applauded, saluted, or pumped their thumbs.

Gazing out his window, Peter felt the amphibian climb steadily to 10,000 feet. Soon, he thought, perhaps before sunset, the aircraft would be cruising at more than 120 miles per hour over the Fiji Islands, then near midnight approaching Tonga, Samoa and the Phoenix Islands. After that, the "hop" would begin, one of the longest gaps in all the Pacific, the distance Palmyra, Washington, Fanning, Jarvis in the Christmas Island group to San Francisco, some 2,400 miles. Not an island, palm or coconut tree, coral reef, rock, or strand of sand to spoil one of the longest distances of blue water in the world.

Despite fighting the persistence of slumber, rubbing his eyes, yawning sleepily, Peter peered eagerly through the increasing small white clouds scudding swiftly beneath the Catalina.

"Vastness, nothing but more vastness," he reflected, "for me to be swallowed up in to think. And, boy, do I need to think things over. Look down there, a sea changing from high and heavy ocean swells to calm, smooth flat as in a glass, echoing the turbulence I carry."

Yearning to slip into sleep, he placed his head on a small pillow against the cabin wall and pulled two Navy blankets over himself. Remaining somewhat conscious, he thought,

"This is good. All is well. I can lay quietly and think things over. During the day I have the drone of the Pratt engines for music, by star-studded skies. Meanwhile, my best friend up here is 'time' and its steady change in the clocks and watches. Also, the varying time zones are helping me get closer to California. Ultimately, up here in the heavens, everything is measured by steady time changes leading me quicker into the future. I love it!"

Initially trundling along like a jumbo but surprisingly elegant brightly illuminated songbird, the warbler heeded to the northeast and balanced itself on a stabilized course straight to the San Francisco Bay Area.

As exhausted as Peter was due primarily to lunching with Chester Nimitz and Douglas MacArthur, it wasn't until later afternoon that he dozed off. Warm and snug under his blankets in his window seat of the empty, dark main passenger cabin, he was nonetheless nagged by his usual uneasy premonition of death.

"They've fixed up a nice bunk back there in the empty main cabin, but I'm too exhausted to get up and walk back there," he thought to himself as he finally closed his eyes. "They did a good job welding that 7-foot metal slab to the ribbed cabin wall. Mattress looks solid, but I'll pass. I'm comfortable under these blankets, sleeping my tired head on the little pillow."

With his languishing eyes narrowing to thin slits and his consciousness losing all sense of reality, Peter laughed to himself,

"Come, warm fairyland! I welcome you with open arms, an open mind, and, especially, an open heart. I will never repress nor ignore any thoughts, images, or emotions that may be conjured up, old but vibrant unconscious-friend of mine. I say that to you without hesitation or equivocation. Daytime memory and nighttime dreams are always difficult. That's why they are so important, especially the dreams. Dreams lead us into the undiscovered, unrealized memory parts of ourselves. Dreams talk to us. I must learn to understand what they have discovered about me, and what they tell me about myself."

After less than a split second, Peter concluded,

"At this point in my life, I am both anxious and depressed. This means, of course, my dreams are going to be just as troubled. How they begin, when they begin, how long they last, whether they are in color, or black and white, what they symbolize are among the unanswerable questions of dreaming. Best I sleep now and enjoy the dreams that are sure to come."

Slipping into deep sleep within seconds, Peter's state of mind soon was riddled with a series of incoherent nightmares.

One of the first fragmented dreams dealt with a terrible midnight violence within a typical pyramidal tent found on Pavuvu Island's Tent City. Dozens or more Japanese infantrymen simultaneously emerged from holes behind the bivouacked tents where hundreds slept, seven marines to a tent on separate cots in their shorts within mosquito nets of the large tent. Grim and silent, each held a Ka-Bar over his head and, reaching the long row of 90 to 100 tents began cutting and ripping squares in the canvas. Without a word or sound, each of the enemy soldiers lifted the long official USMC knife over the open holes and in unison were about to plunge their weapons into the faces of the sleeping Marines.

Although not a sound was heard, Peter screamed and screamed, the other Marines of Tent City rushing forth, firing machine guns, bazookas, and other automatic weapons. Apparently, the Japanese were screaming "Banzai". Unarmed and feeling sickened, all Peter could do was watch the enemy dash in and out of tents in continuous streams, blood dripping from the Ka-Bars. Equally horrifying as he stood and watched, every soldier, with one of three faces, that of Pinoe, Ellen, and Schneidermann, was grinning.

Awakening with a start, Peter was in a sweat under the two heavy Navy blankets. Natural sounds returned, albeit of continuous, monotonous twin-engine droning and other occasional noises of the so-called "ungainly, clumsy ornithological giant". For Peter, the strains, twangs, and tones were welcomed after a silent slaughter of fellow Marines.

With the Catalina PBY-5A seemingly gliding effortlessly due east in the early night breezes, Peter, wide awake from his shocking nightmare, allowed his thoughts to focus upon his favorite friends, one being Mike Masaoka. Unconsciously, he knew that sooner or later, regardless of how painful it was, his thoughts would return to Joan Ikeda.

Peter had been introduced to Mike in the living room of Joan's home on the southside of Stockton, California, less than a dozen city blocks away from where the young future Naval Lieutenant was born and raised. That Sunday afternoon in mid-August of 1941, less than 100 days from the craven attack by the Japanese naval fleet on the American base at Pearl Harbor, was experiencing a temperature of 112 degrees, so normal in the central San Joaquin Valley. Coupled with peat dust storm, fine powdery dirt coupled with decaying plant matter from prehistoric swamps at the base of the Pacific coastal range, the visit was almost unbearable. Only Joan's enthusiastic, loving attendance to Peter's misery made the situation tolerable. He remembered saying,

"As you know, we have a hardware store, and Dad says that soon every house in America will own a new invention called an 'air conditioning machine'."

The Ikeda family, Joan's mom and dad, two sisters, and brother, nodded in approval.

Suddenly, there was a knock on the front door, startling everyone. As Mrs. Ikeda opened the door, there was spontaneous joy among the family members as Mike walked in with his finance, Etsu Mineta.

Peter's first impression of the two as he stood and was introduced to them was "What a handsome pair the two make, she so lovely, almost as beautiful as his Joan, and Mike, handsome with his broad, happy smile, so obviously a man of high intelligence and integrity.

After the introductions were made and Mike and Joan's parents were in deep conversation about Japan's possible threat to America, and what it might mean to the Japanese-American communities along the Pacific West Coast, Joan whispered to Peter,

"Mom is a distant relative of Mike's father. Both families were immigrants to San Francisco, except Dad stayed here in the valley and Mike's went onto the Japanese community in Salt Lake City. But for some reason, they returned to Fresno where Mike was born around 1915. He was the fourth child and third son in a family of eight children. He just graduated with honors from the University of Utah, majoring in political science and history. He is so dedicated to helping our people dispel decades-old prejudices and what he termed 'legalized discrimination' that he is not only the acknowledged leader of all the Issei, but also the Nisei. In 1940, he composed the beautiful Japanese-American creed which was even read into the Congressional Record.

Today, 1941, at the age of 26, he is the National Secretary and Field Executive of the JACL, the Japanese American Citizen League."

Peter adored the man. In fact, Mike was more patriotic than himself. He had a vision to see that the Nisei could best demonstrate their loyalty to America by fighting in defense of their country. He urged them to volunteer for service even while they were confined to internment camps. Mike, himself, was the first to volunteer for the 442nd Regimental Combat Team whose valor stirred the nation's conscience.

The last Peter heard of Mike Masaoka was the year before, the summer of 1943, when his efforts to create a new image of the loyalty of persons of Japanese ancestry earned him the Legion of Merit, Mike was in Italy at the time serving as Public Information Officer of the 442nd Regimental Combat team.

Peter would never forget that afternoon. As hot and sticky as it was, and actually feeling the peat dust on his sweaty body, he was fully aware that what was transpiring, including his involvement, was a rare peak experience.

Mike is known throughout the American armed forces as the 'Father of the Nisei suicide missions' and that he helped our Japanese communities across the nation. He himself was a helper in the 442nd and offered his parents as hostages if he betrayed our troops," Peter whispered back to Joan, who was holding his hand.

Back in his realm of reality, he glanced out the small window next to his seat and thought to himself, "From 10,000 feet in the darkness of night there is nothing to see but the color black. No suspense of enemy flak, no sweating out the unfolding flight with fear of zeroes, and other Jap fighters, chasing them. In fact, he could see no sky, no ocean, no islands, no ships far below, no airports, no bases, coastal defenses, no crisscrossing airplanes, no aircraft flying side-by-side. All that Peter saw was sprawling nothingness, silent emptiness.

Just then, Captain Irving Bobb walked past Peter and asked,

"Hungry, Lieutenant? Food and coffee on the way! Don't give up, but some Big Brass in Hawaii ordered the best food and cold and hot drinks for you."

As the crew relaxed, rested, drank coffee as black as the outside night, Peter's only intent now was to remain awake and consider calmly the heroic men he encountered in his lifetime.

Certainly, this crew qualified. They had been picked carefully. For example, Pilot Captain Bobb himself was obviously a steady, tested, brilliant veteran of thousands of miles of Pacific Ocean flying. He had a reputation, according to the desk sergeant hours before, of being resourceful, calm, yet daring.

Navigator Lieutenant Allan Piercey was another aviator to reckon with. Co-pilot Terry Buttin handed Peter a cup of steaming coffee and recently baked Polynesian-style bread rolls. As he drank his coffee and munched his rolls, his thoughts returned to Piercey, who was busy standing at his counter with his slide rules and calculator.

Lieutenant Piercey was also well-experienced, seasoned in directing PBY Catalinas over thousands of miles of open seawater. Allan was particularly adept at 'dead-reckoning' in vast, unmarked distances. All pilots and co-pilots requested his navigation skills when assigned special, dangerous missions.

Acknowledging one of the first principals in Freudian-Jungian psychoanalytic theory, "Our minds always have a purpose. We have less control than we think," Peter smiled as his thoughts drifted back to Mike Masaoka.

"What a fine man," Peter exclaimed to himself. "And, like Yoshi, my big competitor who won out over me, Joan, you had little respect, although you were always respectful, for the 'No-No Boys'".

Peter had never heard of the 'No-No Boys' until Joan had written their definition down and sent it to him in mid-1943. Peter kept the letter. It read,

"Peter, forwarding info on the No-No boys. I always thought Lance's (Yoshi's) father-in-law, Mits was a No-No boy. I felt the experience consumed his life in camp. But Lance just said, he thought he was just a resister (isn't that the same?). Anyway, my parents feel he's a No-No boy. The JACL did not support them, and I know Mits never forgave the organization for abandoning them. I think many No-No Boys were reluctant to admit they were, but I always respected Mits, because he spoke about it openly, and even went into the camp school to talk about the experience."

"The way I understand them, Peter, is that early in 1943 the WRA, the War Relocation Authority of the U.S. Government released a questionnaire for those men who were over 17 and interned. It was entitled 'Statement of U.S. Citizenship of Japanese-American Ancestry.' Within it was contained the following questions:

Question #27 asked: 'Are you willing to serve in the Armed Forces of the United States on combat duty, wherever ordered?'

Question #28 asked: 'Will you swear unqualified allegiance to the United States of America and faithfully defend the United Sates from any attack by foreign or domestic forces, and forswear any form of allegiance or obedience to the Japanese emperor, or other foreign government or organization?'

There were men who answered no to both of those questions on many grounds, but one of the most prominent reasons for replying with a negative to #28 was the men believed that if they foreswore allegiance it implies that they previously had allegiance.

A number of 'No-No's' openly alleged that those in Internment Camps should not be forced into a draft by a country that had incarcerated them. Those men formed the Free Play Committee that stood to oppose the draft of the Nisei men numbered more than 300 internees at 10 camps. They were all prosecuted, most serving 18 months in a federal penitentiary in Kansas. The bulk of the No-No boys faced three-year sentences in a federal prison.

Most internees were not pleased with the No-No's. But some were angry with the JACL for condemning the No-No's for sticking up for their beliefs. They criticized the characters of the No-No's and emphasized that it was they who were making the Japanese-American population look bad. In a period such as this, one would at least expect those who were equally persecutes and demeaned to stand by them in the defense of their beliefs, but they actively turned against them. This spoke volumes about the environment that the Japanese faced during the Internment. Not only were they forced into those horrible conditions and stripped of their property, they were denounced for resisting, there were no places for them to turn to.

Well, Mike Masaoka would have none of it. he was proud to be Japanese-American and that meant fighting for the country that was so good to him and his parents. Peter almost memorized the words he remembered Mike spoke to him, as Joan sat quietly next to him,

"Although some may hurt me and my family by prejudice and discrimination, I shall never become bitter or lose faith because I understand that not all Americans are this way. I shall do all I can to fight such discrimination. But in fighting the intolerance against a gentle, hardworking, good people, not only the Japanese and the

Japanese-Americans, but all decent, law-abiding immigrants, I shall do it in the American way, aboveboard, in the open, through courts of law, by education, by proving myself to be worthy of equal treatment and consideration. I am firm in my belief that American sportsmanship and attitude of fair play will judge citizenship and patriotism on the basis of action and achievement, and not on the basis of physical characteristics."

"I believe in America and America believes in me. Because of that, I pledge to honor her at all times, to support her Constitution, to obey her laws, to respect her flag, to defend her against all enemies, to assume my duties and obligations as a citizen, cheerfully and without any reservation whatsoever in the hope that I may become a better American in a greater America."

It was so easy to see in that moment why the Ikeda family relished Mike so much, and Joan considered him an "uncle". For all this, Peter bound himself to one of the truly great Americans.

Somewhere east of the Fijis and the Catalina cruising at maximum altitude, Peter's thoughts turned to the other Japanese-Americans, the Issei and Nisei, he was personally devoted to. The one he would gladly have pledged his life to was Kazuo Masai, "the greatest best friend a best friend could dream of having". When he shared his feelings for Joan with Kazuo in the tenth grade, the classmate said, "We are growing up at a time as in the past, the ancient past, of our people, that Japanese marry Japanese, no ifs, ands, or buts. Of course, there have been, and will always be exceptions, but that's what they are, and among the Japanese; the call of the Japanese heritage, culture, traditions prevail. 1939, 1940, 1941 are still too young to make the teenagers give up. For most of the exceptions, breakup is inevitable. The day will come, maybe in our lifetime, when Japanese marrying

Japanese is more the exception. Soon enough, all our Japanese grandkids will be marrying non-Japanese."

Kazuo concluded by adding,

"Peter, I want you to marry Joan, although a lot of my Nisei friends have their eyes on her too. But, you, my friend, in my eyes, come first. I will always hope and will it to happen. It couldn't happen to two nicer friends of mine."

Suddenly, from the northeastern Tasman Sea, a gusty squall crossed the Tropic of Capricorn and slammed the journeying plane, its windy, warm rain drumming the aluminum sheathing encapsulating the tiny Catalina. Although the skies from southwest to northeast were still solid black, an occasional stray storm of wind and rain would arrive suddenly, endure less than minutes, and evaporate just as suddenly. Large squalls swooped past everything in its way, blanketing all; land and ocean alike. Just as certain that dawn would appear in hours, it would disappear.

Amid the short-lasting turbulence, Peter fell asleep again. For some inexplicable reason, his drowsiness evoked thoughts of never forgetting friends--time endured, life never-ending, distances separating, kids changing and evolving, work waxing and waning, hopes and age weakening, deaths of favorites, then death for the self-nearing. But despite life's cycle, true, real friends, never change.

And with such fragments and their images floating or darting through his resting mind, Peter began dreaming of Joan. And, of all the snippets, pinches, slices and bits that flared, flashed, then faded, his most favorites focused upon the love of his life intermingling with children. How loudly he applauded her interpersonal relations, affectionate instinct, with the very young, youngest of the young. Watching her reach out, gravitate toward, then touching them lovingly, was the singular quality that not only defined her character and personality, but also endeared her to him through "infinity to eternity" as he liked to tell himself.

"Joan doesn't just stand before the little boy or girl, or bend over slightly to communicate. She crouches on her knees to be face to face, smiling, eye to eye. Being naturally patient, kind, and gentle, she easily bridges the chasm between adult and childhood. Almost nose to nose, the little one understands the reality of genuine love. She touches his or her shoulder and hand, then ever so slowly and tenderly, she runs the back of her hand down the child's cheek, and there was always the magic of...Oh, dear God, how do I express it, the words."

"And, of course, the dream-memory framed, one after another, in a series of images, an uninterrupted flood of expressions, Joan's face. And, although he didn't hear it in the dream, her little laugh, not a giggle, but soft and pleasant to listen to."

"I'd rather talk to a Nisei girl than any other. And, how he enjoyed gazing upon her while she was unaware. The ragged, but clean, homespun clothing sewn by her mother, fitting her lithe, but vigorous body. Her bare, black-haired head barely reaching his ear, always graceful, physically vigorous reflected primarily by her beautiful wondering eyes."

"There is just no getting around it," he repeatedly told himself, "she is so stunningly lovely and attractive. Her natural alertness and intelligence enhanced the radiance she continually exemplified." He would never forget the feeling of completeness she made him feel every time he saw her.

Finally, punctuating all the disorganized images, appeared a reoccurring steady straightforward dream that never changed. Nothing could resist it, even the deepest, most thankful slumber. Why it reappeared frequently, in precisely the same order, length, and intensity as the original dream when it appeared the night prior to his departure for California from the Rohwer Internment Camp.

Strangely, the persevering identicalness of Peter's dream of Joan occurred in the final hour prior to his awakening at dawn. It always appeared to begin after a long, dark pause, black as a starless night, after a series of "introductory fragments". Usually, at the conclusion of the dwindling fragments, prior to his perceived pause, Joan's lovely features in varying smiling facial expressions seemed to float from some inner depth. When she stood before him during the diminishing fragments, she reached out to Peter, the palm of her hand touching his face.

After the dark pause, he refocused upon her as he entered the Latin 1 classroom in the 9th grade at Edison High School in southwest Stockton. She was 15 years old again, sitting in the first seat of the middle row directly in front of Mrs. Hofmeister's desk. As Peter hurried past Joan to his seat next to the row of windows facing South Center Street in the unfolding dream, he noticed Mrs. Hofmeister was holding a 12" ruler, appeared stern, and the feeling of her absolute dominance permeating the stone-cold silence of the other 25 students. Peter had a sense of the sinister, the grave, suspenseful terror.

Class was in full session as Mrs. Hofmeister moved toward the blackboard where she was conjugating Latin verbs. With notebooks open, the class members were taking notes, all their mouths reciting with their rhythms of speech of the verbs in unison without sounds. Peter, observing all, heard nothing.

Taking his seat, third down from the first, he not only had the advantage of observing the traffic on South Center Street, but also a perfect position to observe Joan, who occasionally turned his way with a quick, broad smile glance at him. To Peter, it seemed Joan did so with all her soul in her beautiful black eyes.

How could any red-blooded, physically and psychologically healthy young man, with all the natural instincts, drives, and impulses of heterosexuality, resist such a glance, the quick grin? Especially when her body posture was one of pure feminine. In that moment, Peter knew for the first moment in his life the emotion of love for a girl of his age. But could it be between an Italian-American and Japanese-American? No one of his ancient culture now so thoroughly Americanized had ever had even considered such a possible union. Especially when a world war was pending with two of the three axis nations.

Wasn't it wrong? He was certain her parents, as well as his, would never hear of "love" between them.

Suddenly, in a flash, the classroom door from the hallway was nudged open by Mrs. Ikeda, Joan's smiling mother holding a large, freshly-baked double-layer chocolate cake on a thick glass platter.

Shocked beyond belief, Joan slowly, almost mechanically, stood up by the side of her desk. Peter was so focused he saw Joan's chin trembling. Without thought or reflection, he stood and walked to her side, reaching out with his hand for her shoulder. She turned and hid her face in embarrassment. He patted her back, and stroked her as she watched, trembling, wordlessly, then sobbing uncontrollable, her mother walked under the weight of the cake to the desk of Mrs. Hofmeister and placed it there. At that point, the angry Latin teacher jumped from her position at the blackboard, ruler in her hand, and literally kicked the cake off her desk, hitting Joan and Peter. The classroom students were aghast, Peter placed his body in front of Joan, while Mrs. Ikeda placed her empty hands to her face. Peter heard Joan's mother struggle to say,

"My old country has hurt my new country. I come to make peace. We cannot make war. I speak for all Issei and Nisei, we are so, so sorry."

Peter put his arm up as Mrs. Hofmeister swung the ruler to strike Joan's mother across the face, absorbing the full force of the blow. When Peter full awakened a few minutes later, amid the continuous droning of the twin engines, a few stars were still glittering stonily from between the broken clouds. The rain and wind that swept the "gooney bird" had long faded. Without a hint of turbulence, the sea below was perfectly smooth. He loved life again, despite having nothing other than his work to look forward to.

Yet, a certain buoyancy had returned. Although the dream of good-hearted Mrs. Ikeda and the destruction of her chocolate cake was unfathomable, he was no longer grim. His inner sullenness and downcast silence seemed to have dissipated as the rain clouds and wind. He was no longer on edge, ill at ease, tense, even angry.

Lieutenant Peter Toscanini was free because he knew the dream told him, if anything, that his love for her was realized, indeed actualized, when she hid her face in his shoulder. That love would never be consummated. Betrayal and jealousy were never an integral part of his months-long shock. Peter truly respected and admired Yoshi. Losing Joan was devastating, but not deadly. He would soon be stateside where he might not survive.

Without Joan Ikeda, he would face his murder naked.

CHAPTER EIGHT

-

"Did I Miss Any Drama?"

Although it had been another near-perfect October morning in the South Pacific Ocean, a dazzling sunrise amid cloudless skies, gentle easterly breezes breeding high visibility and temperatures in the mid-70's, the California coast, from Santa Barbara to Eureka's Lost Coast, was blanketed in heavy fog.

In San Francisco, the murky semi-opaque condition of the atmosphere typically burned off by noon. However, U.S. Army meteorologists stationed at Fort Mason in the Presidio forecast the range of vision would approach zero-zero conditions, along and to either side of an incoming front, as the misty drizzle vapor thickened.

With the Catalina cruising steadily toward the central California coast, Peter had awakened to a brilliant sunshiny morning. Below, waves were virtually nonexistent from 16,500 feet, as was overcast and were cumulus, stratus, and cirrus clouds. From his window seat, the vast expanse of the world was in three colors; the blue-black ocean and light cerulean sky.

Such unrestricted wide-openness soothed a bit the psychological pain Peter had so deeply repressed in his heart. As a welcomed, well-meaning relief allowed thought, he was more reflective, pensive, musing, melancholy, and resolved, compounded by his own possible murder as he went undercover, than at any point in his life. Hour after hour passed.

By mid-afternoon of the second day, as Peter and the crew were munching their final austere meal prior to landing, the pilot announced over the Catalina's intercom that within minutes the descent to 7,000 feet would begin for the approach to the Bay of San Francisco.

"Fellas, we're beginning to cede this immense, calm, solitude of water for the angry fury of the Pacific Coast as we prepare for landing. After flying over the Golden Gate Bridge we'll circle Alcatraz Island for our flying boat's floats to touch down on the Oakland side of the Bay to glide to our Treasure Island berth."

As Peter listening intently, he smiled, "He may be enveloped in fog, but experienced pilots flying these huge turtles always have successful landing, ground or water."

After a short pause, the pilot continued,

"However, men, there is a slight glitch I must tell you about. We may crash into the Bay. I've just been radioed by the Presidio controller that zero-zero conditions, heavy layers of fog blanket the water strip our runway we've been designated to splash down on near the eastern Oakland section of the Bay Bridge. The thin thread of water is smooth enough, but lack of lighting in foggy and night conditions and other safety measures, including warnings to stray, unaware fishing boats, almost guarantees, with the lack of visibility, a collision. Circling before descent, hoping the fog will burn off won't help. We have no fuel to fly into the San Joaquin valley, because all of Northern California is fogged-in. The two of us here in the cabin may be accomplished pilots with years of both commercial and military flying experiences, but that won't help now."

"No boys, we're in trouble. So, with the Treasure Island air staff nervous, the Presidio controller nervous, and the two of us controlling 'Big Breasted Virgin' nervous, I suggest you immediately belt yourselves to your benches, and hope the Treasure Island controller knows what he's doing in talking us down until I can see the water. I believe we'll be okay because both of us in here flew in China over the Hump, then with Claire Chennault and his Flying Tigers. We follow to a 'T' all military airline safety procedures. And most important, a new radar system has been installed in the island's little control tower, which when coupled with our fully-functioning two-way radio systems, reduce the possibility of an accident."

"So again, kids, buckle up, lay back, close your eyes, and see you when we exit after anchoring in our berth, or, for those who qualify, in Heaven."

With that, Peter, uncertain whether to smile or frown, leaned back and watched the weather front's violent rain squalls drum the Catalina. Wobbling over the shoals of the Farallon Islands, some 30 miles from the entrance to the San Francisco Bay, the seaplane heeled directly for the flyover of the center portion of the Golden Gate Bridge.

"Nice to see you, Farallons. No wonder the old fishermen named you the Devil's Teeth Islands. There's no place to dock, the place being nothing but jagged razor-sharp rocks."

As he closed his eyes to doze during the final minutes of descent, he thought,

"Well, if I'm to enter Heaven so young, I want to be asleep when it happens. And, if I'm to have a final thought as I walk up those steps, it'll be of a moment years ago--Joan listening with all her precious mind as Mrs. Hofmeister asked Kazuo to translate from Latin into English the first page of Chapter Four of 'Caesar's Gallic Wars'. Joan's turn would be next, translating the second page. He could see her so clearly as he drifted into a state of "forty winks", wearing a spotless, freshly-ironed white blouse with a Peter Pan collar under a light brown, almost tan, cardigan sweater, the collar showing. Her sleeves were pulled up a bit, over a matching plaid pleated skirt. Especially accentuating her beautiful flowing black hair was a blood-red scarf tied under her collar. She may have only been 15 years old at the time, but Peter knew if he was to marry, it would have to be to Joan. And, it wasn't just because of her beauty. Part of it had to do with her natural shyness, her gentle quietness, and her respectful attentiveness. But the most important was her high intelligence. She was the tenth-grade class president, which meant she was on her way to becoming Student Body President. She was President of the Latin Club; President of Honor E, the honorary "straight A club"; President of the GAA, the Girl's Athletic Association; and social editor of the high school newspapers, the "Edison Hi-Lite." She was academically and socially active simultaneously. She studied hard for her straight A's because she wanted to go to college. All her activities, and quality of input, promised she would be a good mother. What more could a good woman be?"

Meanwhile, as Peter napped during the final few minutes of the journey, the PBY-5A became strangely quiet. Even the reliable motors yielding their monotonous droning, steady and gently vibrating, seemed eerily hushed. The sounds were so hypnotic that Peter slept though the drama about to unfold.

In the Catalina cockpit, the two pilots glanced and grinned at each other as they received clearance from the Treasure Island ground control approach tower to touch down despite the weather conditions blinding the Bay's few visual cues.

By radio, the airmen were now in continuous conversation with the controller. Calmly, and as cogently as he could explain, he said via the radio,

"Gentlemen, I will guide you through the persistent fog. Circling to consume your remaining fuel is useless. Our navigation lights through the Bay are useless in zero-zero conditions. Making practical passovers over the water landing site are also of no value. We hear the spluttering of your engines suggesting the last drops of aviation fuel. Beware that if the aircraft begins to skid, you are less than 300 yards from the Oakland side of the San Francisco Bay Bridge pylons. We have no rescue crews."

With that, the controller, in an unperturbed, composed, confident tone, instructed the two pilots to begin nosing down to 150 feet after circling Angel Island and banking hard to the right.

Flying blind, and as low as they dared, the pilots had no option other than trust the guidance of an unknown official. Meanwhile, the scratchy, radio-statically voice in the headphones aligned the PBY-5A on the landing water-strip correctly. In the final seconds of the splashdown, the two glanced out their plexiglass windows, noting that the nearby high intensity lights were brightly distinguishable.

"My God," whispered the copilot, "he's a cool customer to talk our descent down so calmly. We're not to be killed on impact this day!"

"Yeah, we'll make it. We're not to be counted in the high death rate of our friends. But this approach is the worst of the worst of all that I've made."

As the plane's two-winged landing pontoons simultaneously touched down on the water at the reduced speed of 90 miles per hour within the strip's inner markers, a sudden dull-like sound followed with less than a 30 second silent glide in zero visibility toward the Oakland-side of the Bay Bridge. After it pulled up less than 25 yards of one of the large pylons supporting it, a long silence followed, on the outside of the plane, waves gently lapping it, on the inside the crew shaken, no one daring to admit he had been scared out of his wits.

Within a moment, realizing the landing had been successful, the airmen ecstatically erupted into loud cheers and the stomping of their heavy aviation boots. Although still enveloped in fog, the Navy, Marine, and Army personnel on the docks of Treasure Island and guarding the bridge were heard to be yelling and yelping so loud the hoopla excitement could be heard in both San Francisco and the Oakland-Berkley port facilities.

Of course, the commotion awakened Peter from napping with a start.

"Are we down, or in Heaven?"

Hearing the loud spoken question, the nearby navigator said with a wide smile,

"It's always better to be on the ground wishing you were in the air, than to be in the air wishing you were on the ground. No one wants to die drowning in a sinking plane. That was close, fellas, unthinkably, inconceivably close. Now, let's waddle on over to Berth 4 and, if we're lucky, dodging the seagulls, to moor safely."

"Did I miss any drama?"

CHAPTER NINE

-

Manacled

Although "Fly, Big Breasted Virgin, Fly" was securely anchored in her berth for mooring in the Treasure Island docking facility, all was strangely quiet. Even the late afternoon commute traffic on the eastern span of the San Francisco Bay Bridge seemed hushed, other than the soft lapping of the water around the low cabin section of the Catalina Flying Boat.

Poking his way through the covering of the aft compartment and climbing out of the aircraft's open hatch, Peter, glancing around in the heavy fog, exclaimed,

"Terrific hollering and hoopla, wasn't it? Any left out there?"

Although a cold bay breeze fanned his flushed fact, Peter was pleased by its sting. This sudden vitality somehow softened his tense rigidity, the solitude of dense fog, the strange sensation from fearing pending death by violent impact.

With the navigator directly behind him and the remainder of the crew following the navigator, Peter strode over the gangplank to the ramp leading toward the wharf. Scattered drops of heavy mist fell all around him. The air was colder than usual as the odor of the open ocean was stronger. The only people in sight before them were five or six warrant officers standing around two military automobiles awaiting their arrival. Just then, two Navy captains in the backseat of a jeep pulled up.

"Wow," muttered the pilot, "They've come for you, Lieutenant Toscanini. I know the jeep driver. He's on the Admiral's staff here. The two captains are skippers of destroyers from the Fourth Fleet. Their boats are anchored on the north side of the island."

Slowly, six arrivals, ambling at a leisurely pace on the sloping wooden surface of the ramp, began to whisper to one another.

"They call Treasure Island 'The Bus Stop', where VIPs are dropped off and picked up."

"Easier than flying from the military airfields."

"Look at the berths to the left behind you. Only our PBY is moored."

"Others coming and going all the time."

"What a place to have a sea base!"

"A short bus hop to Frisco's south of Market Street and the bars and accompanying joy palaces."

"Yeah and jammed with every enlisted man of the several squadrons training here."

"You mean the enlisted men who serve as pilots without having the rank of commissioned officers."

"Yeah. They are all housed here."

"You mean the Flying Boat pilots."

"Yup. And everyone wanted shore-leave every night of the week. Lucky bastards. They have the best living conditions. Best mess halls."

"No Tent Cities here. Bet they have the best barracks, too."

"Just look at all those sailors in dungarees lined up over there behind the fence in the nonrestricted area."

"Yeah, most of them are 'pollywogs', so green, so gullible, you have to wonder what's to become of our Navy."

At that point, Peter turned and asked,

"What's a 'pollywog'?"

"Oh, you know, Lieutenant," someone responded. "All sailors in the Navy are first "Pollywogs until they cross the equator. Then, after a brutal initiation, the new recruit becomes a 'shellback'!"

"Well, never happened to me," Peter responded.

"Because you're obviously the best of the USN's intellectuals."

Nearing the awaiting officers, the flight crew, smiling approvingly, began waving at the servicemen starting to cheer again.

Just then, one of the destroyer captains who had climbed out of the backseat of the jeep and walked to the front of the assemblage, demanded in a loud, angry voice,

"What's delaying you?"

Stunned, Peter and the flight crew slowed their ambling gait ever further.

"How rude, after a 20-hour flight," the co-pilot whispered to the navigator.

"Our carry-on bags are a bit weighty, sir," responded the pilot.

After a moment's staring study of the men beginning the ascent to him at the top of the wharf, he retorted,

"Get smart with me, airman, and you'll find yourself overnight in the island's brig. Get cracking."

No one spoke as the arrivals reached the officer who, in the meantime, was joined by two of the six or seven who had arrived earlier in the two military automobiles. Among them, two, in US Army dress had slipped "MP" armbands on their arms above their elbows. All who had arrived were carrying holstered .45s.

"It was a long flight, sir. My fault we're about 30 minutes late. I could blame headwinds, foggy conditions off the coast and in the bay, but I should have allowed time for that. I apologize, sir," the pilot offered.

Without a word, the captain turned to Peter who had placed his duffle bag and small valise on the ground next to his feet.

"Lieutenant Toscanini, I presume?"

"Yes, sir."

Motioning to the two warrant officers wearing MP arm bands, who walked toward Peter, he announced in a cold, somber voice,

You're under arrest and will be immediately manacled and incarcerated in the base brig until delivered to the Fort Mason Presidio Stockade and held incommunicado. Colonel Edward F. Penaat, Port Provost Marshal, has issued the arrest warrant based upon an Intelligence Memorandum forewarned by the Federal of Investigation of Washington, D.C. to the Office of the Acting Secretary of the Navy, James Forrestal. The writ authorizing your arrest was co-signed by Charles W. Dullea, Chief of the San Francisco Police Department; Colonel Murray H. Rapp, Chairman of the Waterfront Security Committee; and, numerous other responsible for the safety and security of the San Francisco harbor, shipping and waterfront activities, military installations, western defense operational areas, the Port of Embarkation and its Intelligence Division. You may peruse the warrant on the drive to the Treasure Island Brig."

"There you will be read your rights under the Rights of the Accused of War Crimes Allegations under the penal code of articles for the Government of the Navy. The warrant specifies Article 4."

"One last point, Lieutenant Toscanini. The port's legal adviser is the Port Judge Advocate. This office will provide legal advice on the claims for the government. At the reading of the rights of the accused, you'll be able to ask, in the presence of your assigned attorney, any questions you'd like."

With that, Peter, in the presence of all the members of the flight crew who were observing the proceedings, stunned beyond belief, mouths agape, minds in utter disbelief, was handcuffed. A pair of connected rings shackling his young wrists, and frozen in thought, he said nothing as he was led to the backseat of the second Buick.

CHAPTER TEN

-

A Secret meeting on Treasure Island

Manacled and slightly manhandled as he was shoved into the backseat of the second military police vehicle, Peter, of course, understood it was all a ruse.

For whatever reason, all servicemen who knew or became acquainted with the Lieutenant, who even casually observed, communicated, or merely smiled or nodded in passing had to honestly believe he was a wanted criminal. Word had to spread, and spread quickly, that he was arrested, handcuffed, and incarcerated in the Treasure Island Naval Base brig. Peter's life as an undercover agent depended on the subterfuge, so meticulously planned and systematized, being believed.

With only a slight nod to the flight crew standing motionless, each man clutching his personal bags, in shocked amazement, jaws still ajar, eyes as wide as the bottoms of beer cans. As the small caravan of two automobiles, a single jeep, and two motorcycle members of the military police who just arrived, sped away. Sitting between two silent officers in the backseat of the automobile second in line, Peter stared straight ahead in absolute silence and lack of acknowledgement. He calmly reflected,

"Regardless of what happens, the systematized stratagem conceived requires my absolute and faithful allegiance. Undercover assignments are created in the shadows of military administrative offices and carried out in utmost silence. I may die with no recognition whatsoever, my body tossed into a garbage drum or dumpster, then burned in some dirt hole full of oil. But I'll do it, so help me God, I'll do it, and do it right."

As the afternoon's first sunlight gently dissipated the damp foggy mists, and he listened to the moaning easterly winds sweeping through the Golden Gate, Peter noted the flurries of Naval activities on the wharves and docks servicing the array of war ships in the Port of Trade Winds Harbor adjacent the Alameda, the broad thoroughfare lived with poplar trees.

Traffic from the side-streets leading to the waterfront yielded the rights-of-way to the speeding four-door sedans, jeep, and motorcycles. Wherever he was being delivered, Peter knew it would be within moments since the Treasure Island Naval Station, the fifth largest in the U.S. Navy, was only a little more than 400 acres of tons of rock and silt dredged up from the Bay bottom.

"Yet," he pondered as he noticed the causeway in the distance to his left that led from the Bay Bridge onto the southern entrance of the island, "look what those 400 acres hold--the Headquarters of the 12th Naval District, three permanent two-story buildings converted from air hangars for blimps and dirigibles; more than 700 units of enlisted men's quarters; over 900 housing apartments, and 90 barracks-style facilities for those in training facilities; a modern Naval Hospital of 500 beds with some 700 patients; several clinics for training medical staffs; the U.S. Fleet Training Center and its accompanying waterfront facilities; the Auxiliary Air Facility Airfield for seaplane salvage, serious repairs, renovations such as new radar installations; plus a variety of hangars, centers for receiving and departure of troops, specialists, and essential officers, and laypeople. Above all, the Naval Air Station at Treasure Island in 1944 was the largest electronics and radio communication training center with a teaching staff of over 1,300 officers."

"And," Peter continued to reflect, "This little artificial island left over from the 1936-7 Golden Gate International Exposition processes more than 12,000 men and women a day. It's the departure point for sailors of surface ships and submarines. Treasure Island, named after the dredged gold-laden fill silt and dirt the rainy seasons in the Sierra Mountains bordering California and Nevada washed down through its rivers to the Bay. More than 29 million cubic yards of sand and gravel make up the island, much of it laced with gold dust. This little treasure dirt was firm enough in 1943 to launch some 4,000 freighter cargo voyages and some 800 heavily-laden troop ships. Who can beat us at war? Some island," he smiled.

The staff car had turned right at the first signal-light intersection that led from the causeway of the bridge after slowing down on what was now a four-lane, two in each direction, thoroughfare named "Avenue of the Palms", and cruising past several small theaters, barracks, recently streamlined, repainted, and attended to by non-military civilian custodial personnel, the green colored camouflaged cars halted in a row before two double-iron gates with shoulder-high columns connected to equally high brick walls.

Despite his excitement of being on the Treasure Island Naval Base for the first time, the San Francisco Bay winds that smacked Peter in the face as he stumbled out of the vehicle with handcuffs on in front of the headquarters administrative building of the 12th Naval District were nonetheless unyielding and annoyingly cold. For a serviceman returning from the Solomon Sea tropics, the shock of the change in weather was commensurate with the bleak, somber gray skies.

Then, as a USMC military police gate officer exited a small wooden guardhouse to stand between the two rifle-bearing sentries at the on-guard behind the double-iron gate, Peter glanced up and down the busy thoroughfare of passing military vehicles of all sorts and varying sizes. Turning toward additional armed Marines trotting toward the gate from across the treeless but well-groomed lawns and flower beds skirting the curved driveway and encapsulating the entire yard, Peter noted the administrative building and the large sign in black letters against a white background which read,

NAVAL STATION, TREASURE ISLAND

Fleet Training Center, Training and Distribution

Peter had actually driven his parents for a day to experience the Golden Gate International Exposition. The largest man-made island in the world had been built on the Yerna Buena Island for it.

The administrative building that served the Treasure Island Exposition between 1937 and 1939 was now serving as the headquarters for the Treasure Island Naval Station, converted in 1941 as a necessary facility should there be war in the Pacific.

Built in art deco, a decorative style of the late 1920s and 1930s based upon the cubism form of painting, it had been streamlined in 1942 in the modern style. Although located on the southern end of the island, the structure was the hub of all activity. It had a matte-white appearance casting a limestone look about it. Blending with the dark waters of the Bay, the structure was quite imposing.

After the USMC gate, the Lieutenant, armed only with a holstered .45, unsnapped the heavy removable lock, passed the long chain through its eye, loosening the iron bar that secured the gates together, and waved his arm in a forward motion, ordering,

"Come ahead!"

As the twin iron gates opened inward, the long chain scraping the concrete entrance way, the caravan rounded the wide-lawned foreground rimmed with flower beds. As he gazed upon four well-positioned sentries on guard at the entrance of the facility, Peter pondered,

"Is a major part of my life, if not all of it, about to end here? Surely, my new assignment will be issued verbally."

After one of the outside entrance sentries pressed the admitting buzzer, and the small party waited, the sound of rapidly approaching footsteps could be heard echoing inside. Then, after the large glass door swung open, no less than an aging USMC colonel, gaunt and lanky, balding with a slightly pinched expression, nodded curtly to the assemblage waiting silently to enter.

"You've been expected for some time, and you may have to explain why. This is the military base of the Pacific and nonsense is punished appropriately," he announced in a loud voice. Pointing, "Go there, past the entrance hall. Follow the stairwell down to the lower level, the basement area occupied by the island's military police. Walk down the narrow passageway until you come to two sentries on duty outside a closed room. A sentry will tell you what to do next. Make haste, latecomers. There's no amount of tardiness allowed here." With that, he turned and ambled off.

Upon descending the stairway, the arriving party was greeted by a naval captain who indicated the officers to follow him. Not once did he acknowledge, or even glance, at Peter. Upon reaching the two sentries, the captain turned and said,

"Thank you, gentlemen. All of you are dismissed. The handcuffed arrested will be relieved of his restraint since he is now in our custody."

With that, and the captain's quick knock on the door, Peter, now unshackled, stood between the two sentries and alone with the captain as the arresting party departed down the hall. As the door was held open for him to enter, Peter slowly strolled, rubbing his wrists, after the naval officer exiting.

"Enter, Lieutenant Toscanini," beckoned a voice in the partially lit, windowless basement bunker.

As Peter adjusted his eyes in the semi-darkness, he initially felt the soft rug he was standing upon. Colorful and thin, he saw that it was larger than the typical Persian carpet. Because he knew such Persian rugs felt good to walk upon barefooted, since they consisted of wool and silk, their knots tied 1,000 per square inch, Peter felt like removing his shoes. But he thought better of the notion.

A quick glance all around showed how austere the room was. The vacant walls were painted a dull gray. In front of him sat someone alone. Behind him was an elongated, highly-polished mahogany table with absolutely nothing on it. Behind it sat three high-ranking USMC officers. Each sat rigidly with his hands folded on the table. no one said a word in the diffused lighting. The seated man, sitting straight up, said,

"Approach, Lieutenant, and sit. We've been waiting for you."

Peter had never seen, let alone met, any of the four men sitting rigidly behind the lengthened bare, well-polished table. Although in civilian clothing, the solemnity of the setting, the formal tomb-like silence in the stark setting, told the wide-eyed Lieutenant he was among the highest level of military leadership.

"I suspect the one in the middle, the frowning old one glaring at me is the boss of this kit and caboodle, probably a major general or a Lieutenant Colonel," he mused. "I sense doom. They going to execute me?"

Suddenly piercing the room's gloom and shadows was a strident voice somehow emanating from the human-like figure resembling a male sitting erect before him.

"No introductions necessary here. You are Ensign Peter Albioni Toscanini. You need know nothing of us. I have two sealed letters to read to you, both of which will be destroyed thereafter in your presence," he said in a loud strained voice.

Peter didn't like this man sitting there bolt upright, facing him directly, hands resting on his knees or his curt condescension.

"Your work," he continued, "is so confidential and unofficial no one knows about it, including the Director of Naval Intelligence, the FME, Fleet Marine Division, Commander, and not even the Criminal Division of the Military Police. Nonetheless, your assignment is top priority to Washington, known only to top staff men. You have no liaison officer, no handler, no surface personnel with whom to reach out in event of discover. There is only one code word to remember from this point to your assignment's conclusion within the stockage, and it's 'almond'."

"Almond?" Peter could hardly restrain his surprise. For the first time, he smiled.

"How'd you come by that code name?"

"Apparently because you're familiar with it. It was selected by the Secretary of the Navy. You need not explain to us. Your life may depend on hearing or voicing that word. Whoever says it is your safety. Otherwise, you're on your own."

"My orders?" Peter inquired, a hint of defiance in his tone.

"In this first of two unopened envelopes," he responded.

From a large sealed buff-colored 81/2'' by 11'' sized envelope, he pulled out two regular sized white letter envelopes with normal gummed flaps. The "orders" were terse. They read simply,

"You are to proceed by way of the Camp Stoneman Stockage as an inmate-prisoner to Camp Elliott where you will be incarcerated for the attempted assassination of the Mad Ghoul of Pavuvu prior to his court-martialed death sentence by firing squad execution. There, while awaiting trial, you will learn the identity of a murderer of Marine recruit inmates. You will retain your full identity, and use when appropriate, or asked, the details and other authentic information pertaining to the crimes of murder by the multiple-murderer, as well as his execution when you served the court-martial board. The code word 'almond' will signify a contact person is at your disposal."

After a short pause, the reader asked,

"Understood?"

"Yes, sir."

"Then, we'll proceed to a letter held until your arrival. It is from your mother, and lengthy. Since both envelopes and their contents will be burned in your presence, you will listen."

"Yes, sir."

Peter leaned forward slightly to listen intently as the five-page handwritten letter described in detail the major war events, and minor civic activities occurring in his Stockton hometown and neighborhood. In her usual chatty, excited manner detailed, for example, how she panicked where she momentarily misplaced the family's monthly ration book. In several pages, she paraphrased the well-wishes from relatives and neighborhood friends. She numbered the variety of clubs, events, and activities in which his brother was involved, and the incidents, some dangerous that occurred in the two jobs his father held down, delivering oil and gasoline to local gas stations and garages during the day, and operating the projection book of the Star Theater on West Sonora Street at night.

"Rarely does Dad get more than four hours of sleep a night," he thought to himself.

Her final paragraph on the last page jarred him back into the reality of Joan's dissolution of their engagement.

"How is Joan and her family doing in the concentration camp?" she asked wistfully, not realizing there was a horrendous difference between "concentration camp" and "relocation-internment camp".

"The gossip around town, and especially the whites in our neighborhood claim they are all doing just fine. That makes me happy," she wrote, "because it will mean a wonderful, beautiful marriage when the war is over and you both return to South Center Street…she hasn't changed her mind, has she, and run off into another concentration camp, has she?"

Suddenly, sharply, a Ka-Bar was plunged into him. Every force of strength, for months, had repressed all thoughts and emotions of his Joan. Now a single question sliced him open again. Peter no longer heard a word that was being said, whether it came from a postscript by his mother, or an official order of instruction. He was so filled with Joan, the woman he loved as much, if not more, than his mother, that he could see her, smell her, hear her, magnificent heart murmuring, her whole soul again alive before him. His eyes welled up with tears, as, in a flash, he recalled every single word she had ever spoken to him, every touch of her on him, every glance, comment, and conversation she had with others in his presence, withered his entire being.

"What's wrong, Lieutenant? Are you still with me, or are you going to throw up and faint?"

"No, sir. And, yes, sir," Peter responded meekly, shifting his eyes.

"Give me the 'yes, sir' part. We have no time for nonsense."

Peter hesitated,

"I was engaged until just recently. To my high school sweetheart. She's a Nisei, interned in Rowher, Arkansas."

"A Jap woman?"

"Yes, sir. And, it's been over for several months. I was just thinking about her from Mother's question, just then. That's all. Nothing more to it, sir."

"I must impress upon you, Lieutenant, the need for utmost secrecy. In fact, within three days, you will be incarcerated in the Elliott brig. Even should you engage in conversation, there is nothing to reveal because you know nothing. You have no knowledge of your handlers, who the victims, and their murdering suspects, are. You can't contradict yourself because nothing has changed regarding your identity, your involvement with the Ghoul. You will improvise your questing both by the brig military police and guards and prisoners themselves. You are intelligent enough to ad lib. Our guess is that unless you are murdered upon arriving, you'll learn something within weeks of being celled. You have no help. Help is there waiting for you, and will be identified with the one word mentioned, a word that none of us know because the order will be destroyed. You have an adequate trail, having been cuffed here a few hours ago for involvement. All perfectly planned, all movements and paperwork perfectly organized. Your trail is covered because all who worked on this project sincerely believe you are criminal. Their paperwork is available to the staff at Elliott. Because it has been so competently prepared, there is not a flaw found anywhere. Your movement sheet is on USMC letterhead because you are on loan from the Navy. Unless there are questions, you are to transfer this moment for the Camp Stoneham Stockage. By morning, you will be in a nonstop troop train headed south, and by late afternoon, admitted into the Camp Elliott reception unit. Everyone from this moment, unless you have a question or two, with whom you come in contact will believe in your complicity with the Ghoul. Your questions, Lieutenant?"

"None, sir."

"You're dismissed. And, good luck, Lieutenant. God only knows how much you're going to need it. Now, put your hands out because I need to put your cuffs back on."

CHAPTER ELEVEN

-

The Daylight to Elliott

In the 72 hours that followed, Peter, tired physically and psychologically, lost himself in a crazy, hurried swirl, pivoting every which way. Temporary detention at Camp Stoneham, with all its orientation, classification, and discipline among military police personnel and both USMC and Army inmates, produced in him such a variegated hodge-podge of impressions and emotions that the young ensign was filled with an unaccountable sense of imminent catastrophe. His very bones seemed to shudder, the blood in his veins frozen into stone.

In short, Peter's mind was a seething ferment as he adjusted to becoming a prisoner. Throughout those hours there was only one firm recollection atop a sad undercurrent, and her name was Joan Ikeda.

"What I'd die for now would be a long, soaking hot bath, but how do I get one of those? And, dreaming of being billeted at the Royal Hawaiian in Honolulu on a honeymoon with Joan, locking the doors behind for a much-needed rest until 1975, in senseless. Now that I am stealth, and that cruelty, bloody, mindlessness will fuel the gloomy vigilance that his begun," he thought to himself.

Peter had never experienced, let alone observed, such a staging center as Camp Stoneman. Although his vision was partially blurred by the 90-minute ferry ride from Treasure Island under an armed guard to the Pittsburgh waterfront wharf leading to the base, Peter later vaguely recalled seeing a 16-foot sign that proudly proclaimed,

"Through these Portals pass the Best Damn Soldiers in the World."

Spread over three million acres, Camp Stoneman was the largest troop staging area on the Pacific West Coast, deploying by late 1944 almost a million troops to the fighting areas across the Pacific Theater of Operations. Not only was it a "jumping off point" to embark on troop ships for overseas, but also it was a medium-sized city unto itself. Named after a Civil War Commander who later became a governor of California, Stoneman was a perfect cantonment area because of its paved highways leading to and from the Santa Fe and Southern Pacific Railroads entering the staging center, and the bay waterways leading to the San Joaquin and Sacramento areas.

When Peter was driven from the Pittsburg landing dock to the Camp Stoneman detention facility adjacent the stockage, Peter recalled the 800 "cream-khaki" colored barracks, 86 additional light gray company warehouses and administrative shacks, three motion picture theaters, eight infirmaries, nine post exchanges, 14 recreation halls, 13 mess halls, a post office, and chapel. Somewhere along the way, he heard Stoneman boasted 75 phone booths. Apparently, over 2,000 long-distance phone calls were made each day by base personnel and departing troops.

During his three-day orientation phase of looming incarceration in the Camp Elliott Stockade, two images would remain indelibly engraved in his mind. The first dealt with a seven-hour full medical examination in which he was riddled with innumerable inoculations for a variety of disease, either as prisoner or for his return to combat duty in the deep Pacific areas. In addition to updating his immunizations, he had to undergo half a day of dental work that had been long overdue.

The second was a USO show that the 100 or so detainees had been allowed to attend as a group under armed guard by the military police. On his second visit in the detention center, Peter watched Lucille Ball don a swimming suit to dedicate an enlisted men's club. Later, Groucho Marx, Gary Moore, and Red Skelton, on their way to the baseball field to perform before some 10,000 servicemen awaiting deployment, stopped unannounced by the detention to say, "Hello to the boys who have been naughty."

On the early morning of the fourth day of his "detention", Peter was issued newly-washed and pressed clothing for prisoners, gray with a large "P" for prisoner embossed in yellow paint on the back. After updating his personnel file, he was issued into lecture hall where other passengers for Southern California were assembled. A mean-looking staff sergeant entered with a clipboard and without introducing himself, launched into a lecture on proper prisoner train travel, its etiquette, and potential security and safety risks.

"You'll be traveling south with the Marines' 2nd and 86th Infantry Divisions deploying for maneuvers in the Mojave Desert sands for preparation of invasion on some small island of nothing but volcanic rock and ash."

"Your conduct is to be impeccable. Conduct is everything, or you'll hear loud and clear the 'why' of it. You're lucky about one thing: You're boarding a shiny new Southern Pacific Streamliner."

And it was true as Peter watched in amazement as he waited with the other prisoners on the small station platform. The clean streamliner seemed to shine in the gray overcast, slightly foggy morning as it steamed directly into the installation on the spur from the Southern Pacific's mainline shared with the Santa Fe. Then he, for the first time, noticed the recently established German-Italian prisoner-of-war camp everyone was talking about. More than 500 POWs lined the barbed-wire fence to watch the streamliner ride by at less than 10 miles per hour and the boarding of the passenger-servicemen.

Equally interesting was observing a contingent of military police also waiting to bard from the 720 Military Police Battalion that had recently established a school for the highly-selected members. Standing at attention, looking smart in their freshly-laundered uniformed, they, like Peter and the other inmates, awaited their Pullman seats. In addition to guarding the prisoners-of-war, the MPs performed sentry duty at the Pittsburg wharf, docks, piers, tracks, utilities, waterworks in and around the base, and the highways and back roads leading into and out. The MPs at Camp Stoneham referred to themselves as the "red-headed step-children of the U.S. Army". More than 300 MPs were instructing more than 3,000 of initiated, who, upon completion of their training, were to be dispatched to all occupied territories for policing, criminal investigate work, and security details.

For three nights while in detention, they heard trains whistling as they slowly rolled in and out of Camp Stoneman. During the day while on exercise day, he saw through the heavy wire mesh fence trainloads of troops bound for "somewhere in the Pacific", to say nothing of the steady stream of trainloads of tanks and heavy guns.

The West's biggest railroad was the Southern Pacific, headquartered on Market Street in San Francisco. Although its public relations office dubbed it, "The Friendly Southern Pacific", the railroad company was totally mobilized for war. All railway lines converged on the Pacific Coast, especially California and Oregon, the main springboards for the offensives against Japan.

And, the greatest pride of the "friendly Southern Pacific" company was the passenger train, the Daylight Limited, in the eyes of just about everyone, the most beautiful passenger train in the country. Like in peacetime, the Daylight ran in two sections, the regular Daylight left Oakland, then, Camp Stoneman in the afternoon for San Diego by tracks along the Pacific Ocean above Santa Barbara, then inland all the way to San Diego. The next morning, it would leave for Los Angeles, Oakland, and Camp Stoneman.

Hearing the burst of a whistle shriek, Peter turned from observing the M.P.s standing at attention to watching the new train advance. With the engine in its two-tone orange red and black, and a train of 15 passenger nightsleeper cars, including a beautiful, shiny new observation car, Peter was impressed.

Almost immediately, GIs in fatigues heading for nearby San Joaquin Valley field maneuvers began disembarking and unloading their packs and equipment. Then, without a pause, the assembled MPs and Camp Stoneman detention inmates boarded and prepared for a long train ride. The MPs were ushered into their seats, passenger car by passenger, three to a bench seat facing three, their gear in backpacks hanging from ceiling hooks. No sooner were all seated and the Daylight began to inch its way out of the camp when their early dinners were served in small box containers at their seats. Although every solider on board knew that each time the streamliner stopped, the MPs knowingly ran to the station's canteen entrance.

Since the Daylight did not stop long, everyone knew there was just enough time to be serviced with fast food bites and beverages, almost always coffee and Coca-Colas, by the railroad's canteen service women. But, you had to move fast (run was the word) to the canteen, then get back on board, or get left behind.

With the sun slowly descending into the Pacific, and the shadows growing longer, the MPs and detainees began to wrap themselves in blankets and fall asleep where they sat. Those luckily assigned to Pullman-type berths had to sleep in pairs, two in every lower berth, two, or more rarely, one, in the upper berth.

Although Peter sitting without cuffs or chains with the other prisoners in the 12th passenger car with MPs at each end of the coach, realized this was no ordinary journey, he also knew it might be his last. Within a few days, the MPs would be on the high seas. He himself would be behind bars, assigned to finding a killer of young Marines. He was now wide-awake, listening to an MP in the next car playing an accordion, staring outside his window seat into the darkness.

That night, he knew he was leaving behind a way of pre-war life-- the taste of well-mustarded hot dogs and hamburgers and "pop" soft drinks, Cokes being the most painful to abandon. Would he ever again drive a car over a two-lane highway? See or pat the neighbors' dogs named Shucks, Spot, and Barnacle Bill? His mother and father, and grandparents he loved so much? Southwest Stockton where he was born and raised? St. Mary's Church where he had served as an altar boy for six years?

That night, he thought a lot of issues over, Joan, of course, being the most critical. There was a lump in his throat, and certainly a tear filled an eye. It didn't matter, he thought to himself, because no one would see it in the dark.

With everyone breathing heavily, many snoring loudly, Peter decided to pull from his backpack his Armed Services Edition of a western by Charles Alden Seltzer entitled, "The Range Boss," written and published in 1916. Not a digest, but a complete novel, the small pocket-size paperback was no larger than 3 ½ wide x 6" long. Thousands of titles in this format were known as "Overseas Editions" and were distributed by the Special Services Division of the Army, Navy, and Air Force. A non-profit organization, the Council on Books in Wartime, published and distributed them in American bases and camps stateside and occupied and friendly territories.

All night long, the Daylight rumbled and rolled south, toward San Diego, stopping frequently to drop-off and pick-up military police passengers. The incarcerated Camp Stoneman detainees remained intact, under guard.

Traveling at less than 35 miles per hour most of the journey, the Daylight paused, after exiting Camp Stoneman at Camp McQuaide, Fort Ord, the Presidio of Monterey, the Hunter-Liggett Military Reservation, Camp Roberts, Camp San Luis Obispo, Camp Brooke, Camp Santa Ana, Fort MacArthur, the Naval Station Reeves Field Maritime Training Station, San Clemente Fleet Training Base, Camp Pendleton, Camp Gallan, where they disembarked and boarded busses for Camp Elliott.

All that Peter could remember on that long stop-and-go journey from Camp Stoneham between Pittsburg and Antioch to Camp Elliott on the outskirts of San Diego were blurred images, overheard incoherent rumors, fragmented and nonsensical, and an endless series of brief doses and short naps. Furthermore, from the afternoon of the day before to the early morning hour of the next day, Peter sat along at the window seat, his backpack on the seat next to him, and spoke nary a word, even to the three Marine prisoners in endless chatter or the harsh sounds of snoring.

During that more than 15-hour train ride, he read three Zane Grey novels, "The Last Trail" (1909), "The Lone Star Ranger" (1914), and "To the Last Man" (1921). But despite his love of Grey, his favorite was Seltzer's "Range Boss" which told him the story of Ruth Harkness, a lovely Eastern girl who comes west to claim her inheritance, a cattle ranch, The adventure begins when the range boss protects her from vermin rustlers, assassins, and the corrupt political and banking officials.

Where the major rumor that circulated among the Daylight's cars was concerned, only the "red-headed step-children of the U.S. Army", the special unit created in 1942 of the 720th Military Police Battalion was concerned--and in anguish.

Word got out that the 535th contingent, most of the MPs on board also on assignment to Camp Elliott was going to guard Axis prisoners of Germany, Italy, and Japan, at home and abroad.

"What the hell is that?" Peter overheard an MP shout. "And for 'the duration'? That means we're being converted into Rangers. I'm all geared up to kill Krauts, Japs and I-tyes."

While Peter was prepared to read his four romantic westerns, one by Seltzer and the other three by Zane Grey, he was mesmerized by all the military routines and activities of the Pacific Coast, specifically California, at war. Before sundown that afternoon, as the Daylight slowly rolled and reverberated on railway sidings and railroad spurs south through eastside of the Bay Area, namely Carquinez, Richmond, El Cerrito, Berkeley, Oakland, Fremont, and San Jose, Peter believed the entire population was engaged in one form or another of military production.

Everywhere he glanced, there were Army and USMC convoys in various stages of movements. Whether on tracks, or highways and roads, adjacent to tracks, short clusters or long groups, small four-wheeled vehicles or large half-tracted carriers, all were either in transition, or preparing for journeying. And, behind the convoys on ramps and mounds, built as billboards or natural weeded lots, were signs, "To Hell With You, Hirohito, You Son-Of-A-_____"; "The West Coast Has Rolled Up Its Sleeves. Have You?"; "Stay Put For The Duration. You'll Be The First to Know When The War Is Won"; "America Needs You--Don't Let Her Down. Do Your Part Today And

Every Day"; and "Lest You Forget, Remember Pearl Harbor" and "Jinx To The Japs." What brought a smile to Peter's lips was how large they were, all in black bold-faced letters, usually in a variety of colored backgrounds.

Since the Southern Pacific tracks ran along the shores of the East Bay, shipbuilding facilities were stretched from Richmond to East San Jose, every one of them operating around the clock. In the western distances of the Golden Gate Bridge were barrage balloons at varying heights, and high above them further out at sea, Navy blimps on the lookout for Japanese submarines which could easily surface and fire a dozen or so shells from their forefront cannons, then submerge, all in a matter of less than 10 minutes. Far below beneath them were lighthouse ships, permanently anchored to guard against enemy infiltrators rowed to shore from the submarines.

Equally fascinating were the shoreline assembly plants of "who-knows-what?" operating in three eight-hour shifts. And, almost in every one of their yards were large piles of gravel, cement, ferro-silicon, small tin can depots and old rubber tire and rubber material dumps.

The activity of the Alameda Naval Air Base and Coast Guard Air Base opposite Newark north of San Jose were also fascinating.

Leaning back in his seat, Peter had no idea how the state of California alone was studded with bases, camps, schools, and training centers there were for the U.S. Military establishment, especially in the San Francisco Bay Area for the Army, Navy and Marine Corps. And, he thought to himself, I can't even see the Bay's elaborate and extensive fortifications grid of harbor defenses and hidden vital anti-invasion artillery and mortar point.

With twilight, the streamliner was riding along past Mountain View, Watsonville, and Salinas for a long stopover at the Monterey Presidio Selectee Reception Center. In both locations, members of the High School Victory Corps Girls Riflery, along with mobile canteen unit staff served hot coffee, doughnuts, and other pastries and fish-tasting snacks.

Between reading and napping, napping and reading on the way to King City and the Hunter-Liggett Military Reservation and Morro Bay submarine base, Peter noticed air raid wardens and citizens with small flashlights maintaining strict blackout conditions in trailer-court encampments outside small towns and larger cities. At the Camp Roberts Army Replacement Center, a two-hour layover was necessitated for the disembarkation of three-fourths of the 720th Military Police Battalion's 535th contingent of Special Forces.

Near Santa Barbara, after at least an hour's uninterrupted doze, Peter noticed sandbagged oil well pumps, beach oil fields, and oil derricks, the first he had ever seen in California. All were near and around Goleta, where on February 23, 1942, the Japanese long-range submarine, I-17, lobbed 25 shells from deck guns into the oil fields and Ellwood Refinery. Now, two long sentinels walked posts around each individual unit.

Although Peter pretty much was napping on the journey between the Fort MacArthur Selectee Center at San Pedro and the Fort Rosecrans Naval Base and Training Station-Destroyer Base near San Diego, he was wide awake as the Daylight pulled into Camp Callan and Camp Elliott, some 20 miles due east of San Diego.

Fully alert, listening intently to any comment or description someone in the coach was uttering about Camp Elliott, Peter leaned forward to study every structural feature he saw on the outskirts of the camp.

Suddenly it dawned on him.

"Well, you young, garlicky fart, here you are. Now, we'll see what you're made of, iron or nothing more than an offensive smell."

CHAPTER TWELVE

-

Sunny, No More Than A Kid

With dawn's first sun-surges bursting over the rims of the eastern San Diego hills, Peter grinned at how the recently activated 29,000-acre Army tank and infantry training grounds known as Camp Elliott, bleak and gray, was suddenly mantled under a mosaic of vivid colors and clearly distinguishable structures.

As the Southern Pacific Daylight slowly crept across the trestle over a dry creek road lined with a dozen black buses, it pulled up to a railroad siding adjacent a small station next to the main entrance of Camp Elliott.

Even before the streamliner rolled to a complete stop, several Marine officers jumped aboard, including a tough-appearing staff sergeant ambling down the aisle of Peter's coach, yelling continually,

"Move, get moving, you bastards! Wake up! Outside, you miserable, disgraced sons-of-bitching Marines. Double-file! And, with your bag of turds over your shoulder, you yellow cowards."

Grumbling by the drowsy inmates swept through the coach from entrance to exit, then back again. Peter heard someone at the front end of the car shout,

"Come over here, you miserable piece of shit. I want to show you something. And, when's breakfast?"

Everyone chuckled as the staff sergeant, oblivious to any or all insulting responses, ambled out and into the next car.

As the uncuffed prisoners exited the coach, stepping down onto the siding platform, more than two-dozen white-helmeted MPs, each holding a polished baton, standing shoulder to shoulder at attention, awaited them.

Not one smiled.

With the last inmate descending from the coach, and the staff sergeant behind him slamming the passenger cab door shut, the men lined up in two rows, their bags and gear slung over their shoulders.

While Peter stood at ease as the others formed the second line behind him, he noted from the large clock atop the station entrance roof that it was past 7:00AM by six minutes. The early morning weather was already hot and unusually humid. Yet, in the distant hills and plains, all was a grassy green.

"Well, cowboy," the prisoner next to Peter whispered under his breath as everyone, prisoner and MP alike, remained stone-cold silent, "I suppose the great sport of waving at everyone as we pitter-patter through Los Angeles is over."

Peter, glancing at him, sized him up. The nice-looking 18 or 19 year old, blond wavy hair, medium sized, well-built, although somewhat plump, continued, "The railroad workers in their filthy, oil-soaked overalls, along the tracks waving at us, the ranchers, farmers, and farmhands in the fields, waving back as we wave at them, and best of all, the girls with no blouses and thin see-through skirts, because of the heat, standing on house steps waving back at us, some bending over on purpose, as we waved at them, what fun, Lieutenant, buddy, what fun. And now, we're off to some shithole jail."

The staff sergeant, the last to exit from the passenger car at the end of the train, waved his baton at the stationmaster waiting patiently near the streamliner's forward engine, who in turn signaled the engineer looking down at him from the cab.

As the Daylight slowly pulled away with hundreds of troops still seated within, peering out at them, the silent prisoners heard the staff sergeant shrill in a high, thin, piercing voice,

"No cuffs, you shitheads. But try to make a run for it, all those fine, unsmiling champion redeemers standing in front of you, their batons at the ready, will catch and pound you into Gehenna, the bottomless Valley of Refuse."

With that, the staff sergeant beckoned for the long double-lined inmates to follow him, the MPs positioning themselves alongside every dozen or so prisoners. Peter and his young "partner", were the eighth twosome in the long row. Trotting to the edge of the ravine, the doubles slid down with their bags and gear into the deep hollow where the large wide buses, motors waiting for their boarding.

Observing the line-up buses observing up close for the first time, Peter, amazed, exclaimed, "Just look at those troop-carrying monsters! Belching thick smoke from their overheating engines at varying throttling! What grim sorry-looking Black Marias! Huge, fat police or prison horses! The ugliest, most melancholy looking tubs the Army and Marine Core have to drive us to the brig in? Probably our coffins for our last rides."

"Oh my God," Peter heard someone murmur behind him. "The Provost Marshall is talking to a bunch of officers near the lead truck right under the large sign "Marine Recruit Depot".

"Who's he?" another asked.

"He's the guy you don't want to meet because if you do, it usually means you're in big trouble, big-time trouble. He's the head of the Military Police on a base. He's the Big Cheese, basically the Chief of Police, and he's got the power to throw your ass in isolation, or give you any other punishment he thinks you deserve."

Seated next to each other, their bags under their feet, the young soldier commented,

"I heard that beyond the creek bank we slid down, and that bridge under, the outer camp fence marks the beginning of the relocation camp that was thrown together in early '42 to move the Jap-Americans to the centers."

"Oh, really?" perked up Peter.

"That's what I heard."

"I know we're in Area One, the Prohibited Zone in which the Alien Exclusion Military Area Act is enforced."

"What's that mean?"

"Enemy Aliens, such as Japanese-Americans, are prohibited from residing here, and working these fields, in which wonderful crops were grown for decades by hard-working conscientious 1st and 2nd generations; these so-called 'enemy aliens' who tilled the soil and grew vegetables and fruits for the American people."

"Really?"

"I grew up with the *Niseis*, the second-generation Japanese-Americans. And, by the way, they are not 'Jap-Americans'. They are Japanese-Americans, as American as you and me. The family of this place, the *Satos*, I believe, bought the large acreage in the early 1920s with hard-earned money they earned in Japan and here. No one wanted this land way out here from downtown San Diego. They revitalized and made over the part dirt-part sand with new vines until they had nearly 10,000 of them by 1930. They cared for each one. The family of sons and daughters tractored the land, irrigated each row, pruned every vine. All with their bare hands. Their joy wasn't in the money the earned, but watching their labors blossom for hungry, appreciative people. And, their prices were always fair."

"Grapes mostly?"

"Yes, Zinfandel wine grapes and a second, Tokay table grapes. Tokays are a northern California grape grown around Galt and Lodi. They are a Galt-Woodridge-Lodi specialty. They contain seeds, have crisp reddish-yellow skin, and the taste is a nice full fruity flavor."

As the line of buses, each filled to capacity, with some troops standing in the aisle, began to rattle away, the young man asked, concerned,

"And our government made that family leave their own property just because they had ancestors buried in Japan? Who could stand that? I'd be so mad!"

"Yes. And, almost all Japanese-Americans survived, pretty much, with the exceptions of the elderly suicides in the camps, and those who died of broken hearts. Those who survived had a wonderful attitude akin to '*gamon*', which translates to 'never giving up', 'continue to go forward' through the seemingly unbearable. The word '*shouganai*' also guides their lives. It means 'always endure with dignity all hatreds and discrimination'. It's an idea that pervades every Japanese and Japanese-American family."

"Well, you sure made me rethink how I feel about them. I can understand relocating them if they lived around oilfields, armories, railroad lines, reservoirs, power stations, harbor defenses and other specialized and restricted zones. But ranching way out here in the boondocks? What threat are they to us out here?"

"Well, next time you have lunch with Lt. Gen. Dewitt who instigated the mess, you give him a piece of your mind."

"Before Pearl Harbor, all was well, wasn't it? We were all having a good time without knowing it. Oh, if we could only jump forward for a quick tomorrow," concluded the young private.

To reach the brig-stockade, the caravan of Black Marias had to drive through the heart of Camp Elliott toward the east.

Once again, Peter was lost in a mad swirl of events. Despite not knowing what awaited them after the 25-minute bus ride to the Camp Elliott brig, the prisoners were surprisingly jovial, happily chatting, joking, teasing, throwing paper balls, etc.

"Ah, remembrances of boot camp experiences!" Peter's new friend exclaimed.

"With a large, ugly, belching, supperting transporting us," chuckled the Lieutenant, as he gazed out the window at all the camp activity. Part of the Treasure Island sit-down concluded with a short briefing of where he was headed.

It seemed that by September of 1942, Camp Elliott had become the home of the Fleet Marine Force Training Center, West Coast Sector, with the main mission of training individual replacements for combat duty. Over 10,000 Marines were in the San Diego area, under the banner of the 2nd Marine Division and leadership of Major-General C.F.B. Price. Peter know that he had served in World War I, and, with his considerable experience, was assigned the responsibilities of coordinating and supervising all the training there. Although more than 50,000 Marines passed through Elliott en route to Pacific duty in late 1944, the area could not meet the expansion needs for the training and deployment of the overseas replacements. The Training Center consisted of over 30 schools that taught a wide range of subjects, including individual combat and modern infantry.

"What a base," Peter said to the private sitting next to him who was listening intently. "Apparently, there are five large separate commands quartered here."

"What, for example, are they?"

"Well, let's see. If I remember correctly, the Headquarters for the Fleet Marine Force Training Center; the Troop Training Unit, Amphibious Training Command, Pacific Fleet, the Marine Barracks, and Base Depot. Few bases in the world, Allied or Enemy have such."

"Yeah, I heard. And, each command is separate, and distinct with specific responsibilities. Four of the five commands here fall within the jurisdiction of the Fleet Marine Force, under old General Clayton B. Vogel, a good man, I've repeatedly heard. Of these four, the largest and most complex operation is the Fleet Marine Force Training Center."

"Wow, young fella! How do you know all that? I'm your superior and can't articulate the detail you know."

"We're going through the two-story temporary, wood-frame barracks, officer's quarters, and their necessary utilities, such as the water supplies stored over there to your left."

"Yeah, and on the other side, the mess halls, storehouses, non-commissioned officer and bachelor quarters, recreation areas, and additional magazines."

After a pause, Peter continued,

"A city unto itself, completely self-sufficient, boating mess and recreational facilities, post exchanges, classrooms, outdoor theaters, shops, medical services, and maintenance facilities to teach how to maintain tanks in combat. What a base, youngster."

Even for the sunlit San Diego area, including the Camp Elliott area, the morning seemed extraordinarily brilliant and bright. As the caravan slowed even further, maneuvering through incredibly busy grounds, virtually all flooded with raw recruits hustling in groups or individually to one area or another. It was a little more than 7:30AM, and, as Peter noted, a Training Center reaching its peak of personnel movement among five separate major commands. Although Lieutenant Toscanini was apprehensive when he reflected about the unknown demands of his undercover work, and the very real possibility he would be murdered before a final word to Joan Ikeda, he felt himself in a whirling, unsteady sensation.

"When do we eat? I would love to have a cup of Java."

"Soon, kid, soon." Peter smiled, "By the way, what's your name?"

"Daniel Michael Marino. Supposedly I'm part Viking, part Irish, part Portuguese, and 100% American, the part I'm most proud of."

"Where you from?"

"Astoria, Oregon, at the mouth of the Columbia River."

Peter gazed upon him and smiled again, "I know Astoria, like it a lot. Been there often because before the war I enjoyed driving the Coast's Highway 1 during summer vacations."

"And you stopped in Astoria?"

"Best fish restaurants of the Pacific Coast."

"I was a dishwasher in three of them. That's how I earned my keep. All my earning went to Mom and younger sisters. Dad was killed working on a branch line of the Southern Pacific. We all took it hard, real hard. But I know he would be proud I signed up, although Mom was harder than hard to persuade to sign for me."

"How old are you then?"

"Ah, 18. Well, I'll be honest with you, 17 ½. But I can fight."

"Peter again allowed a slight smile to cross his lips. He liked Daniel Michael Marino. The 17 ½ year old was young, intelligent, sincere, honest, sensitive, immature, and most important of all, good. Peter, with all his natural warm, protective instinct aroused knew he would allow no harm to come to the teenager.

"How on earth did you get mixed up with us? You're no criminal, are you?"

"I have no time to be a criminal. My mom needs my earnings! They're first in my life. No, I'm no criminal. Let me explain what happened. But, before I do, Lieutenant, what's your name? Oh, and please call me by my pet nickname Mom and Dad always called me, which is Sunny."

"Okay, Sunny, and, somehow that one fits you. Well, my name is Peter Toscanini. In fact, it's Peter Albioni Toscanini."

"Where have I heard that name before? Before the war, were you some kind of big-shot ball player or movie star? Or politician?"

"Hardly. Although I feel I should have been. I'm better looking than William 'Bill' Lundigan, far better looking. Even better looking than a new kid that just arrived on the Hollywood lots named Greg Peck."

"Never heard of them."

"Of course not. Bill is my friend resting, recuperating, and refitting after fighting for six months on Guadalcanal. He's now on Pavuvu Island, getting ready for the next island happening. My friend, a good guy. Being assigned to camera, motion picture taking duty. In real life, he's actually a movie star."

"But I know your last name. I've heard it before."

"My dad's grandfather, back in the northern Italian mountain village named Suzzi, was related to a Toscanini there. Who? I don't know. If I survive this war, I want to honeymoon there to find out who my distant relatives are. I'm temporarily out of fiancées. So it may be awhile. But you've heard of Arturo Toscanini, a conductor, a classical musician the whole world knows. He grew up a cellist-turned-composer, and he fled Italy in 1931 to get away from Mussolini. By 1934, millions, almost 10 million Americans, men, women, and children, tuned into the radio on Saturday nights to hear the New York

Philharmonic concerts. May family and I listened faithfully because, after all, he is a relative. Our favorites were 'Pagliacci', 'La Boheme', 'Cavalleria Rusticana', 'Rigoletto', 'La Traviata', heck I can name them all."

"Never heard of them. My family likes old-fashioned cowboy music, Okie music, singing, stomping, and strumming. That's my people. And, your middle name. Who does that belong to?"

"Another Italian composer, but of an earlier time. SO, we're music people and proud of it. Now, it's your turn. How does a nice kid like you wind up on this fat bus sitting next to me."

"Well," Sunny blushed, "I'll try to get my story in before we arrive at the stockade, which we must be near by this time…Look there…"

As Sunny paused, Peter quickly glanced out the window of the Black Marias. At the corner of one of the camp's main thoroughfare in "Barracks' City", two dozen Marine inmates wearing white uniforms bearing the word "BRIG" written in large black letters across their backs stood at ease in three rows facing the street.

"Jailed for various infractions at Stoneman and other bases, but who opted for an infantry assignment rather than remain incarcerated in the brigs, near the bases where the infractions occurred."

"Camp Elliott serves as the advanced training base, as well as the headquarters for the West Coast elements of the Fleet Marine Force."

"Wow, 24 of them, probably waiting for these buses to drop us off, then return to pick them up. And, if you look out there behind the base, the landscape offers a unique combination of gently rolling hills and steep hills and mountain slopes that are ideal for infantry conditioning as well as weapons and field maneuver training."

"Well, we still have a little time before we pull up at the stockade."

"Okay. I was not your usual typical teenage errant Marine. After Mom reluctantly signed for me, and I went through training at the Fort Cods Bay training facility near the Oregon and California border on the Pacific, we stepped off the troop train at Camp Stoneham to board a transport at Fort Mason in San Francisco for ferrying to Honolulu, then straight to Guadalcanal, we think. I knew nothing about brigs, military police, stockades, Army discipline and court martials. In my young life, I hadn't even watched a single guardhouse, prison, or jail movie. For me, the shock and fear of such words was greater than any near-death experience I would encounter wherever my battalion was going in the Pacific."

After a pause, looking down at his folded fingers, Sunny continued,

"While undergoing additional training, I wound up serving a short sentence in the brig we were in together the past week or so. I had served slightly more than a week of a 30-day disciplinary sentence for being AWOL three days after a leave for completing the additional training. It was a non-escort by Military Police sentence."

As Peter listened intently, oblivious to all the outdoor base activities, Sunny continued,

"We were about to complete the boot camp addendum at Stoneman when our outfit was granted a 10-day leave to go home, or fool around in Frisco. Well, naturally, I hitchhiked to the Oregon border, then hopped a freight to the Portland area, and hitched again to Astoria. All in only three days! Mom and the girls were so surprised, so happy to suddenly see me walking from the main road to the house. I got more hugs in those minutes than in my whole life, and I was only gone for less than a few months. You'd think the war was over."

"Well, Mom prepared a dinner you'd think it was Christmas! She didn't have that much money, but she bought a whole chicken for us.

That evening, I strolled to downtown Astoria and saw one of the girls I vaguely remember from the 5th or 6th grade and lost track of for a while because she had moved away, then moved back again."

"I don't have to tell you what happened next, but to make a wonderful story short, let's just say I lost track of time. By the time I got back to base, I was three days late. Hitching rides and finding the fastest freights didn't go well. Besides, the distance from 1027 South Suisuin to Antioch-Pittsburgh, California, and Camp Stoneman is long, very long, more than a thousand miles. And, even if you could afford a passenger train, no point in trying to get a seat, what with whole units of troops traveling hither and yonder."

"Okay, so I was late. At the time, I laughed, 'So what? No big deal. They going to throw me in the brig when the battalion was preparing to ship out?' Heck, I meant no harm. I didn't plan on staying out. I just went home to see Mom and sisters, while the Corps filled out all the paperwork for our movement. After all, it was a 10-day leave. But a curfew is a curfew and, as you better than anyone knows, the USMC is strict about those kinds of things."

"Well, the battalion shipped out a few days before you arrived. I saw you come in. And, I saw you come in because they left me behind. Can you believe that? When I finally stumbled in, dreary and dirty, embarrassed and angry at myself, sheepish but hopeful, I was escorted by four MPs past the whole battalion to the base detention center. And, for what? Look at me now. I just hope I didn't get Agnes Dobbs pregnant. That's just about all I need."

After a long pause, Peter offered somber, downcast Sunny a slight smile.

"Well, let's hope she's not. It would hurt your mom and her mom. Marriage, yes. But not that way. And, for what? Oh, well. Life goes on.

Now what's important is for us both to get through what we're about to face as safely as we can."

"Damn," Sunny uttered softly.

CHAPTER THIRTEEN

-

The Stockade

"Nothing froze me in my tracks more than Mother warning me from time to time, 'Now, you behave, young man, or I'll call for the Black Maria to come and take you away,'" Sunny said weakly, smiling. "And, who would have predicted that now, in 1944, I'd be leisurely riding along in one of those dead meat wagons to the blackest Black Maria of all, the Cape Elliott 'Calabozo', as the Navajo boys call it."

Peter grinned,

"That bad, huh?"

"Maybe worse. I've never see it, or obviously been in it or any house of detention, for that matter, but was told by my Indian friends at Stoneman who did time there for being drunk all the time, or innocently being AWOL without realizing it, that inmates would occasionally be found dead on the yards, or simply disappear. 'Oh, he was shipped out', or 'He went home last night' was the explanation. They all knew it was a lie. But they figured the guy was so badly beaten he was put in a van and sent to a prison hospital. But they claimed that soon enough, a strange, peculiar smell, faint yet strong enough would come from the outdoor furnace and open dump area. No one knew whether any of it was true, or their imaginations running wild after a little drink or two. All they knew was what they warned me, 'Be careful. You're going into hard times in the worst of the baddest, most evil calabooses in America, a black monster in the middle of the desert, ugly, screaming for more of us defenseless to devour'. 'Be real careful, or you'll wind up a clump of roasted meat thrown into an open garbage pit'."

With the caravan weaving its way through the main 2,500 acre camp cantonment, past barracks, satellite tent cities, auxiliary structures, and classroom buildings, acres of tank training yards, grenade courts, bayonet assault ranges and trenches, it soon merged onto Murphy Canyon Road. Less than a mile later, it turned off upon the old dirt and gravel Escondido Road leading directly to the stockade's outer entrance, less than a mile away.

"That large dreary, dismal blend of black and white mass down the road there much be there brig," Peter said quietly, pointing.

"Yeah, sticking out of a rattlesnake hole in the hot desert, like a fat middle finger," returned Sunny, disgustedly.

Peter recalled being told the stockade grounds were on the fringes of the Jacques Farm located at the extreme southern corner of Camp Elliott. Originally, the area was used as a bivouac and training area for the 2nd Tank Battalion and 2nd Marine Raider. Since it was so isolated, the bivouac had to be self-sufficient. Easily accessible was slate, a bluish-gray hard, five-grained rock, suitable for building temporary stone warehouses. Evacuated from nearby newly designated slate quarries, large blocks were cut to construct the stockade, originally used as a tank maintenance center, and other minor facilities.

"Lookie yonder, Lieutenant. We're coming up to the inner stockade entrance, the so-called Westgate Entrance where they'll dump us off. More important, out to my right, you can see what appears to be a large furnace, and next to it an open pit."

"Yeah, I see them."

The caravan slowed to a crawl through the wire-mesh fence with razor sharp edged wire topping it off, two armed Navy sentries standing beside their smart-looking guardhouse waving them forward. Less than 50 yards across the desert floor, at a roundabout before the sunlight-lapped triple rusty iron gates, more than 20 feet high tall, the Black Marias pulled up, then switched their motors off. Waiting outside the gates was a contingent of some two-dozen unsmiling MPs waiting for the prisoners to disembark.

As the doors of the large buses opened, and the suddenly docile prisoners began to slowly and orderly descend the steps of the opened doors, a shrill cry rang out from someone, obviously an officer, hurrying past the MPs lined up, now standing at full attention.

"In double rows, convicts, double rows! No talking! Your bags at your feet!"

Since Peter and Sunny sat next to each other near the front of the bus, they were among the first six to disembark.

"The air is oven hot," Peter whispered.

Ambling to line up in the first row alongside of Sunny, Peter noted how stone-cold silent the roundabout area before the stockade's entrance was. In addition, not a single inch of shade was anywhere to be seen. He continued,

"I can see why they call this outlying area of Elliott the 'Silent Region'. Hot and no shade. Perfect."

As Peter glanced around, he could hardly believe what he saw.

"Pure medieval," he muttered quietly, recalling the photo images the students were shown in the graduate pre-Renaissance classes he enrolled in at the University of California, Berkeley years before.

"Not exactly a splendid Renaissance style edifice," he thought. "If any one word comes to mind to describe this gray ghost, it has to be 'dilapidation'."

Sunny, who had remained silence since, he, too, had alighted the bus, whispered,

"Should be leveled, totally completed, without any vestige it had ever existed."

Turning half-around to study his new friend, Peter whispered in return,

"Amazing your vocabulary, young private. I'm impressed."

So, there it was, the ominous and hideous weather-beaten two-story cage of countless iron-barred casemates and casements. Protruding from an old abandoned drill ground, the infamous "brig", the so-called "living tomb", or "tomb of the living dead", the most dreaded place on the Camp Elliott grounds had an "aura' of mystery about it. Not only did it appear as a hodge-podge of dull 15th and 16th century architectural facades, but also an engineering construction monstrosity of what a prison in America must have looked like a hundred years before.

From ground up, the lower half of the single building was erected with large slabs of slate, old brick, and stone blocks, the entire facility surrounded by double barbed wire fences.

"Eerie, huh?" Sunny whispered.

"Damn," Peter reflected wide-eyed, "Not only does it look merciless, but even out here in the open desert air, the whole atmosphere stinks pre-World War I fortress. What kind of another world am I being locked away in? And, just look at those lined-up lifeless MPs, as frozen zombie-like graveyard statues, adding to the overall stench of decaying flesh."

"Wow!" exclaimed Sunny, "Just look at those modern metal guard towers!"

At every 75 yards, rose what appeared to be spanking-new glass-enclosed cabin campaniles without bells, all more than 50 feet tall. Within, the towers looming over the stockade each contained two heavy caliber machine guns, two large search lights, a telephone, and two guards, three shifts, 24 hours a day.

"Kinda doesn't encourage you to jump the wall, do they? And, by the way, what's the big stink, Lieutenant?"

"Yup. Dunno. You could smell it once the Black Marias entered this part of the country. I have no idea, Private," Peter responded, adding, "The scent of breathing corpses, I'm afraid."

Indeed, a pungent, puzzling reek suffused the air, an odorous smell unto itself suggesting peril if solidification occurred.

"DOCUMENTS! TRAVEL PAPERS! IDENTIFICATION PAPERS!!" screamed a pudgy little officer in his mid-50s as he exited the stockade entrance and hurried around the lined-up MPs standing at attention.

"SHOW ME YOUR PAPERS CLEARLY OVER YOUR HEADS. FORM ONE LINE TO ENTER. ONE LINE!! PAPERS IN ONE HAND OVERHEAD. HAND TO OFICE AT THE GATE."

As the prisoners gathered their papers and lined up, one hand holding their bags, the other overhead holding the documents and IDs, Sunny, standing behind Peter, whispered,

"I never understood the difference between a 'brig' and a 'stockade'. They're used for the same place, right? I mean, a brig is a stockade, and when you're told you're going to the stockade, you're going to a brig. Correct?"

Peter smiled slightly.

"A military brig is basically a jail, a guardhouse. It's not like putting you in Alcatraz or San Quentin with a bunch of gangsters, rapists, and ax murderers. We're supposed to be going into a minimum-security facility with other Marines who have also done things that are violations of the Marine code of conduct. Nothing violent. Just things like being off base longer than you were supposed to be. Drunkenness. Fighting. Shoplifting. These kinds of petty crimes."

"Well, if so, what's a stockade?"

"Well, it too is a 'holding area' or place of brief incarceration for minor offenses. Colloquially, that temporary jail is called the guardhouse or stockade. 'Brig' is the historic term used by Naval and Marine forces. Down the road there, over at Miramar, is the huge Naval brig. Generally, though, the brig is the term used for barred confinement aboard any vessel."

As the long line of prisoners slowly tread its way toward the main entrance gate of the high-walled stockade, Peter marveled at how unsightly the windowless entrance appeared. A poorly sculptured false arch over the formidable black steel door dominated the facade.

"Just like a western cowboy movie fort. Some imagination. All this place needs is moat. Yes, it should be dismantled and leveled."

Just then, after Peter and Sunny handed over their travel documents and identification papers, the screaming figure startled Peter by walking up to him, saying with a sarcastic smirk,

"Ah, so you're here at least, Mad Ghoul!"

Stunned, Peter stepped back in a japer of surprise and wonder, acknowledged the greeting, but more to observe the arrogant officer. And, what a sight greeted him.

"Oh, my good-humouredness, St. James, Heavenly Protector of Principle and Patriotism, who is this?" Peter asked in a mixture of amazement and surprise.

A plump, smallish Captain, tight-lipped and sallow-complexioned with a short, carefully trimmed mustache dominating his putrid face, glared up curiously at him through enormously thick-lensed pince-nez eye glasses. With a whistle on a thin cord dangling from his neck, the

USMC officer referred to the clipboard and list of arriving inmates and said in a high-pitched voice,

"You are placed in solitary confinement. All VIP prisoners are treated thus. Tomorrow, I'll call for you to meet with me. Inside you'll be escorted to the isolation unit and fed there, Mr. Mad Ghoul."

Just as Peter was to respond, two truckloads of newly arrived Southern California prisoners drove up behind the parked Marias, the drivers turning their motors off.

"To be processed after us," someone in the line commented.

"Then shipped off to nearby labor camps, for sure," someone else added.

Peter was more fascinated with the Captain who was hurrying away to line up the additional hundred or so inmates for special movement processing.

"Just look at that appendage to the Marine Corps. Mousy little creep. It has to be over 100 degrees this morning and the idiot is wearing yellow Navy foul weather clothing," Peter whispered to Sunny, also thunderstruck with the encounter. "He's got on a long waterproof coat, waterproof trousers and arctics, large waterproof overshoes! Ever seen anything like that? He looks like a Canadian rodeo clown! All that's missing on him is a sou'wester, an oiled canvas cap with a flap at the back worn in stormy weather! Holy cow! Don't know whether to laugh, cry, or throw up."

Sunny, wide-eyed, mused,

"And I bet he's wearing woolen undies, woolen socks! And, undoubtedly suspenders for his trousers!"

"Suspenders AND a belt!" Peter said softly.

As the two chuckled, Sunny added,

"He strikes me as the type the more you tell him, the louder he laughs. And, look at how far that stout snout projects out of that homely face."

"Aw, poor guy, we've got to stop laughing at him. After all, he's a human being."

"Like hell," Sunny concluded the ridicule.

As the single-file prisoners were led into the stockade, the first impression Peter had was one of an unusual concentration of power and terror confined narrowly in one stockade structure.

Upon entering the stockade, and signing the Log of Admittance, the single file of prisoners entered and exited the prison's sally port, the rear gate of the short underground passage from the outer world to the inner core of prison, then locked into a communal cell that was under point-blank gunfire.

After being counted for the third time that morning, and responding to a fourth roll call, the large assemblage was handed week-old bread, a container of drinking water, and a packet of jam. This would suffice until afternoon mealtime the following morning.

From the communal cell, the troops were led by triple sentries of statue-like MPs to the stockade main courtyard, then to the basement where the cells were located. Peter immediately noticed that if an officer or MP closed the main basement door forcefully from the outside steps, the air pressure affected one's ears. The corridor, and long aisle or passageway between individual cells in a row was deathly silent. Sunny turned, glancing at Peter, and noted an expression on his face, suggesting intellectual interest mixed with suppressed anger. It was very dark.

As the men were led down the passageway, and assigned to cells, most two to a cell, then one to a cell, Peter suddenly realized how cold it was. Assigned one to himself, next to Sunny's, Peter could barely tell its content in the dark. For a long moment, he stood like a shadow, motionless. Its width was measured from the tip of his right hand to the full length, plus an additional 12" to 15" of his left hand. His metal bed with a single blanket and no pillow was bolted to the stone wall.

The happy chatter the prisoners engaged in on the journey from Camp Stoneman to the Camp Elliott stockade ceased the moment they disembarked single-file from each of the Black Marias in front of the entrance.

Now, not a sound could be heard in the brig's windowless cells, every Marine sitting or lying back on his narrow metal bed. Most were suddenly confused and frightened, never having been incarcerated in such dreary conditions. Since no one knew when he would eat again, most conserved his bread, jam, and drinking water. Furthermore, it hadn't escaped a single prisoner how undisciplined and unruly the prison guards appeared to be. All wore MP uniforms, smoking on duty, playing cards, their feet on tables and desks, talking and laughing loudly, cursing, their dress unkempt and slovenly.

Although the interior rooms, floors, corridors, stairs, stairways, and stairwells were neither littered nor desultory, all were unclean, almost filthy. No matter where one looked, the area was forlorn and somehow disheveled.

Peter, meanwhile, lay down on his narrow steel bed, his blanket serving as his pillow. Staring into the pitch darkness of his putrid cell, wondering what his invisible ceiling looked like, his thoughts were too vibrant for a short nap. He knew MPs were posted at every cross-corridor, that not one was armed, that the door to his cell was heavy ironbound, with a small peephole.

As he lay there in the cold with his eyes open, fixated upon the blackness of his small cell, Peter half-smiled. He was always felt an uneasiness when duty called him to deal with prison personnel. It certainly wasn't fear from possible physical dangers that perturbed him. No prison inmate ever scared him, even the most violent in solitary confinement that he had to interview. He knew what all prison guards know: If you show respect, you receive respect in turn. No, his reluctance was a mixture of awe, curiosity, and nausea. It was due to his realization that the state and federal government were unable to provide the necessary rehabilitation to reduce human suffering of the criminal. Peter certainly didn't excuse criminal behavior, but was upset by society's indifference to it. What was so sad was the indifference of the American public to provide psychological relief for those in locked up cages of steel bars behind thick concrete walls.

"I'm now alone, totally and absolutely along," he reflected. "There's no one in here to look to, no one to tell me what to do. I'll never hear a friend whisper 'almond'. I have to figure all this out by myself. Once I learn what I have to, I'll have to bust out all by myself."

Although it was mid-morning, and much too early to be forced to bed, Peter found there was nothing he could do or say. He was a prisoner, a nonentity, and unless he behaved himself, might not eat again for a few days. Gradually, his thoughts returned to those he loved the most, his parents, grandparents, and extended family, and, of course, Joan, whom he believed he had lost forever.

After a few moments of struggling to bring himself back to reality, Peter failed and slowly fell into a long deep sleep that lasted well into the early hours of the next morning.

CHAPTER FOURTEEN

-

The Interview

Upon gradually awakening in the wee hours of the following morning, Peter, after an almost 14 hours of solid sleep, yearned for a hot cup of Java. Pan-fried eggs, sunny-side up would be nice, but not as critical as a large cup of steaming coffee. Maybe prior to or immediately after his pending meeting with Captain Hofmeister. He still wondered why he had been singled out for a one-on-one session with the Stockade's warden.

As he lay back, eyes wide open, on the cold metal cot bolted to the wall, all he could do was wait patiently until summoned, and reflect upon how he would carry out his assignment. He was fully aware that the only way to survive as he moved forward was to keep his wits at their peak.

To do that successfully, he had to have a daily routine, every minute of which was devoted to ensure not being detected. He had to remain flexible, lest he be recognized as the USN Lieutenant who thwarted the attempt on Bob Hope's life and captured the Mad Ghoul. His assignment depended upon confounding the approach of anyone who knew him personally.

To prepare for such an eventuality, he had developed friendships with a number of the prisoners who would willingly serve as lookouts. With sufficient warning, he could clear the area. He simply had to be adept at switching behavior if an emergency surfaced. Most importantly, he had to trust his first impressions of all strangers, and act upon them accordingly, without reservation or qualification.

By 7:00am, Peter heard the sound of footsteps along the corridor. As he quivered, he quickly roused himself, and then followed the MP from the near-freezing condition of the cell upstairs into the sweltering heat of the first-floor corridor to Captain Hofmeister's office. There, continuing to shiver slightly, he gratefully stood under a cooling ceiling fan fanning the hot stockade air. Patiently, he waited to be admitted into the captain's office.

Within minutes, the door swung open and Captain Hofmeister stood silently studying Peter. And, all that the hungry Lieutenant saw in a glance was a freshly shaven, mustached little man wearing funny-looking glasses. As the captain stood rigidly in the doorframe, unsmiling and eyes glaring, he was dressed immaculately in his starched, recently pressed USMC military police uniform. Again, Peter saw a face that looked old, sensing that beneath the imposing appearance of freshness, cleanliness, and the smell of starch, was a neurotic fussiness, an inherent nervousness based upon fear.

Peter sighed, "This nervous-looking donkey isn't going to be of help in a pinch, and he's more of a cheap carnival clown than a respected Marine officer, more a buffoon than a systematic murderer."

Nothing, absolutely nothing, neither a scintilla of a moment, nor a single detail of the captain and his office escaped Peter.

A long, large office, barren with the exception of two framed photographs, one of General Dwight Eisenhower, the other of General Douglas McArthur on the wall behind his desk, greeted Peter as an MP ushered him in. Austere, walls and ceiling painted the same stark white, a single window opened out on the small, enclosed winter garden. Standing there in the dazzling sunlight flooding the room was Captain Hofmeister, his hands clenched behind his back. The only sounds Peter could distinguish were the Captain's heavy breathing, and a horrid low hissing from a small bulging potbellied stove a few feet from his desk, emitting thin peels of white smoke from a smoldering fire.

"Well, look at that," Peter mused. "It's over 100 degrees outside, even hotter in here, and this florid fool has a fire-burning stove next to his desk! If this isn't something. The stove's smoke is spiraling around MacArthur and Eisenhower, Oh, if I only had a camera!"

After another long minute of silence, Captain Hofmeister slowly turned around. Although he looked placid, Peter sensed the man was ill in some way. With an expression of deadly seriousness, he waved his hand, motioning for Peter to sit down.

As Peter sat down, the aroma of fresh brewing coffee reached him from an office or workroom next door.

Another 30 seconds of silence intervened during which time the captain studied the young Lieutenant in a glaring manner.

Finally, Hofmeister said in an almost high-pitched, squeaky voice, "So, Mr. Mad Ghoul, you enjoy the killing, I see."

The question was so innocuous, so meaningless, Peter didn't even hear it, as he focused on the warden's haggard, troubled eyes.

With an additional 30 seconds of silence slipping by as the captain awaited a response, Peter finally asked, "Huh?"

"Well, Mad Ghoul, we have an army of convicts here to choose from. Kill as many as you like."

"What?"

"Oh, I make merry. I wisecrack with you."

Peter thought, "This man is so senseless, so stupid, so silly. In God's name, what sort of murdering conspirator are you?"

Suddenly, Captain Hofmeister was standing very correctly, very stiffly. Then, with his hand clasped behind his back, he walked around his desk, stood over Peter for a moment, and then leaned back on it, half-sitting on its edge.

As the captain gazed grimly at the lieutenant for the second time, Peter sensed there could be no doubt that something unusual was going on in the stockade. And, the intentional dehumanization of soldiers with minor offenses was the least of the stockade's offenses.

"Mad Ghoul, our favorite trick around here for those who misbehave badly is injecting them with a scoop of aviation fuel. After one injection, no more trouble."

"And meanwhile," responded Peter, "prisoners are beaten, humiliated and terrorized into obedience."

"Why, of course. What's wrong with that? And in this prison, we intersperse endless shouting of orders, endless punches in the solar plexuses, endless insults in names, accusations, and catcalls. We shock, here."

"Most sobering, most sobering!" Peter said as an afterthought. Looking up into Captain Hofmeister's tight-lipped, sallow-complexioned dark brown eyes, protruding and enlarged three times their natural size by the thick lenses of his French spectacles, the Lieutenant understood he was now incarcerated in a model of authoritarianism. And, the man's deep wrinkles, mouth tightly closed with determination, and eyes burning with pyre-like intensities, testified there was neither a spark of human graciousness about the man nor a hint of a soft smile.

"No," Peter concluded, "This is a place of terror and blood, and blood and terror."

Suddenly, the abrupt opening of the office door behind Peter startled him. As he turned to the sound, two hefty-looking men in civilian clothing hurriedly approached him. Although neither was armed, one carried a thin black briefcase.

"Lieutenant Toscanini," one demanded loudly. "The Mad Ghoul? Let's go!"

Peter, who had foreseen such a moment, remained perfectly still and expressionless. He reflected as he studied them. "Smiling, frowning, or expressing fear may suggest I have no idea what he's insinuating. Remaining completely composed, admitting to nothing, pretending automatism, being slumberous, or a somnambulist, may suggest I am indeed am the Ghoul and don't care if they know it or not."

Of course, the Lieutenant understood instantly who they were, and why they had come. Glancing at Hofmeister, he noticed a smug smile crossing the captain's lips.

"The secret police of the Military Police, akin to the Gestapo. No badges, no uniforms, no paperwork. Only cold, silent, unfeeling intensity, the sons-of-_____s. They have no formal name. Their only responsibilities consist of monitoring all court martial proceedings and corruption or illegal activities of the MPs."

Yet, Peter was ambivalent.

"If these guys are the secret police of the military police, where are their usual telltale signs?"

First to appear was demanding impatience:

"UP! You're coming with us! Now! Let's go! RIGHT NOW!"

A second sign was the other "civilian" sitting arrogantly at Hofmeister's desk calmly, coldly, and methodically thumbing through a small pile of military personnel records from the thin briefcase he was carrying as the captain stood meekly a few feet away without comment.

As Peter was hurried out of Hofmeister's office and escorted down the corridor to the end of the stockade's administrative unit, a number of armed MPs flanked the entrance to a door without a sign bearing its purpose.

The civilian knocked, while clutching Peter's elbow. Someone within shouted, "Enter."

To Peter, the large windowless was being used as some sort of a conference room by the captain. In the center, stood a wide table capable of seating eight. Peter was ordered to sit across from the other side where the two civilians and Captain Hofmeister sat, the file from the briefcase on the table in front of the middle man. No one else was present.

For more than several minutes, the three sat staring at the Lieutenant. Peter stared back, expressionless. He understood exactly what was happening. They were highly suspicious of him. Was this the notorious Mad Ghoul associate who was soon to be court marshaled and, in all probability, sentenced to death? Even with careful examination, the three couldn't make up their minds. It was an ancient technique, designed to both instill fear, and produce feelings of anxious inferiority while measuring his reactions for further interrogation methods to be employed at later sessions.

At this point, Captain Hofmeister, with a friendly smile on his lips, stood up, and, as he replaced his eyeglasses with a monocle in his eye, began to speak in a surprisingly soft, almost human tone.

"We have questions. Answer the truth. This is not the Spanish Inquisition. They are inquisitors. We have no tribunal. Just give the true answers and we'll learn if we have work for you. Or, you wait for trial in isolation, solitary confinement. Tell us the truth."

While thoughts raced through Peter's head, he listened, but remained silent. He said nothing. Hofmeister whispered something into the ears of the civilian who had been thumbing through the personnel files on the table, then walked out without so much as glancing at Peter.

"So, Mr. Ghoul," the civilian-leader said soothingly, "Let's begin this interview with your thoughts about Pavuvu Island."

"Certainly. The Japanese didn't even want it. Malaria-carrying mosquitos, worthless kunai grass with razor-sharp bandsaw edges, capable of cutting men into long vertical strips, coconuts falling on you, sometimes, if head-hits, pure bush, a wilderness, knee-deep mud, devoid of anything valuable, always hot, steamy, smell of death, billions of land crabs, trillions of rats, etc. etc. Frankly, I'd rather talk about my impressions of 'Jimbo's Bop City Jazz Club on Fillmore Street in San Francisco, and what it was like between midnight and 6:00am."

"We have no interest in 'Jimbo's', Lieutenant Toscanini. Tell us, instead, how gastroenteritis sneaked into your gut and racked your bowels with enervating dysentery, which, in turn, led you to ghoulish murders. Right?"

Peter remained stone cold silent and expressionless. If anything, and as difficult as it was, he feigned indifference, as if caught in guilt. In reality, he was seething with anger at the insulting arrogance of two military police members posing as civilians who may indeed have been the murderers themselves.

"The stockade, Lieutenant, is divided into three different camps, A, B, and C, within the walls. On the main yard, barbed wire fences separate the three spaces. All are guarded by strategically placed machine guns and sentries placed in perfect detention positions. The three areas are the maximum-security yard and housing; the minimum protection recreation area, and the General Infirmary compound which is the closest to the road and beyond the barbed wire adjacent to the other two camps. Because we understand your training, Mad Ghoul, is medical, you'll be assigned work duty in the infirmary, where staff is desperately needed. The offices of the doctors and nurses are there. The 'maximums' never leave the stockade. The 'minimums', the workers, form groups every morning and are sent out to supply labor in San Diego County, but mostly on all the main surrounding bases. Some go in buses more than 100 miles away for special military jobs, returning a week later. They work in a variety of jobs supplementing paid civilian help in quarries, roads, and odd construction sites. Those prisoners are allowed canteen privileges, especially purchasing cigarettes."

Peter hoped the civilian was correct indicating he would be working in the infirmary. From past experiences, he knew the General Infirmary was the only place where the prisoners of various camps could meet for a few moments.

Suddenly jolted from thought, Peter heard a horrifying, piercing shriek followed by a succession of rapid, loud screeches, ending with a long, painful howl that faded into silence. Peter looked past the two seated civilians as if his eyesight could penetrate the room's walls and see down the long corridor. The two MPs facing him remained stoical and impassive. Peter had never before heard such a desperate, blood-curdling scream. Only someone being tortured beyond human endurance could have emitted such a sound.

Only one word came to mind, "Torture!"

Unfazed by the sound and concerned whether Peter was shaken by it, the lead MP continued abruptly,

"Answer when asked, after considering that the least resistance will be answered by harsh methods. Before I begin, is there a question you care to direct to us?"

"When do I eat?" Peter asked, nonplused. "Or if you won't feed me, how about a cup of coffee?"

The two civilians stared at the Lieutenant incredulously.

For a moment, Peter stared back, then said quietly, "Oh for Christ's sake, it's been over 30 hours since I've had a meal or coffee. Or, maybe it's true, what the prisoners are saying about this so-called 'simple guardhouse', this harmless 'minimum security brig' for irresponsible young men who went AWOL for a few hours, that the way you treat prisoners but for soldiers who have been condemned to punishment by and at the whims of their own officers--brutal, sadistic, cruel, inhuman. If so, inhumanity is not unique with or restricted to the Japanese or Nazi SS and Gestapo."

Again, the two civilians, with the hint of fury in their eyes, stared laser holes through Peter. After a long moment, the one leading the interview said in a low, slow, dull voice, "We may be stiff, controlled, tough administrators. But I assure you, Lieutenant Toscanini, we are not sinister or evil. Like all stockades, there is much noise here, shouting, screaming, and babbling. But, there is no murder here, as has been rumored. There isn't even bruising brutality or special torture, as far as we can see. Never have we witnessed suffering torment, other than the occasional complaint of not having a cup of coffee for 24 hours."

Peter sat back and glared at the civilian. Then, he asked quietly, "Can you tell me your names and ranks?"

"No, we may not."

Then, after a short pause in which the civilian glanced down at a file he had before him, he said, "In this interview, I ask a few questions, primarily about your medical background and experience. Be specific in your responses. If you do not lie or exaggerate, this will require only a few minutes. You'll then be determined for work or remanded to your cell until the court-martial. Either way, you'll then have your coffee and eat. So, let's begin."

Again, a pause, as the interrogator looked up at Peter with the barest hint of a smile.

"In one statement, describe where and how you grew up; why you chose to join the Hospital Corps, hoping to be a corpsman; then, after that, pharmacist's mate third class; how you wound up in the Naval Hospital in Seattle, learning first aid and minor surgery; the understanding you gained of difficult autopsies; the amount of exposure you had of everything in the hospital environment; and, in this phase of the questioning, why you believe you were selected for the Fleet, Marine Force back at Camp Pendleton."

For a brief moment in time, Peter was quietly pleased. In responding to questions about his early years, he pleasantly reminisced about favorite people and significant events and changes that impacted his life. He responded, "Well, from Corps School, I went to Hospital in Seattle, as you know. The Corpsmen were interns there. In those days before the war, they moved you from ward to ward knowing you would be doing a variety of medical functions. So, it was a good teaching process. I learned first aid and minor surgery. I even did autopsies."

"It was at that point they began selecting the people for the Fleet Marine Force. Somehow, after spending 10 or 12 weeks at the hospital, I was transferred to the FMF at Pendleton."

"I was happy about it. I felt it would give me an opportunity to learn more than I was learning in the Naval Hospital. I wanted to get out in the field and have a little independence. I looked forward to it, especially since I had taken a course as a junior college freshman in Introduction to Psychology and I loved reading Freud and Jung's concepts about the unconscious mind and its motivations. But, to get back to the point, in pre-war times, the independent corpsman was a doctor without a license and you could do just about what you had to do in the field. I never felt that I was at a loss as to what to do in certain situations or conditions."

"On my transfer to Pendleton in the summer of '42, I trained in what is the Field Medical Service School. The training was terrific. They were trying to put into our minds enough information to be able to do our jobs in the field and the instructors were very dedicated. It certainly wasn't near as polished as it is today. In those days, the theory was the same but we didn't have the high-tech things. We didn't have the dummies to practice with that you find today. However, there was enough there to do and we had enough accidents to patch up so we got the message quite loud and clear."

"So you see, it was basically aid and minor surgery. We had had all the schooling they could pump into us at Corps School, and it was trauma training mostly. If you had to encounter illness or disease, the training for those was pretty basic because there was only so much you could do for that. During each phase of my activity, I had the opportunity to work at sick call, setting some Thompson leg splints, and doing some things that later would become very important."

With such enthusiastic responses, the two civilians leaned back in their chairs and actually chuckled, surprising Peter.

The leader of the two commented barely audible, "You're doing fine, Lieutenant. Just a few more questions, then you'll have your breakfast. But, now, we're going to bypass your weapons training, assault unit medical work, and your reassignment from the 11th Regiment of the 1st Marine Division to G Company, 2nd Battalion, 5th Regiment, 1st Marine Division. What we're most interested in is how you were most certainly going to be killed by the Japanese."

"Yes. We had a complete briefing before the Guadalcanal assault. The night before, on board our troop transport, our company commander, Colonel Bill Desrosiers, told our entire company that we were expendable, but we already knew that. It didn't make for too good an evening."

"In the meantime, the Zeroes were doing their thing. We were a small ship, so they weren't trying to get us, but I stood on the top deck of that LST and watched one of them 100 feet from us trying to make a turn into a capital ship and one of the guys on our LST knocked him down. His name was Pocani. He was running a 20mm hand-operated gun that doesn't carry too many rounds. When the Zero was hit, I saw the pilot try to open his canopy, but he couldn't or three nights before we were ashore."

"The day of the assault, we discharged from the tank deck. I think mine was the fourth amphibious tractor out. I didn't know what I was doing in the front row. When we hit the beach, we were very surprised to lose only one man early that morning."

"Then, you went ashore on Guadalcanal to do your medical work?"

"Yes. I went ashore with the full pack of medical supplies, my .45 pistol, and rations, pretty near everything to survive for a week or 10 days in the event we weren't resupplied. We were pretty well equipped.

"When you came ashore, did you have a 'snooperscope', which was just recently developed?"

"Yes, we were among the first to test it."

"I'm curious. Not for the record, but to satisfy my own curiosity, how did you use the 'snooperscope' and how do you judge it?"

"Well, you could mount it on a light machine gun and snoop at night with infrared and see things moving. You could also mount the scope on a springfield that had a backpack sniperscope and batteries for power. Enemy soldiers would show up fuzzy and once you got them in your scope, you had them. It took the Japanese a long time to figure that one out. We also had the rocket ships that could fire ashore and they did a lot of damage."

"For your work here in the stockade, tell us about the care you took with your actual first casualty."

"Well, during our advance into the near jungle off the Henderson Airfield, a sniper shot the lead man in our company with a small caliber Japanese rifle. I thought I could save him because he was talking to me, but he was just too far gone and as hard as I tried, I couldn't bring him back. He was lying on his right chest and was drowning in his own blood when I knelt next to him. While I was working on him, I came the closest I ever came to being killed next to when I got myself hurt later on. I literally looked down the rifle of a Japanese and he did not fire on me."

"In that company had replacements with us and a number of Marines who were unfamiliar with warfare. They were well trained, but it takes a little while before you get to be a veteran out there. An elderly Japanese woman had come out of a nearby cave and pulled the sniper in after we wounded him and he fell from a palm tree. We did not fire on her and I think that was because we looked upon women differently.

Later in the Guadalcanal and New Georgia campaigns, we changed radically when we saw women, young and old, shooting at us. But at that time, our group didn't fire on her. A few hours later, when I went after another of our boys, the Japanese didn't fire on me."

"Interesting. You say you looked up and saw a Jap aiming his rifle at you?"

"Yes. I could tell the caliber of the rifle, maybe as close as 20 yards. And, I knew what I was up against. I thought, 'I'm in deep trouble now.' But after I couldn't do any more for him, I calmly covered him, turned around and walked behind a big rock. And then all hell broke loose. But I didn't even get shot at. I suspect that they didn't fire on me because we hadn't fired on that elderly woman."

"There's no doubt in my mind that I never came as close to death as I did that morning because they had me and there was no place to go. The dead Marine had a BAR and if I picked up the automatic rifle, I would have been dead in an instant. Had I gone for my .45, I could never have hit that soldier in the cave or the one down the path looking at me. So, I just walked away. We ended up closing that cave with a satchel charge and kept on going."

"And, after that?"

"Well, I was always, in one way or another, in a full-scale war. For months, it was an absolute continuous battle. My exposure was in every fight. In those days, if someone was wounded out in front of the lines, as a corpsman, I had important things to consider. If I exposed myself and was nailed, the rest of my company lost their corpsman. So they were not too happy to see me go out any more than I was happy to go out. But the decision was mine, not the sergeant's. I always said, 'I'll go. Give me someone in front, and someone behind me. We'll bust getting to the wounded guy.' Once there, I did what I could."

"Well, Lieutenant, here at Elliott, you'll be assigned to the infirmary to continue your corpsman work. No surgeries, no heavy-duty medical work. Guys in medicine rarely come through and when they do, they do a little time, and are then quickly scooped up and sent to the front lines, usually in the Pacific. No, you'll be put to good use here until your court martial."

As Peter gazed at him, the civilian interrogator said, "Go get your coffee and something to eat. You start tomorrow. You'll be awakened at 4:00am, breakfast, and report for duty under the watch of an MP. Since you're facing the death penalty if found guilty, 24-hour surveillance is ordered. Even at work in the infirmary. We'll escort you back to your cell where you'll spend the rest of the day."

After being escorted by the two mysterious civilians to the stockade's kitchen for his first meal in more than 30 hours, Peter was unceremoniously turned over to three surly, gruff-looking MPs. Without so much as a word or glance, the sergeant pointed down a long corridor to a door that led down the steps back to his windowless basement cell.

Halfway down the dim-lighted stairwell, Peter heard his second bloodcurdling screams from somewhere in the basement.

"Only some poor fellow in abject, wretched terror of pain or terror was capable or releasing such a sound," Peter thought to himself. Glancing at the three MPs, he saw that none of the three were moved in the least.

Reaching the basement corridor, Peter heard a louder, more intense shrieking that appeared to emanate from behind an iron-bound door where a grimacing armed sentry eyed the passing four-member party with disdain.

"Stoical bastard," Peter thought to himself. "Not a civilized military man in the whole lot. Seeing him, I must be dreaming or in some Gestapo moving of the 1930's."

As the MP sergeant shoved the massive, weighty master stockade key into the cell lock, swinging the iron door, and firmly pushing Peter in, the Lieutenant once again was sickened by the terrible suffocating odor. Then, the door was swung closed and the lock clicked locked.

For several minutes, Peter sat on his metal bed in the coldness of his cell, staring into the darkness. Then, he rose and peered through the door's peephole into the empty, smelly corridor. Of all his possible thoughts, he focused upon his new friend and train-partner from Camp Stoneman, and now Elliott Brig cell neighbor, Private Daniel Michael Marino, from Astoria, Washington. Peter hadn't heard or seen neither hide nor hair of Sunny. Not a hint of a whisper from his cell neighbor. All the undercover Lieutenant could reflect upon was, "God only knows how many mouths opened in excruciating painful screams in this basement that no one ever heard."

CHAPTER FIFTEEN

-

The Infirmary -- An Abyss?

That afternoon, Peter lay on his back, dozing off intermittently as his mind was flooded in a myriad of thoughts, half-dreams and reminiscences. For hours, faces and events floated past him, some hovering and lingering longer than hours. Despite feeling strangely emotionless and detached, he couldn't sleep.

A deep silence had settled over the stockage, the air so still he could hear the heavy breathing of napping nearby neighboring prisoners. One thing was certain, he thought feverishly, "Serving as an undercover agent, living under the same conditions as the inmates, deceiving fellow incarcerated Marines who trust me, is the greatest challenge of my life. The die has been cast. All I can do now is learn what I can and ride out whatever's coming. Meanwhile, I wait for someone to whisper 'almond' in my ear, that magic noun describing an edible, nutlike kernel. Meanwhile, I live a silent nightmare."

The following morning, as the first rays of sunup ascended the eastern hills of Camp Elliott, Peter was an unbearable specimen of human tension. In additional to being hungry and yearning for a cup of steaming hot coffee, he was disheveled after a sleepless night of twisting and turning and dismayed he hadn't had a haircut in over a month or a shave in three days. He felt as awful as he thought he looked. Endless thoughts of little or no consequence only made matters worse.

Precisely at 6:00am, Peter, hearing the lock of his cell door double-click, then swing open, jumped stiffly but quickly to his feet. Standing unannounced on the threshold was Captain Hofmeister, hands clenched behind his back, the hint of a grin hesitating around his lips. An armed

Marine accompanying the captain stood behind him, partly in the corridor, watching, appearing mean and hard in a lipid sort of way.

"Come, you Ghoul, you Mad Ghoul!", ordered Hofmeister, harshly. "You'll eat, shower, shave, and dress, instead of a tramp, a U.S. Navy Corpsman."

Peter studied the captain decidedly.

"That silly, stupid, son-of-a-bitch is dressed immaculately in his stiff, starched military uniform, weighed down by varying insignias, medals, emblems, and decorations. But, oh God, he is still as homespun and homely as when I first laid eyes on the freak."

"What are you looking at?" demanded Hofmeister angrily. "Put your shoes on and COME!"

Peter, shoving his socked feet into his Camp Stoneman-issued shoes, thought to himself, "I'll tell you what I'm looking at. An ugly reptile recently removed from a bottle of mothballs."

Led leisurely back down the corridor to the stairwell leading to the main floor and General Infirmary, Hofmeister reminded Peter, "The kitchen is next door to camp where you will be henceforth quartered with the patients and convalescents you in a special single cell. There, you have canteen and cigarettes. The dentist has his offices there, although all we have here is a pair of pincers for extracting with a little anesthetic. Prisoner sits down and dentist, who comes here twice a week from Pendleton, asks, 'Which tooth hurts'? 'You sure that's the one?' And before the poor prisoner knows what's happening, he suddenly howls in pain as a tooth goes missing!"

With that, Captain Hofmeister giggled. "By the way, you see black market activity going on, pay no attention. It's none of your business. Money exercises attraction and, Mr. Bad Ghoul, you are to pretend you see nothing, or you will be in a big pain."

"What do you specialize in, in case you want to purchase?"

"Food, always, for prisoner watches, fountain pens, tobacco, a few other things. Special food requests by the convicts make the MP sentries of the guard are non-commissioned officers. You talk about what they are doing, you will pay dearly, perhaps the removal of an eye or leg or arm."

"I get it, Captain."

"No one is scrupulous around here, not even the doctors and corpsmen, like yourself. However, faced with the iniquities of rogues and criminals, we react as one body. We don't both with justice, legal military etiquette justice. We prefer to punish our black sheep ourselves."

The Camp B dispensary, first-aid infirmary was next door to the stockade kitchen, less than 50 feet down the main corridor between their two entrances. As Peter completed his second cup of steaming hot coffee, after a reasonably good breakfast, Captain Hofmeister said as he stood up from the kitchen table, "Ready to assist with minor surgery in the sick bay?"

Surprised, Peter responded almost inaudibly, "Sure. It's been a while, but I'll help. Of course!"

"Good, Ghoul. I understand you'll scrub down there to help with an incision and the drainage of an axillary abscess."

As the two exited the kitchen entrance, and Peter was led down the short hallway, Hofmeister hurriedly described the infirmary's chief physician, Dr. Simon Fisherly.

"He's a big man, very precise, cautious, and unhumorous. A West pointer, he practices medicine by the book. We laugh, and he will nod as we do so, 'If in doubt, go by the book! Every pain, every disease, every sickness is described and taught how to heal in the six-volume set of the Navy's Internal Medicine. Just go find it in the index and follow the instructions."

Entering the infirmary, a voice boomed out, "Yes, come in, Captain and Lieutenant."

I was Dr. Fisherly. Standing next to him was a small in stature, frail, thin warrant officer, a clipboard in hand. As the physician pulled his Zippo lighter from his pocket and fumbled with a cigarette, he studied Peter in a sweeping glance.

"So, you are part of the infamous ghoul team the whole Pacific is talking about. And, now you're going to pull duty with me. Well, you may be famous out there, but in here, you're little more than an orderly, and a toilet orderly at that. Newcomers are always assigned night duty first, 7:00PM to 7:00AM. You, plus Officer Campbell here. Tonight, you two get the isolation ward. Between now and then, smoke cigarettes and drink gimlets. For now, Campbell will tour you through our work areas, then show you your more basement cell, Mr. Multiple-Murderer."

With that, Campbell threw Peter a pair of olive-drab "snuggies". And, with bare-faced skepticism, he said in somewhat of a snarl, "Government -issued. Comes in two sizes, large and colossal. Giving you a 'large' because you look skinny to me. So, it'll be like wearing a blanket. And, trust me, you murderer, the 'snuggie' will keep you warm in this freezing tomb."

As Peter slowly began to reconcile the dangers of this undercover assignment, assimilate into his new hospital environment, and confirm, then coalesce a new friendship with a fellow Navy medical officer, he simply smiled at the rude remarks and ignored the epithets characterizing him a multiple-murderer.

In addition to immediately recognizing the sickbay infirmary would serve as a perfect base from which to conduct his probe, Peter, with his usual extraordinary intuitive sense of judging men, knew the chatting, incoherently, indeed, foolishly jabbering warrant officer would be a buddy for the duration of the assignment.

As the duo began the tour of the medical facility, Campbell, continuing to eye Peter skeptically, couldn't stop talking, "Generally speaking, Lieutenant, as you might imagine, healthy young men who wind up here with much gut crud, mind rot, and otherwise crap. The one thing they are all riddled with here at Elliott, especially in the stockade's Promised Land infirmary, are the nuisance symptoms of adolescences and the behaviors they spawn. The scrapes and minor cuts and wounds they come in with are not from bullets, shell fragments, and knives. They are wounds of penetration, perforation, and laceration. Almost all are fighting, as boys do, each other or being attacked by our people. We pour a little sulfanilamide powder into the cuts and tie on small Carlisle bandages. After kissing the bandaged wound, we send them back to their cells."

Peter smiled. He knew almost from the first he would like this feisty man who appeared a few years older than himself.

"Hey, you've got a little pluck and spunk in you," Peter interjected appreciatively, if not admiringly.

"Don't mind admitting I do. Not enough to go around murdering people like you, I hear. But dad did say I had enough in me to fill a thousand turd holes."

Peter again grinned slightly. The warrant officer, despite his grossness, was clean, decent, honest, cautions in manner in fact. He was thankful he had been assigned to work and bunk alongside of him.

"But, in seriousness, Lieutenant, what sticks in my throat day in and night out is seeing men crippled and disfigured and permanently impaired, every one of them in pain even before they face their first Kraut or Nip."

Peter, suddenly alert, debated how far he would go with his questions if his first was answered.

"How is that?"

Campbell, realizing he may have spoken too long and too much. He hesitated, then said softly, "Maybe later…"

Peter knew friendship in a confined entity where there was so much suspicion, distrust, and dishonesty took both time and nurturing to develop. He felt, and appreciated, the impact Warrant Office Campbell made on him, especially since he had never encountered a military officer raking above a noncommissioned officer, but below a commissioned officer sounding so rowdy, brawling, fiercely spirited, and funny. Because Peter knew the man would give him far more than he could return; he wanted nay, needed, to have his affectionate presence near him.

"As you can see, Lieutenant-mad-killer, this crappy wanna-be emergency medical in a penitentiary hole-in-the-wall is part clinic, part bedridden ward, part operating room, part staff sleep quarters, part classroom, and part center for crafts, rehabilitation activities and prevocational skill training center. On some days, we may have as many as 50 inmates in here. Unlike other military infirmaries, outside-of-uniform volunteer personnel are not allowed. We have to do all the work ourselves. So, you and I do the whole show, with me supervising you. One guy ahead of you who disappeared last month, and I printed a sign and put it up at the rehabilitation open space wall. It read, "Cpt. Hofmeister says, 'No bullshit rehabilitation time wasted here. We offer broken knuckles, smashed kneecaps, cracked and missing teeth, and assorted broken head wounds. No empathy, no sympathy, only hard knocks without. 'Rehab' is squarely for the effeminate, timid, and cowardly. Stand up and be a Marine or sit down and be a sissy.

Captain 'Adolph Hitler' Hofmeister'."

Peter chuckled, "How long did it stay up?"

"Until the old bastard came through a few days later. He was furious. I don't know what all happened, but my corpsman Rawley Shipley disappeared that night."

With that casual statement, Peter knew there could be no doubt something akin to murder was going on in the infirmary itself. He tried to think as he was led on the tour. For one thing he noticed, there were more MPs than usual around the corridors. And, having cat-and-mouse conversations to elicit answers from Campbell seemed fruitless. There was more than usual saluting going on. Laughter and idle chatter were missing despite the increasing number of patients being admitted. Peter said nothing as Campbell busied himself with introductions and explanations. The unusual tenseness and officiousness persisted. The patients being escorted in from the stockade cells seemed to carry a wide range of illnesses, injuries, and treatment needs.

With the staff of corpsmen having grown to seven, and physicians to three, Peter heard one medical man say, "As usual, this time of day, they're coming in by the trainload."

"So what?" another responded. "We'll passively treat them quickly and send them back to their cells. No room in our tiny wards. Who's on duty as triage officer today?"

"Felix," someone said.

"That's good. You know how totally imperturbable he is. Like he says, 'Can't save them all.'"

As Peter leaned back against a wall to continue listening in, as well as watching the increasing activity, the warrant officer standing next ot eh Lieutenant, said casually, "This is even better than a tour. All these men with their varying types of needs for recovery need rehabilitation. You can see for yourself. But we think it's phney-baloney stuff for getting out of work or taking required classes. You may know that not until recently, this year of 1944, in fact, the term 'rehabilitation' emerged due to a wonderful program of conditioning and retraining established by Dr. Howard Ruck in New York. Now, months later, 'Rehab' is the focus of treatment in all hospitals, whether military, prison, or general medical in states and cities."

"What about advanced cases of respiratory and intestinal diseases, like the two obviously have sitting and waiting for one of the physicians to see them?"

"They'll be on our afternoon bus to the Camp Pendleton Hospital and their staff will take care of them."

"That's good."

"No, Lieutenant, what you see before you is little more than a clearing station, a first-aid center, to lance and patch everything from blisters to smashed faces, black eyes, and broken noses. We give aspirins for head colds, and merely watch over the ones who cry out in pain. If someone cries out 'medic' or 'corpsman', you run to him, usually for the bedridden it's because they want water. You'll hear men yell at you such things as 'Wait until Ernie Pyle hears about the lousy jobs you corpsmen are doing'. That's the ultimate threat!"

Peter chuckled.

"By the way," continued Campbell, "you'll receive your corpsman badge to wear on your frock front. So, the most you'll administer will be sulfa drugs. In the safe, we have a small amount of life-giving intravenous plasma, just enough, just enough to keep a patient alive until Pendleton is reached."

"When do I start?"

"In a few minutes, actually. Your first assignment is to keep clean and keep in order the medical cupboards across the room, there--with continual use, they're always untidy. All new staff have to do it. In emergencies, I may need to call upon you to apply tourniquets or inject pain-killing morphine or life-saving penicillin."

"Well, Officer Campbell, I'm ready. Just give me a damp rag, cleaner, bucket of water and dry towels. Bring on as many cabinet shelves as you need cleaned."

The warrant officer glanced at him with a slight smile.

"Haven't had someone so overqualified as you serve as a mere orderly."

"I see four coal-burning stoves in here. Anyone bother to clean them? I'll do it. Anything at all to help the sick and injured."

"Let me show you what's in the cabinet. You can get started while I hail a corpsman to bring the towels and water," Campbell said as he led Peter to the closest cabinet.

"Look," he said, as he opened the lock with one of his belt's keys. "Note the contents, all scrambled and in disarray. We have 2"x2" gauze, bandage compresses, acetaesone tablets, sulfurous acids, amydol tablets, atabririe tablets, bile powders, benzidine camphor, calcium chloride, atabrine, DDT, instruments for small wound bandaging, two mortars and pestles, a number of centrifuges, and a dozen or so bottles of anesthesia. Hooked to the wall adjacent the cabinet are a dozen or more stretchers, skeletal traction devices, laundry equipment, and floor to ceiling wall shelving containing several lamps, boxes dental equipment, food trays, bed candles, a medical library.

Each of the infirmary's rooms contains several locked refrigerators, the lead physician-director's office holds the prison's only safe."

"Wow!" exclaimed Peter, "A whole lot of supplies, I'll say."

"Yeah, but not the heavy hospital iron. That stuff is only in designated U.S. Army 'Fixed' Hospitals, for us, the nearest being Camp Pendleton. There, four general hospitals, including convalescent, evacuation, and surgical, are grouped into a single administrative and clinical organization known as a Hospital Center."

After perusing the contents of other wall cabinets in preparation for his initial infirmary assignment, Peter and Warrant Officer Campbell sat down at a small table near Dr. Fisherly's office. For a long moment, both men remained silent as they relaxed, observing the normal sick-call activity, prisoners arriving and departing, and listening to the surmising and speculating of physicians and corpsmen of varying illness, aches and pain complaints. All the while, Peter reflected that the quality of medical attention and response left much to be desired.

Just then, an MP walked up and without comment, handed the warrant officer a sealed envelope. Quickly tearing it open, and scanning it in seconds, he turned to Peter and said, "It's about you. From Headquarters. It reads that for the rest of the day, you're free to relax, settle in within our sick halls. You can't enter the corridors or wander about. You violate those orders and you'll be confined to your basement cell 23 hours a day. But later this afternoon, you're to complete a full physical, then visit our barber shop before being escorted to the supply depot for the standard issue of Corpsman pants, shirts, socks, boots, and hygiene kit."

Peter responded as he continued to gaze at the infirmary activity, "Well, I'm here. No worries about me straying down hallways. I don't do well in isolation cells 23 hours a way, one hour out to jump around. No, sir, that's not for me."

"Well, smiled Campbell, "whether you're who everyone says you are, or not, you've been delivered through the gates of a notorious, nefarious stockade. No, penitentiary is the correct noun. Plenty of guards, gates, barbed wire fences. Whether a stockade or prison or penitentiary or county jail, it's all the same thing: Plenty guards, gates, and barbed wire walls and fences. An abyss for a young solider who's committed a minor crime."

"Oh, Officer Campbell, I don't know if I would refer to it as that," Peter reproved mildly.

"Oh, yeah," waved Campbell, "even a Mad Ghoul murderer will see the extent of an abyss this place is."

Time passed so quickly that Peter all but forgot his stockade surroundings, and the purpose of being there.

As Fall began to break, and winter beginning, the first rains began. On the prison yards, normal standing pools of water overflowed, and minor flooding was the excitement of dull gray days. The first cold snap of the approaching new year had arrived overnight, and the thermometer dropped throughout the Camp Elliott facility, turning the infirmary into a refrigerator.

Peter's enervating regime began to tell on him soon after being introduced to Dr. Fisherly and his Warrant Officer Campbell. For days, even weeks at a time, he worked in a state of semi-consciousness.

"What's wrong with me?" Peter repeatedly asked himself. "Does all confinement turn you into a state where dream and reality blend into each other, or is it only the result of being in this one?"

Then, there occurred a chain of events that seemed so totally disconnected yet flowed so violently that he felt his undercover assignment was bearing fruition.

To remain eagle-eyed focused, Peter carefully scanned the faces of all who entered the infirmary assembled in groups or individually escorted by an MP.

His search for Sunny had commenced on the first day of his new position as Corpsman as sick-call. He had heard nothing of Sunny for more than a month now, other than a rare, occasional glimpse of him entering or exiting the stockade basement isolation cells. Of course, he was in no position to greet his friend, let alone talk to him. And, as the days passed, Peter's undefined premonition of death for him, as well as himself, increased.

Meanwhile, in both the sleeping quarters and infirmary halls, Peter and Warrant Officer Campbell were inseparable. Continual conversations and communications, where one sentence, questions, comments, and acknowledgements or long bulletins of sharing information, were obvious to everyone. Whether in the hour they spent together on the recreation yard, or during the minutes they lined up for meals, they talked. In fact, they lined their cots up in the infirmary staff sleeping quarters to debate, argue, agree and disagree, and simply share random thoughts about provocative issues. Two or three other corpsmen joined them in order to listen in. Everyone, including Dr. Fisherly and Captain Hofmeister, listened in, appreciating the lively and vociferous repertoires Peter and Campbell so obviously enjoyed performing.

In short, Peter became almost a brother to Campbell, and vice versa. The warrant officer stared what war news was available, as well as all the gossip of the stockade. He criticized whom he considered was the worst MPs, and stockade administrative staff, and praised whom he felt was best. His contempt for Captain Hofmeister knew no bounds. Fisherly, he felt, was the only tolerable official in all of Camp Elliott. His admiration and indignation were irrevocable. And, of all that was shared, pointed out, and confided in, it was the escape routes from the facility that interested Peter the most.

If questioned regarding the unusual screams emanating from the basement heard throughout the institution when the door to the lower stairwell was inadvertently left opened, Campbell suddenly angered, shaking his head decidedly, "NO! Off-limits! We don't discuss forbidden subjects!"

While a cold teeming rain pounded the Camp Elliott stockade late one afternoon, Peter and Warrant Officer Taylor Campbell found themselves together quietly taking inventory in the supply closet of the infirmary. But each bolted upright when two burly MPs, led by an Army Lieutenant, dragged in a bloody, virtually unconscious prisoner.

For a long moment as Peter and Campbell froze observing the scene, the beaten prisoner sagged in the arms of the MPs who unceremoniously dropped him in a heap. An Army Lieutenant who followed behind them walked past them and shouted loudly, "Who in the goddam hell is in charge here?"

Patients on cots, capable of ambling from their cots in the sleeping quarters leapt forward as best they could and hurried to the open waiting room. As Dr. Fisherly emerged from his office rubbing his eyes from a nap, he asked loudly, "Why bring that man here?"

"Basement is flooding. He's yours now," answered the Lieutenant as he turned, and with the two MPs, exited the infirmary. In a high-pitched, but calm voice, Fisherly said, "I hope this doesn't mean the lad has to sleep the everlasting sleep because of a few mean American boys!"

Glancing at Campbell holding the inventory clipboard, he added, "Warrant Officer Campbell, take charge here. We know that Lieutenant and his MPs It's likely they give this man their iron heels. Even the Nips aren't this brutal."

The last of the three-man escort party exited the waiting room, one turned and glanced back, bellowing, "Wipe your nose, crybaby, and learn to behave. Good thing our work area in the basement flooded or you'd be on your way to Purgatory."

Kneeling before the young Marine withering in pain, Peter heard Campbell whisper, "The two omnivorous, almighty forces of the Elliott stockade at work: painful punishment and sadism."

Peter remained silent as he clutched the hand of the young Marine who so obviously appeared tortured. He thought to himself, 'Such a frightened, pitiful boy.'

Looking up at Peter, tears in his eyes, he mumbled hoarsely, "Why? Why? What did I do?"

And with that, while clasping Peter's hand tightly, he died.

CHAPTER SIXTEEN

-

Navaho Six-bits

"Who is the poor kid?" Peter asked gently, sensitively, a tear welling up in his eye as he continued kneeling and holding the boy's hand.

Campbell, leaning over Peter to study the face, responded quietly, "Not sure. But whomever he is, the fellow took a hell of a beating. One of the sons-of-bitching MPs repeatedly smashed his fist into the side of his head. The second MP probably joined in using both, plus his baton. They beat him mercilessly. Such a sad death."

"Why? Why?" demanded Peter, angrily.

"Who knows? But I've seen these kinds of beatings before around this place. At this Elliott hellhole, the only arbiter is the Almightiness power of the fucking fist. Some survive and leave here deranged. Others either disappear or die in here, in that spot on that floor," Campbell relied calmly, his own fists clenched. "It looks like they even stripped off his clothes to better beat, no, torture him. Look at all the welts and cuts and bruises. They sure enjoyed themselves, the dirty bastards."

Peter, remaining silent, finally looked away. Barely audible, he whispered, "No wonder our infirmary is given the sobriquets, 'Death's Favorite Depository' and 'The Carnival Satan Loves Most'".

At that moment, Dr. Fisher opened the door of his office, stepped out and yelled, "You two stay with the corpse! Hofmeister is on the way with MPs and a stretcher to get it out of here and over to Pendleton."

Peter turned back to the deceased Marine and asked "How old do you think he is? 18 or 19?"

"Barely 17, I'd say. Undoubtedly, he got his mother to go with him to the nearest Marine recruiter and lie that he was 18 or 19."

After a slight pause, the warrant officer concluded, "He's a Navajo Code-talker. Wasn't too long ago when he arrived. Don't know his name. Check his dog-tags. Will try to get word to Navajo Six-bits."

With that, Campbell walked over and knocked on the doctor's office door. When Fisher acknowledged his officer, Campbell explained he and Peter would like to visit Navajo Two-bits in his cell to inform the leader of the Code Talkers of the boy's death. Fisher readily agreed. Since Captain Hofmeister was due at any moment to retrieve the body for autopsy at Camp Pendleton, he would ask for permission for one of his MPs to escort the two to the Code-talker's cell.

As it turned out, Hofmeister consented to send Campbell and Peter to the stockade's second floor attic where a dozen or so windowless isolation cells were housed. While waiting for the MP to be assigned to escort the two naval officers, Campbell took the opportunity to explain who the Code Talkers were and why they had been assembled at camp Elliott.

"There are some 25 to 30 Navajos in classes at the camp. Here in the stockade we have their leader, Navajo Six-bits, and maybe two or three others, the boy, there, being one. Rarely do they come to the infirmary, because they never get sick. If they do, they suck it up. Anyway, all good men, I hear, never causing any problems."

"Why are there three or four in the brig?"

"Real minor problems. Ignoring rules, restrictions, maybe some drunkenness and fighting, but small stuff. I have no idea what he did. Six-bits will tell us."

With the assigned MP pointing the way, Peter and Campbell were led up the flight of steps of the heavily locked stairway, then escorted then down a short corridor past half a dozen grim helmeted, rock-like sentinels.

Campbell continued, "Weren't you on Guadalcanal, Lieutenant? I heard the Ghoul didn't begin his filthy business until he arrived for refitting on that Pavuvu. He and you were together on the 'Canal', right? You must have seen and comingled with the Navajos there. Right?"

"As a young Navy Doctor, I had many duties. One of them was to handle dispensing the malaria pills containing atabrine. In my sector each evening at a designated hour, Marines reported to my tent for their routine pill. So typical, he walked up with his mouth open and I threw the pill as far down his throat as I could. The Navajos arrived as a group, polite, kind, patient good man. I knew of their work, but only by rumor."

"Yes, I thought so. Well, at Camp Elliott we're very proud of them. The Code-talking program, the creation of the Navajo code took place here. The trial demonstrations in 1942-43 were impressive. Guadalcanal proved beyond a shadow of a doubt the Indians of the Southwest, specifically the Navajos and their unique non-translating language, would work. The Japs had no idea what they were listening to. We brought in hundreds of Navajos and they all became 'specialists' in the Signal Corps as Code Talkers. The original 29 Code Talkers were in the 382nd platoon."

Peter interjected, "I learned in one of my courses that during World War I we used Native American language to code secret messages."

"The idea of the Navajo language as a code for the Marine Code was conceived by Philip Johnson whose parents were Presbyterian missionaries. As a boy, he moved with his family to Arizona. He went to school with and played with Navajo kids and learned much of the language. Years later, after attending UCLA and working as an engineer for Los Angeles, Pearl Harbor saw him contacting the USMC signal office to explain the complexity of the never-before-recorded Navajo language. Its fluency could only come from exposure to it beginning at birth. He himself was one of the rare exceptions learning it. No went outside the reservation could speak or understand the language."

"Never knew any of this," Peter murmured.

"Very few do."

"How do you know so much of their story?"

"Navajo six bits is a close personal friend of mine. He's not fully Navajo. In fact, he's a despised half-breed.

His Navajo mother was from Northwest Arizona. His father, white, works for railroads. He was born on a reservation hospital. It's a long, involved story I'll tell you about later. But like himself, native speakers were easy to recruit within weeks of December 7. By March of '42, Major General Vogel, the Commander of the Amphibious Force, Pacific Fleet, among a number of other generals, lined up to watch the presentation of proof Code-talking could work. Some 200 Navajo young men were enlisted as Marines at Fort Defiance, Arizona. All were required to be fluent in English and Navajo. They were not informed of the reason for their recruitment, only that it was a 'special' assignment."

"I remember. Of the 200, the first 29 enlisted men, placed in the 382nd Platoon went through boot camp and were highly praised at graduation. That night, without the customary 10 days of leave, they were flown to San Diego from Fort Defiance, and from the Miramar Naval Air Station where they piled out of their C-47, lined up, and marched for hours to Elliott. They got here in late June 1942."

"Never heard any of this, and I rub shoulders with high Navy, Marine, and Army personnel."

"Well, that's only part of the story. The following morning, the 29 were roused by 5:00AM, breakfasted, and still unaware of the status of their duty, were escorted to a classroom where they learned they would play a new but critical role in the war history of America."

By this time, the trio had reached the corridor to the darkened isolation cells on the second floor of the Administration Unit. The MP, who had remained silent on the ascent steps, yet listened intently to the amazing story, turned and said quietly,

"My buddy was saved by the Code Talkers on Canal. Could you continue your account, Warrant Officer Campbell? It would mean a great deal to me personally."

"Of course, Sergeant," Campbell smiled. "Well, in that first session it was explained the Marine Corps believed a code based upon the Navajo language could be created and utilized during battle. Therefore, the list of assembled men was super-secret and their forthcoming task, super, super task was to construct an alphabet and find accurate equivalents for military terms not found in the Navajo language."

"So, the 29 original recruits invented the code with limited direction from command. Meanwhile, Philip Johnson, who never developed a single word of the code, served as an administrator for the new language school, acting as a liaison between the Navajo instructors and the commanders."

Peter chuckled. After a few seconds of reflection, he said, "I remember hearing the field test of the code was conducted in mid or late 1942 and it shook up all the military post along the Pacific Coast! Apparently, the Coast Guard intercepted the field test transmission, and alerted everyone they heard a new form of the Japanese language and an invasion was imminent. The entire California Coast was put on Red Alert! Well, it wasn't long before it was all cleared up and a new policy was established required everyone up and down the coast to be informed before the Indian code was used during field exercises."

The MP and Campbell smiled in wide grins. The warrant officer added, "Yeah, that incident is well-remembered, especially around here where the Code-talking originated. The Navajos of that original team are still laughing about it."

Then, after a pause, Campbell said, "Well, let me continue the story."

"Six-bits will tell you that at least 250 young Navajo recruits have gone through the Code-talker program with another 100 scheduled for 1945. The original 29, as you may know, were assigned to the 1st and 2nd Marine Divisions, including the famed Raider Battalion. They saw action on Canal, Bougainville, Peleliu, Saipan, Tinian, Guam, Leyte, and other islands. As you can imagine, the Navajo code has saved, and is saving lives, of our men. It's proving indispensable, allowing secret military message information to be sent and translated in minutes compared to the hours, even days, of the code machines."

"I suppose the boy who was beaten to death was going through the program when he was ordered into the guard house."

"Probably," responded Campbell. "We'll ask Six-bits."

After the MP thanked the two for the cogent history of the Navajo Code Talkers, the blond, colorless man with a tendency toward stoutness led the way to the far end to cell number 8. Peter had not visited this area of the stockade before, surprised the isolation cells were on a second floor rather than in the basement.

Pulling a chain of keys off his belt, he unlocked the iron door and entered. Peter and Campbell followed. In the dim light from a single lightbulb, the three looked upon the single occupant standing next ot his cot. Peter silently noted the prisoner's somber features.

"The strain of long days in solitude certainly have beaten this poor guy down. His mental state may be gone."

No one said a word.

The only acknowledgement the incarcerated man offered the three was a cold, suspicious stare.

"Hello, Six-bits," Campbell said softly, "How goes it?"

"…There's no pity here."

"How so? What's your meaning?"

The imprisoned said nothing.

"Well," continued Campbell, "Yes, I agree. That's why we've come. One of your boys died in our arms a few minutes ago."

For a 30-second moment, long and graveyard silent, no one said a word.

Then, in absolute silence within the small cell, Peter heard the man say gravely, without emotion or surprise,

"I know."

"You know?" asked Campbell, stunned.

"Yes."

"How can that be? It happened less than 30 minutes ago."

"Bad news always travels fast."

"Did you know the boy?"

"Like a son."

"I'm so, so sorry."

Turning his attention to Peter, Six-bits asked calmly,

"Is this the partner of the Mad Ghoul?"

"I suppose so," responded the Warrant Officer. "I don't see it in him and I work with him every day. But we're assigned to hold him for this forthcoming court-martial. He couldn't step on a bug. He almost cried when your Navajo went down a few minutes ago."

Peter blushed slightly as he studied Six-bits. The man was approximately 45. An unusual age for a recruit. He appeared as if he had slept in his fatigues for a month. Six-bits urgently needed a shave and a haircut.

Despite his dishevelment, his eyes were steely cold icy blue. His face seemed to have been chiseled from granite. Six-bits stood in a calm, dignified manner. He asked,

"You said you were there when he died. I already know how. Tell me."

Campbell began by saying, "He was a sacrifice to human justice. He was beaten and kicked to death, although he was still breathing, barely, when he was dumped in front of us in the infirmary. His last words broke our hearts…"

"And, what were they?"

Campbell hesitated, as Peter looked on, then lowered his head and said,

"Why? Why? What did I do?"

With that, Campbell, with a look of extreme anger in his eyes, lifted his head to search the haunted face of Six-bits. He said,

"I hoped to spare you those words of a young Marine, a Navajo kin to you and the others."

Leaning against the cell door downcast, an assortment of keys dangling on a ring chained to his belt, the MP ever-so-slightly recoiled. Both Campbell and Peter saw the flinch and each, noting the eyes of Six-bits, knew that the prisoner saw it too. All three then watched the guard cough, a hand raised to suppress it. The stockade MP turned away.

Campbell and Six-bits understood.

"He probably dropped a pent-up tear, too," the warrant office smiled at Six-bits. "The Navajo prisoner knew the MP had listened to every word, thinking hard when it was said, feeling every emotion of its impact.

Six-bits nodded.

"Scarce. His skin is very white, the kind that can never brown up. Yet, he knows his own had no cause for that and enjoyed it. No, that one there is too soft for killing his own. My people know if nothing else, how to read the nature of an animal, or a man. We do it fast and without failure. He is with the others, but he is of human heart, feelings and straight words."

"Officer," Campbell called out to the MP now standing in the middle or the corridor, "Come in for a few minutes."

As he did so, somewhat startled to be included in the conversation, the MP was asked,

"Aren't you the man guarding the holding pen just outside the brig area, away from the rest of the camp?"

"Yes. I worked that detail. The new recruits were all placed there at one time or another," answered the MP.

"Yeah," responded Campbell. "And, they all had to run the gamut of the inner yard."

"When they planned that, and I was assigned to duty at the 'holding pen', I refused the assignment. Got into hot water with people..."

"And why was that?" Peter interjected. Campbell glanced at Navajo Six-bits, who nodded with a slight smile.

"Initiation ritual that was unauthorized," responded the MP, stonily calm, pretending indifference to hide angry disapproval.

"How so?" Peter demanded. "I may be incarcerated awaiting court-martial, but I'm still an officer of the United States Navy, one of our Nation's armed forces."

"Yes, sir. It's a game the other MPs like to play, except it's not funny. Marines get hurt, putting some in painful conditions, others in the hospital."

"Goddamn it, officer, HOW SO?"

"Me, when on duty, or the others on rotation duty would love to open the main gate of the brig, escort us into the pen, about 10 other MPs following us. When me, or the others, were given the signal, I would release the bolt that locked the recruits in the pen. One man was released, and someone would scream, 'Run! Run, Marine! Run! Run! Run! Run your ass back into the brig gate, about 15 yards away.' Guards were on the walls, or inside from the windows, watching the fun as the poor Marine started running as fast as he could toward the main gate."

"Where was the amusement in that?" Peter continued his questions.

"Well, without interferences, and it being deep into the late-night hours, the 15 yards normally would require 20 or more seconds! As soon as the Marine began his dash, running as hard as he could muster, out of nowhere, he was blindsided by an MP waiting in the dark shadows of the stockade walls. Knocked flat on his back, most suffered damage, some serious. The MPs always enjoyed themselves."

"I imagine they did. Defenseless men, unknowing, trusting, but picked on by the base MPs," Peter said angrily.

"And," added Campbell, "when questioned by our officers, the MPs who took turns broadsiding the men would respond by saying, 'Well, the son-of-a-bitch was making a break for it, SIR!'"

"You left out the part of the MPs enjoying kicking, punching, kicking and punching the poor man. I heard that as many as seven MPs would be involved in beating the Marine to near death. Boot and fist marks all over the head and body, by six or seven brutal MPs, each trying his best of beat any pulse of life from a kid who is too weak and defenseless to protect himself. If only my looking at them could kill," interjected Navajo Six-bits.

"Exactly," continued the MP. "I would watch each Marine instinctively cover his head and face with his arms. It seemed the guards deliberately were aiming their blows above, not below, their shoulders. The MPs didn't care if marks and wounds were observable. There was nothing any of the victims could do, except take it, and then shut up about it, even to fellow Marines! This is the standard routine for most prisoner incomers. The MPs looked forward to every incoming shipment of prisoners because they could get their exercise running and tackling the Marines sprinting toward the gate. The harder the hit, the better, they figured."

"Did that happen to you, Peter?" asked Campbell, turning to the Lieutenant.

"Didn't happen to me because I was taken out of the incoming group early. But vaguely I remember hearing someone say, 'Our violent introduction was just the first hint of things to come.'"

"Well, that boy who died today wasn't killed by tackling guards. He was kicked and beaten to death. Not outside the prison walls, but in the prison basement."

"And, by the way," continued Six-bits, snappishly, "are you aware there's one job nobody wants in here?"

"What's that?" Campbell asked, peering intently into the incarcerated man's red-slitted, weary eyes.

"Working at the incinerator next to the garbage dump."

"Yeah, I heard that," the warrant officer responded morosely. "If the guards think you deserve extra punishment because you've done something to piss them off, you're sent to the furnace dump."

The MP bent forward slightly to listen intently, suddenly interrupted,

"Yes. There are not too many words around here that strike fear into the hearts of the prisoners like 'furnace dump'."

"What? Why is that?" demanded Peter. "I don't understand. Is it dangerous work, possible sharp object, diseases, wild animals? I imagine it's a disgusting job, being around it all day. But life-threatening?"

Campbell, patiently, looked at Peter and said calmly, "The thing that scares the inmates the most about the dump are the stories."

"What stories?" Peter persisted.

The MP, moving from the cell door, joined the three for the first time, commented,

"The dump is away from the main camp, away from the stockade, so no one can see or hear anything that happens over there. But rumors have been heard in the deepest part of the stockade of Marines getting weights dropped on them, of young Marines being sodomized with broom handles, beaten with thick boards, all kinds of horrible things.

There are stories of Marines being killed at the dump, intentionally killed. I heard accounts from other MPs of a few Marines actually beaten to death at the furnace site. I refused duty there after being assigned. My superiors had no problems with my refusal."

"So," concluded Peter, shocked and dismayed, "you mean that our own Marines were…"

"Yes," Six-bits said loudly, taking a step forward, fists clenched. "Marines murdered, then thrown into the furnaces. The smell of burning flesh reached us here, almost a mile away."

With that, Six-bits turned away, and lowered his head. He would say no further word.

As the MP exited the cell with Campbell followed by Peter, right behind him, they bumped into Captain Hofmeister, with two MPs batons in hand. Immediately, Hofmeister walked up from a few feet away, and looked into the faces of the three men.

"Oh, no! What's this? A cell search or cell extraction? Speak up MP, speak up."

"I escorted the two corpsmen to the provident leader of the Code Talkers to inform him of the death of the young Marine downstairs on the floor of the infirmary."

For a very long moment, Hofmeister studied the three, grimly determined. Since the steel cell door was still open, Six-bits stood back in the shadows listening to every word of the unusual proceedings coldly. Finally, addressing the MP,

"Any other words you have to spill?"

"Yes, I do. But I need not bother to say them of everyone in here, you know the cruelties that happen in here."

Hofmeister stiffened visibly. His face fixed in a grave expression of angry defiance, the Captain said slowly, almost stoically,

"Report to your quarters this very moment. Await for my summons. I will deal with you later."

The MP, in a defying, bold response of resistance to authority, said quietly with a sly smile,

"To prepare me for my burial place among the forgotten, unnamed, vanished Marines in the furnace dump?"

"I don't even know the boy's name and he died at my feet, one hand in mine," Peter said angrily. "He died as he was speaking."

"Six-bits referred to him as 'Smelly'. Why, I don't know," responded Campbell as the two continued walking back to the infirmary, unescorted.

"So, when the MP said there were others…"

"Yes," answered Campbell, "there were without question. I saw them when they invariably wound up in the infirmary. Given the opportunity, as he often said, Six-bits would personally clip the wings of the killers, and, he knows who they are, I'm certain. he may have already set the killers in motion."

"How would he know who, and then plan their deaths?" Peter asked, realizing this was the first time since arriving that someone was finally talking, informing on the brutal Elliott staff.

"Explain why Six-bits refers to himself as a 'providential' leader, a half-breed. When he breathed 'half-breed', if you recall, he actually growled. Such an incongruous way to talk about one's self."

"I'll explain. You've become a friend, and you should know even if you face death by firing squad," the warrant officer said as he halted before the entrance to the infirmary. "Let's sit on the waiting bench there before we go in."

As the two sat quietly, Peter barely breathed, thinking it best to remain silent lest he spoil the opportunity to learn about the Navajos, specifically one of their unofficial leaders. Finally, Campbell said,

"Because Six-bits is a half-breed, he has no right to lead. He is half white. His father was white, the mother of the northern Navajos. If there's a 'leader', or 'spokesman', of the 30 or so Code Talkers, it's Mr. Johnson, whose idea formed the program. Willie 'Silver Eagle' Notah is supposedly head of the group. Some of the staff know him as Tkal-kain-o'-nei, 'run-on-water'. Another leader is Red Soil. I don't know his name, or how the Code Talkers."

"I don't' get it," Peter said, frustrated. "What's wrong with being a half-breed?"

"He says being a red-skinned white, or red-skinned black, makes no difference. You're neither nor. People, society, culture, even history has no use for you. I think that since his father was white, he wanted to be accepted as white, treated as a white, loved as a white. But whites see him as all Indian. He may be lean and tough, fearless, and living for something to die for, like his fellow Navajos, but in his heart his great need is to be better than the whites, and therefore finally be recognized. The Navajos see all this. They see, as the whites see, a strange, friendless."

The two men sat side by side in silence, their heads bowed. After a few minutes, they both stood and upon entering the infirmary, immediately resumed their responsibilities. Since both were physiologically drained from the day's activities, each was quietly relived not one patient was in need. Furthermore, the rain had ceased and a late afternoon sun had broken through, engulfing the isolated stockade in golden slightly.

As long as Peter could remember, he had heard from family relatives and friends that there was no calm as peaceful, no peace so idyllic as that which was to be found on a Southern California landscape when neither windy nor raining. Watching a sunset in such an environment is as beautiful as it can get, especially when fused with good companionship and neighborliness.

As prized corpsmen privileged to sit and relax on a recreation yard bench at sundown, weather permitting, Peter and Campbell felt and saw nature at her gentlest. The shocking day was over, the two sitting idly, and their appetites healthily assuaged, the contented men and their untroubled minds were suddenly recalled to their sleeping quarters. The entire stockade population, prisoners and staff, were in the process of being notified that inmate "Six-bits" had within the hour been found in his isolation hanged to death.

CHAPTER SEVENTEEN

-

"...the sorriest sorry son-of-a-bitch in the universe"

That night, neither corpsman slept much. Each was so deeply troubled he couldn't speak a word to the other. Both knew Six-bits hadn't hung himself. He was lynched. A perusal of his body would have revealed welts, lesions, bruised areas, and assorted painful raised ridges on and around discolored skin tissues resulting from powerful pummeling.

Adding to their mental torment was a howling wind reverberating throughout the stockade that had replaced the day's downpour. And, despite the smell of Pacific Ocean salt mingling with the aftershower humidity, a stench of death seemed to pervade the infirmary staff sleeping quarters. Peter, sick at heart, occasionally napped, dreaming spasmodically of the same scene: the same three who had been at the cell of Six-bits standing beneath a gallows, whose thick spiral-threaded rope had just extinguished a man's life in the name of human justice.

As vivid and with the clarity of a high-resolution photograph, he saw himself from different angles dropping to a kneeling position at the side of a uniformed man whose face he did not recognize. Although he appeared still-calm as the other two remained standing over the body, he saw his face flooded with tears. the face of the deceased man had been brutalized. Then Peter watched himself pray in the midst of tears streaming down his own face. Then, Peter turned to the two men beside him bowed in respect and reverence and said,

"We must take him with us."

Where to?" asked one of the men who appeared, upon closer examination, to be Warrant Office Campbell.

"To the San Joaquin Catholic Cemetery on Harding Way in Stockton, California, the city where I was born."

Handling the unknown corpse with infinite gentleness, the three then carried him off in silence across an endless sea of grass. And, throughout their journey an endless silent procession three-astride followed them. Upon reaching the entrance to the cemetery, one of the oldest in the state dating back to 1849, the height of the California Gold Rush, Campbell turned to Peter and said, "It's in your nature to love all suffering humanity."

Peter saw himself smile, and respond, "I've never had anything but kindness for the oppressed."

Then, still carefully, kindly clutching the body, they turned past the first row of graves, the oldest section of one of the oldest graveyards in the state's nearly century old history and approached a large open pit next to his grandfather's grave. Standing at the edge of the massive bottomless pit, the three men still holding the dead man nodded to each other, and with wonderingly glances down into what otherwise appeared to be an infinity, placed the body on the edge of the abyss and stepped back. Peter saw himself remain at the edge gazing silently down. Then glancing across to the next grave where six to eight feet below the surface, he saw the side of an 1880's coffin in which his grandfather on his father's side rested. Peter knelt, brushed the waxen face of the hanged man, took hold of the body, and leaped in.

This, the final of a series of short dreams, awakened him. He sat up, and, for some moments, he trembled slightly. Never once in his entire life did he dream of any form of death. What was the interpretation of this one? Out the small, barred window of the infirmary sleeping quarters, he saw a razor-thin light creep over the eastern horizon. Dawn was near.

As he sat up rubbing his arms in the cold room with several others, he considered his own situation. It was entirely possible that he might be the next target. After all, he and the warrant officer had been observed with Six-bits in what appeared to be sympathetic conversation. Did the MP inform whomever it was signaling the victims for murder? More likely, it was Captain Hofmeister who stumbled upon them together in the cell. Where the killers fearful Six-bits had informed on them? No matter how he cut it, he was in an extremely precarious position and he neither had a defensive weapon nor anyone to help defend him.

As he sat there shivering in the darkness watching the gray of early morning fade into the first rays of sunshine to inundate Southern California, Campbell awakened. For some time, he said nothing as he studied Peter. Finally, he whispered a hoarse whisper so the other staff asleep under their thick Navy blankets could hear,

"Worried, aren't you? So am I! They know I know what a cesspool of unmilitary inhuman acts and conditions occur in here. They know I'm not going to rat out the MP guards who deny medication, savage for the joy and sheer fun of it, young defenseless Marines, and even sexually abuse them. I've seen heads stomped, permanent injuries leading to disabilities, guards refusing to stop fights. I don't even want anyone to tell what other injustices take place here, especially in the basement and out at the dump."

Peter was dumbfounded. At least the opportunity presented itself to ask the ultimate question he dared not ask before.

"Unreported beating deaths that wind up in the incinerator and the after remains in the dump?"

Campbell, suddenly wide-eyed, lifted slightly, and leaned on his elbow, staring in utter disbelief.

"What kind of a question is that?" he asked haltingly in a soft voice. "What do you know?"

With eyes narrowing, Peter gazed calmly at the warrant officer and responded bitterly, "Only what I overheard a few of the Stoneman inmates whispering in the seats in front of me on the train ride down here. I hardly paid attention, thinking deaths and disappearances of the bodies were impossible in a modern Army stockade. If nothing else, the inmates would go berserk rioting."

"Last year, a few, learning a buddy went missing, smashed some furniture, threw their tin dining plates at windows and the MPs, and that night they all were shipped out. Who and where, no one knows," Campbell said with a sneer. "The Hofmeister group posted a list of names of those sent to 'punitive segregation', but no one ever saw or heard of them again. The hue and cry lasted a few hours and young Marines disappeared. End of story."

"Plotted murders?" Peter asked, fearful he was pressing for answers too forcefully.

"I don't know. I doubt it. Just too many involved to get away with it. One thing is for certain. That martinet of strict discipline, Hofmeister, always puts out official memoranda, 'Today's Suicides'…oh, Peter, I'm kidding. He doesn't do that. Today, when we see the bulletin on the board stating Six-bits death was a suicide, we'll need to hold back our smirking. We'll know a clean, open, honest, friendly, but burdened man who was murdered for talking to us."

Suddenly, the door to the infirmary sleeping quarters swung open and two burly baton-carrying MPs entered, along with Dr. Fisher.

"Glad you both are awake. Hofmeister wants you two in his office in an hour. Better come and eat something. We're to escort you. Let's go, and right now."

After a hasty breakfast on a back table with Fisher and the two MPs joining in, the men relieved themselves in the corridor restroom, next to the Captain's offices, then, unannounced entered the outer office of the Captain's suite. His door open, Hofmeister, looking even more dumpy than usual in a hodgepodge of military clothing, glared past an MP sitting at the entrance desk plucking a typewriter at the arrivals.

Squatting on an undersized chair, a sullen expression on his face below slitted red eyes, he yelled,

"Sit here."

Entering the inner office, as sterile and lifeless as when Peter first entered weeks before, the Lieutenant and the warrant officer seated themselves before the Captain's desk. For a long moment, he studied the Captain. His skin was very white, the type that never browns or burns in the sun. Like his barren office, the man appeared empty of thought or motion. A broad forehead capped a wide-open pair of black-green eyes, stubbed nose, and clenched mouth.

"Of course, this measly military man, condones murder," Peter reflected. "Sure, he's always alert and his eyes move quickly, occasionally stopping to weigh whatever catches his attention. Even with a midday shower or bath, he never seems fresh, his unnatural paleness never leaving his body."

With a slight harshness in his voice, his overall bearing hinted an exultation from a false sense of command leadership. Seated, nay, squatting, his overall countenance appeared grotesque. "Adding his toadying demeanor to higher-ups, he is a freak. Well, the comedy is over."

After another moment of studying each other in silence, Hofmeister leaned forward across the desk and said with a satiric smile,

"What did your dead friend the so-called, Six-Bits, tell you?"

"He said your tongue is not straight and his heart, as well as all the hearts of the Code Talkers, are not good for you," Campbell said slowly, somberly. "He said you are a burlesque, a parody, a travesty wrapped in a single pot belly. He said that the Japs will surly win this war if the top brass are all caricatures of you."

Eyes bulging, fists clenched, and flabby facial flesh beginning to swell, Hofmeister flushed.

"Damn it all," he sputtered, attempting to sound manfully,' We'll get the truth out of you, if it takes great pain. We already know the difference between truth and lies. You will pay dear for your drollery."

With that, Hofmeister folded his arms, and, glaring at Campbell with pure hate, Peter thought, leaned back in the frail chair.

"That fat, flaccid ton of crap is going to collapse his throne, for sure," he snickered.

But then, the Captain nodded to the two, stood up and abruptly left the room through the door behind his desk.

Then, without warning, and what appeared to be a single movement, one of the MPs smashed a powerful fist into the side of the warrant officer's head, nearly toppling Campbell from his chair. The second MP stepped forward with his long black baton to mercilessly batter the corpsman in a systematic manner; they stripped off his clothes and continued to pummel as they screamed, "Tell us everything!! You are covering up! No lies, here!"

Peter, shocked, stood up in disbelief. He had never seen such a continual beating. Campbell, doubled-up on the floor, whimpered in agony. Peter know that fists, boots, and batons pounding his face and body would not cause Campbell to give them information, even if it meant his death.

With blood on their knuckles, fingers, and hands, the MPs turned from the warrant officer's bleeding body to Peter standing back. Shouting curses and insults, they raised their batons to strike the Lieutenant, when the back door of office opened and Hofmeister emerged, shouting loudly, "The murderer will tell me. Step back."

Grinning a little as he glanced at the warrant officer clutching his stomach and writing in pain, the captain motioned Peter to resume sitting in his seat.

Now, once again seated and leaning across his desk, Hofmeister nodded to one of the MPs, who resumed his standing position behind Peter and smiled,

"Hit him again. Not too hard that it hinders his vocal cords…"

Peter stiffened, repressing the compliment of a sneer, while gravely locking his teeth. And it came, a stunning smash to the right side of Peter's face. It was so hard; Peter was sent spinning from his chair. Bleeding, and barely conscious, the Lieutenant found himself on the floor face down next to Campbell. The two MPs leaned down, grabbed Peter, and lifted him up. But instead of continuing to strike him, the two introduced a new means of torture. While one held him up, the other twisted one of his arms behind his back.

Hofmeister eyed Peter suspiciously, musing, "Will you tell the truth before losing your arm? No tales. Only what the Redman said. That, or the bloody work on you continues. You'll wish you had told the truth after your body is broken all up."

Peter's agile mind thought hard how to respond. He nodded. Hofmeister waved the MPs aside, then leaned further across the desk in anticipation.

"Well," he grinned.

"To tell the truth, Captain, all I can remember is that Six-Bits said you were the sorriest son-of-a-bitch in the universe."

Hofmeister remained motionless, neither leaning back in his swivel chair nor shifting his feet. Although he appeared impassive, he was stiff, including his face muscles. Without changing expression by so much as a flinch or wince, he appeared to Peter carved in stone.

For what seemed an infinity in time, Hofmeister focused his cold eyes upon the Lieutenant's lips. Then, suddenly, he squared his shoulders. Remaining immobile, he asked slowly, almost measuring the impact of each word, "What did you say in response?"

Peter, tight-mouthed, answered, "I told him, to his delight, that I agreed with his every word, and then some. Where he labelled you 'an ordinary graven sorry son-of-a-bitch', I held my feelings and description of you back."

With that, Hofmeister leaned further over the desk to shake Peter's hand. With a shy grin, he stuttered, "Oh, for crying out loud, Mad Ghoul accomplice, share with how you view with increasingly wrinkling USMC officer. Don't worry about little ole me coughing up a tear or two."

In the tone of his statement, Peter sensed Hofmeister was growing, despite his veneer of civility, angrier and more vituperative. Again, the Captain broke the silence by raising his voice, shouting, "Tell me how you picture me, murderer. TELL ME EVERYTHING! YOU'RE GOING TO DIE ANYWAY AFTER YOUR TRIAL AT THE STAKE BY FIRING SQUAD! TELL ME!"

Yet, another pause.

"Well, I told him the truth. You, a full-fledged Marine Corps Officer are not an ordinary graven son-of-a-bitch. You are the sorriest of all sorry sons-of-a-bitches in the universe".

Peter, about to shake Hofmeister's hand, refused. In doing so, he thought he saw the barest glimpse of a cynical smile crisscross the man's face. It was so fleeting, it seemed to occur in less than lightning speed time.

One of the MPs, baton in hand, walked from behind Peter in his chair around the prostrate Campbell, to the side of the desk, and whispered a few words in the Captain's ear. then, with a glint in his eye, Hofmeister looked at the second MP guard, shifted uncomfortably, grunted, and, as Peter sat studying Hofmeister, rammed his baton at full force into Peter's stomach. He hit Peter so hard he went flying backwards, the chair hurtling almost all the way to the office's entrance. Peter, virtually swooning from the powerful force of the blow, laid smothered in pain on the floor. Utterly defenseless, he wanted to regain his feet and balance to hurl every criminal epithet and obscene vulgarism known to man at him. But as Peter struggled to get back on his feet, several other MPs rushed through the back door, grabbing his arms, restraining further movement. Peter, in a state of painful delirium, fell back. His final recollection was hearing Captain Hofmeister shouting something about being "…the sorriest sorry son-of-a-bitch in the universe."

CHAPTER EIGHTEEN

-

Pipsqueak

Tired of their bloody work, the MPs, now numbering seven, lifted and carried Campbell and Peter Toscanini from the floor of Captain Hofmeister's office down the corridor and main steps leading to the several dozen cells, including the solitary conferment "hole".

Both brutalized corpsmen, barely conscious and bleeding from a multitude of wounds and fissures, lay in a heap, shivering in the near-freezing cold, on a flat piece of wood serving as the bare cell's bed. Their bodies tangled within each other, the two friends, groaning while slowly emerging from semiconscious conditions, tried to sit up. Neither spoke, although each was riddled with pain.

Peter, managing a slight grin, nodded to Campbell and said hoarsely, "Chicken-shit punches and beatings."

Before Campbell could sit up and smile, all but one of the MPs left the large darkened "hole". As they did so, both Peter and Campbell managed to raise themselves on all fours. As the single MP stood between the two corpsmen, he suddenly bent over and grabbed Peter by the throat and began choking him.

"Tell us what the Redman said! Or, in less than a moment, you'll stop breathing. Now, talk!" he pleaded implacably, his eyes narrowing.

Pretending to remain unconscious, Peter remained silent as the MPs finger tightened around his throat. With a wry smile, the nameless MP then stepped back, dropped Peter and paused to catch his breath. Again, the Lieutenant was back down on his knees. He could barely breathe. The resistance Peter maintained all day was waning. He was so weary, he could barely open his eyes. No matter, he thought, he would stick to his story. According to Six-Bits, the captain was one sorry son-of-a-bitch.

"I will be back soon, and your pain is nothing compared…" the MP shouted, his rage increasing the man's intrinsic banal brutality. Hardly conscious of his plight, Peter sustained another noisy bombardment of blows.

"I will break you in half," the MP again scowled furiously, rubbing his hands together in delight and self-satisfaction.

As the solitary confinement steel door slammed shut behind the exiting MP, Campbell was up on all fours with enough energy to crawl toward Peter.

"Chicken-shit or not, are you okay?" Campbell asked Peter.

"Hell, yes," Peter struggled to answer. "It wasn't his baton, or fists, or boots that punished, it was looking into that big bastard's bully looks looking straight in my eyes, the sorry son-of-a-bitch."

Campbell smiled weakly. Then, crawling even closer to Peter, he whispered, "There are things I must tell you. Things I kept from you. But they may string me up as they did Six-Bits. As early as tonight."

Peter nodded, "Whenever you're ready."

Glancing around, he said as Campbell lay back again.

"Look at this dungeon! No windows, a gloomy, airless tomb, so dark I can't even see how far back it goes."

Suddenly from somewhere in the black darkness of the "hole's" depth, a voice startled the two corpsmen.

"Welcome to our ghastly Death House!"

Peter, still dazed, and yearning for the comfort of deep sleep, opened his eyes wide. "I know that voice!" he thought. "I know it! But whose?"

The unidentified voice continued, "You two will undoubtedly want to freshen up after your comfortable arrivals. We have plenty of room, and more to come since some of us are going to die anyway."

Struggling to regain his sensibility to respond, all Peter could respond was, "Who's that? I know you, friend. But who are you? Are you a victim, too, like us?"

"Are you hurt bad?" the voice asked, as it grew louder with approach.

"We never have visitors down here in solitary confinement. So, when the other guys come in from the exercise yard, they'll surround you for news. But, how badly did they punish you?"

Campbell looked up and smiled. He recognized the visitor. Peter, continuing to see through bloodied facial cuts, his vision gradually gaining clarity, saw the figure of a young Marine approach, stand before him with a wide grin, then kneel face to face. Peter gasped.

"Sonny! Sonny, is that really you? What are you doing in this hellhole? I've been looking for you since the day we arrived together. Why? Why? God, you look well. This is my partner in the infirmary. But why?"

"Being the angry smartass that I am, I could say that it's because of bliss one feels in the darkness, day after day, week after week, month after month. I'll tell you a lot of things about this horrible death-house. Later, we'll catch up on things after I care for you and your friend."

Peter, in pain, clutching his stomach and ribs, reached up and gently stroked Sonny's face. His eyes narrowing, he was relieved to see whatever stockade and brutalness he endured did not affect his handsome face. No contusions, black-and-blue spots, or bruises. Appearing intact, his height was unchanged, as were the colors Peter remembered of Sonny's hair, eyes and complexion. He had no idea how long his friend had been swallowed in darkness and loneliness, but the teenager had survived thus far. Even Sonny's clothes had the appearance of freshness. Tight-lipped, Peter said so softly they were barely audible,

"The silence of isolation and dark gloom didn't leave your face expressionless. Your eyes are exactly as I remember them, bright and black."

"Yes. Death hasn't reached me yet. But it's on the way. For weeks I've seen nothing, and heard even less, except for one thing--one of us being grabbed without warning hauled away. When other prisoners began surrounding the guard MPs as the frightened Marine wondered why and where he was being taken, one would laugh, 'Why, to the dump, of course.' That's why we must talk."

As Peter studied Sonny, weighing his words, he heard the tramp of heavy footsteps walking down the corridor to the solitary confinement cell. For a long moment, he, Sonny, and Campbell listened intently, especially when a heavy key was inserted in the lock of the steel door and it was shoved open noisily. Entering, three guards holding their batons tightly swaggered in. The one strutting ahead of the other two shouted,

"Toscanini. Which one is Toscanini? The Captain wants you now. Let's go!!"

"Oh, shit," whispered Sonny, as he stepped back a few feet. Then, he walked forward and whispered,

"When you return, we'll talk about this year's 'almond crop'."

At that exact moment, the lead MP guard walked over, and said,

"There you are! Get up, goddamn it, or I'll show you what being on the floor is really like."

"But…," responded Peter, stunned beyond belief, by both the "almond" noun from Sonny, of all Marines, and the MP's threat. As the guard yanked him to his feet, Peter fainted, buckling under his own weight back to the floor. His face darkened to a blood red, he was again lifted to his feet, and, regaining consciousness to a certain degree, he felt all bewilderment, dispersion, puzzlement, and relief, culminating in an overwhelming urge to vomit.

Together the three guards led Peter up the one flight of basement stairs, one step at a time, to the first floor, then down the corridor back to the Captain's office. As they passed numerous frozen-faced MPs leaning back on the walls or chit-chatting one-on-one or in small groups, Peter managed to place a hand on his low thumping heart to check his heartbeat. As beaten and weary as he was, he worried it might be the first organ to give way. Although he felt his blood pressure had reached a dangerous level, he was more concerned about the punches he was taking on his torso and head. those could kill him.

After reaching the door of the Captain's office, knocking, then being summoned to enter, Hofmeister, dressed as gaudily as ever, sat alone behind his messy desk with his thoughts. Seeing Peter disheveled, crippled, and in pain triggered a slight smile. Some lacerations were open, either still bleeding slightly or in dried blood. After motioning to the MPs to sit Peter in the chair before the desk, he signaled the guards to leave. he then stood up, walked around the desk to sit on its edge before Peter slumped down, pretending to be totally disoriented. He was damned if he would be the first to break the silence.

Then, as Peter slowly looked up, Hofmeister, clutching a knee, leaned back, and with a slight shine in his eye, he sneered,

"Well, hello, Mad Ghoul! Welcome to our last talk, before I abandon you to the hole at night, and the dump during the day."

In his state of enormous pain and swelling, Peter, struggling to fathom the Captain's words while weighing how to respond. Again, that face so obviously chiseled from granite was less than a foot or two from his nose and the eerie smell that hit Peter like a ton of bricks was suddenly returned.

Peter, slit-eyed, gazed upon the homely face impassively without comment. Instead, he reflected, "Dare I tell this loathsome sorriest of all the sorry son-of-bitches in the world that when he gets close, he reeks of death. I've had to examine corpses. I know up close the smell of the dead. But this pig's stench is worse. What's floating from his filthy carcass is shrinking up the thin, soft membranes of my nostrils, clogging up the passages. It's not body odor. It's worse than the smell of not having bathed in a year. I've only experienced it near him, and especially in this locked up, windowless office. He obviously likes it. All I can compare it to is the appalling malodorousness of charred corpse remains up close. All that's missing in that sibilant monstrosity of a man are hissing sounds. Oh, for the feel of winds of fresh air.

"Are you thinking evil thoughts of me?" Hofmeister uttered in a snarl. "Oh, I know you are! Worse than, what was it you called me? Something about 'Sorry, sorry, catch my pants on fire'? Well, smart-alecky Marine murderer, no more infirmary for you. No more physicians, no more medicaments. No more wounds washed, disinfected, and dressed. You'll enjoy the gangrene before the furnace."

"That's what you believe, eh? And for you to mention furnace…that's all I need to know!" Peter thought, expressionless.

"Like all the others, and their peculiar iniquities, you are trivial, a hick, jerkwater, smartass and we of the prison staff know precisely how to react as one body to the likes of you. We don't like military justice with all its stupid legal rights. We prefer to punish our black sheep ourselves. There is order here in this stockade."

Peter, sensing the Captain having unleashed a string of invectives at him might reveal more if properly prodded.

"Why Hofmeister, you old bastard, you dumbfound me! I'm astonished there's a 'body', a select group, to handle Marines the likes of me."

"You'll see. Before you know it, like others, you'll commit suicide. I'm not saying my little squad is going to brutally torture you during interrogations. Just because the Camp Elliott brig and stockade has the most dreaded address of all the military stockades that are homefront. We enjoy helping those who won't bend appreciate that bending is much easier on the body than beatings. We have no issue, in fact rather enjoy, remanding delinquent Marines to solitary confinement for days, weeks, months, and even years on end, if necessary. The accused must, and will, answer to my interrogator's questing, or else. Yes, indeed, I have a team, a 'squad', if you will, of special men who, together with me, selected, plan and administer our punishments, some small, some more severe. Concentrating on the orderly processing of soldiers in wartime for any or all infractions of military law rules, regulations affecting the safety and security of the armed forces. Yes, sir, you despised wretch, I have my own 'special unit'."

Peter, in a moment of almost uncontrollable wild excitement, refused to believe what he heard.

"Was that a confession, or what?" he demanded with an intense glare at Hofmeister. "This fool, probably figuring they'll kill me at the furnace so they won't have to physically haul my body out there, felt free to tell me exactly what I need to know. All I need now are victims, names of victims, names of the missing, just names and names and names! Then, to get out of here, taking Campbell and Sunny with me. And, soon, maybe tonight. All three of us are certain to be murdered."

Suddenly, the telephone on Hofmeister's desk rang loudly, startling both Peter and the Captain. As the warder abruptly swung away from Peter and returned to his chair from where he answered it. As Hofmeister engaged in a long conversation in which he did most of the listening, Peter attempted to follow the dialogue the way he could. As he did so, he became more and more nervous about his situation. His bones ached and his stomach began to hurt from hunger. He continued to churn over ideas to get out of the stockade. In addition, Peter felt that since Sunny had been imprisoned almost since arrival he had no idea of available escape routes. As for Campbell, the issue of escape never once surfaced in all their friendly discussions. He would not know a way out.

Peter watched Hofmeister closely, as he finished listening to whomever it was delivering a monologue. Even before the Captain hung up, the back door opened and two MPs entered.

Turning back to Peter, the Captain, in a soft, pleasing tone, announced,

"Mr. Ghoul, Mr. Mad Ghoul, that will be all for today. We'll resume all this tomorrow. Meanwhile, you'll be locked in the special cell next to be office. You'll be more comfortable there than in solitary."

Peter, suddenly alert, knew this was most unusual. Something was up. At first puzzled by the first friendly sentences he had heard from Hofmeister, it now dawned on him that the cell next to the Captain's office might be the holding cell prior to the walk toward the furnace. Peter was now convinced the three friends were going to be killed that night or in the morning. They had to escape within hours. But if he was locked in a cell on the first floor, how would he reach Sunny and Campbell in solitary confinement in the basement?

Nodding to the MPs, Hofmeister terminated the meeting by turning to a report or document lying on his desk in front of him. Without so much as looking up or even a slight grunt, the Captain dismissed Peter by simply pointing to the door. Obediently, the two MPs pulled him up out of the chair.

"No manacles," shouted the Captain. One of the MPs with a barely audible guffaw as he cast a sidelong glance at the warden. Then, on each side of their prisoner, the two MPs led him out of the office, down the corridor to the next door, the holding cell, almost opposite the stairway to the basement's solitary confinement cells.

As one of the MPs was unlocking the cell door, Peter thought he overheard one of the MPs say to the other in a low voice,

"The Captain doesn't like this idea. Earlier, I heard him trying to persuade whomever he was talking to, possibly the head of the Special Unit that moving the three upstairs was a mistake. 'Best to leave them down in the basement', I think Hofmeister insisted."

"Well, it shows who's boss around here," the MP unlocking the door responded.

Shoving the prisoner through the door into the holding cell, Peter, in the dim light, laid down on a normal bed, rather than the usual raw boards substituting for typical prison cots.

After resting on what was a surprisingly comfortable mattress, he lifted his head slightly to scan the cell's contents. Despite the semidarkness, he noticed nearby a number of Army sleeping bags stacked halfway to the high ceiling, several positioned neatly in a row on the floor, a sturdy table, five or six stiff-backed chairs, and a few assorted small pieces of furniture, his eyes, fell, and then focused, upon what appeared to be a body sound asleep in a far corner bed similar to his. He was obviously a Marine and somehow appeared familiar even in the dull lighting.

Almost simultaneously, the man turned over, yawned, stretched, looked around, and peered at Peter, who was smiling at him. Staring squint-eyed, he asked, "Peter is that you? They threw me in there. Someone said you and the other corpsman, Campbell would soon be joining me. Are you okay? I'm fine, but worried. Doing this, putting the three of us up here in what they call a 'holding cell' is ominous. I've seen it before. Several times. The guy never came back."

"Sunny, the question is whether you are all right. Let me get over there and we can talk."

Struggling to lift himself on his elbow, then sit up, Peter managed to get to his feed. In pain, he ambled across the room, using odd chairs, the table, and other furniture as support. Reaching Sunny, who was indeed hurt, Peter gazed for a long moment into his friend's face. He was shocked. His face was like a fleshless skull with a thin white sheet of paper stretched over it. He was that gaunt. His eyelids were almost black and tired. "How grave and grisly he looks. Why is it I hadn't noticed these facial features before? It's only been minutes since I first saw him after our arrival at Camp Elliott," Peter reflected. This young man now sitting on the edge of the bed, his friend, was in great pain.

Raising Sunny up with his two hands, Peter asked, "Where's Campbell? Is he all right? And safe? And, 'almond'! You said, 'almond', right? We have much to talk about and quickly. The bastards may separate us again. And, most important of all, we've got to escape, if not in the next few minutes, then certainly tonight. I've got enough of a rambling admission of murder to court-martial the monster now. But how do we get out of here and make it to the base authorities?"

During that moment of joy, of sheer excitement, the two friends huddled, Peter with his arm around Sunny, who was trembling in pain. Peter, in low whispers, tried to reassure him that help was nearby, that once Corpsman Campbell was in tow, the three would find a way out, that all was really well since his priority now was to return him to the Corps safely. "After all," Peter smiled, "soon after this damn war is over, I want you and whomever your wife-to-be is to take me on a tour of the beautiful Oregon coast. So, kid, I'll watch over you."

Sunny responded sadly, "We must get out. We must. I've heard too much screaming, seen too many beatings, know too many disappearances. I was assigned to watch over you, and it turns out you're going to watch over me. I was supposed to hear from an MP in here, but as yet, haven't. I have no idea who it is, but supposedly, he knows me."

Just them, Peter and Sunny heard the bolt in the cell door lock click open and a Marine sergeant entered, followed by two MPs holstered with .45s dragging Campbell in a semiconscious state.

"Not that damn pipsqueak! He's the night basement sergeant. Everyone in solitary wants to kill him."

"Yeah," Peter acknowledged. "I know who he is. They say he's more of a brute than the Captain. Nothing funny about his nickname. Everyone calls him Pipsqueak out of pure abhorrence and loathing."

But it wasn't the 5'4", pudgy sergeant who caught his attention. He was white, and "...as sergeants go, as ordinary as any floor scrap of paper," Peter thought. What instantly interested him were the two dark, taciturn MPs, well over six feet, extremely powerful, whose swart coloring and hawk's features of face. Although at first glance they appeared more like Sioux or Cheyenne, the two were obviously Navajo, possibly part of the Code-Talker contingent.

"The real articles made of real stuff" was the colorful expression that crossed his mind. "How could such honorable men be a part of this murderous travesty?"

"Up!" screamed Pipsqueak. "No time for nonsense. Hurry up!"

Peter and Sunny stared at the sergeant blankly. Neither moved. They both sat there for a moment, blinking from the corridor light suddenly illuminating the cell by the open day. Momentarily disoriented, Peter could only muster,

"We're not moving."

"The hell you're not. Stand up!"

Without looking up at him, Sunny echoed,

"We're still on our hands and knees. Like the Lieutenant says, we're not moving. We've both been slammed in the gut by your MPs waving bullies. We can't, you f------ idiot."

The sergeant whispered, "Well, you two and that one my boys are carrying, have thrown us for a loop in our planned escape for you!"

Turning to the Navajo MPs, he ordered, "Drop him. Let these two snots handle him. They can go to the furnace, for all I care. Let's go."

As the MPs literally dropped Campbell in a crumbled heap, the three started for the door.

"Wait!" Peter said, hoarsely.

The sergeant stopped, turned, thought for a split-second, the said,

"If you are in that much pain, lie down. When they come for you in an hour or two, you'll be in a whole lot more pain as they march you to the burning oven."

"Is this another Elliott Stockade trick, sergeant?"

"While you lurch around trying to decide to follow my instructions, consider this: You, Mad Ghoul colluder, are 'almond', and Kid Sunshine there on your lap is 'Mr. Almond Eyes'. Now who would know that other than a friend. And, this 'Pipsqueak Hardy' or 'Pipsqueak Lou Costello', or 'Pipsqueak Gildersleeve', is all that stands between you, the furnace, and the Death Squad on its way to get you this very moment."

CHAPTER NINETEEN

-

On the Run

The Camp Elliott stockade was near-midnight dark when Pipsqueak and his two Navajo MPs led Peter with Sunny's feeble assistance, carrying Corpsman Campbell nonchalantly out the admissions lobby to the outer entrance gate. Sergeant Murph O'Laughlin, well-known to both Pipsqueak and Campbell, was on duty that night as the main-gate officer.

"Hey, sergeant! Open up!" hollered Pipsquak at the small office sign-in attached to the gate wall and administered by O'Laughlin and two MP guards.

Sliding the sign-in window open, the sergeant poked his head out, "Are these the guys?" he inquired.

"Yup," responded Pipsqueak, "going about our business."

"Well, get back quickly. I want to go have an early breakfast."

With that, the entrance gate officer pressed an interior button and the large steel double gate swung open. As the outer double gates slammed shut, and the stockade's light towers atop the battlement walkway engulfing the cellhouse and surrounding yards in bright illumination, Peter stared blankly at Pipsqueak.

Was this half-pint sergeant leading the three prisoners to their deaths?

With his uniform filthy, torn and blood-stained, hair matted, and eyes wide and alert, Peter whispered curtly,

"Who on earth are you?"

"For me to know and you to find out."

"Huh?"

"Sorry for being so snappish, but no time for proper introductions. You did your duty, Lieutenant, and now it's incumbent upon me to save your asses from the furnace. We'll be on the run, dodging and deceiving all the way across the 'boondocks', through the edge of Camp Elliott itself, past the water supply tanks, the new training areas at Camp Holcomb, across roads and streams, through 15,000 Marines, all the way to Building 6317, at the Marine Corps Air Station in Miramar near San Diego, some 20 miles from here. We trust no one, NO ONE. Hofmeister with his Death Squad will stop at nothing to find us. If he doesn't, at least a dozen of his staff and squad face court-martial murder charges and certain executions. We have a sack of dry bread, biscuits, and cookies, plus cheese and water. We're headed for an underpass electrical and tool encasement rarely opened about seven miles from here. Now we must get into the fields and travel by night. Any light on us in the darkness will mean death. Let's go," Pipsqueak ordered fiercely. "Of all the routes to safety at headquarters, I've chosen the only one that will work given they have multi-terrain vehicles crisscrossing the open lands. At daylight, they'll follow our tracks. More, I'll inform you about as we go along."

The following few moments were a strange combination of critical thought and warm emotion, puzzlement and giddiness. A full realization swept over Peter like a powerful surge, inundating him in confusion. Yes, they were free. But to what extent? No arrangements had been made by Pipsqueak to bring them to the ultimate authorities other than to walk some 20 miles to them while being pursued. They were left to shift for themselves in the midst of extreme danger.

Peter, Campbell and Sunny were grateful for having been rescued, even if they had been dumped in their dirty military clothes. Suddenly, they were men again instead of numbered punching bags. Triumph, relief, and fear surged through them. But would their exultations be short-lived? This was the real thing!

Suddenly, there were sounds of confusion back within the walls. Although no sirens or alarms had been sounded, something was underway. All ears were cocked.

Recovering his wits, Peter asked, "What now?"

"Shut up, all of you, and follow me, single file, without a word, quickly into the black night, off the main road, across the fields, irrigation ditches, ground crops."

As Pipsqueak turned, and began to tred his way into the darkness, he added tersely, "The moonlit night is more of an enemy than the dozen MPs Hofmeister is making ready to dispatch. Listen for shouts from search parties. Walk low. No profiles in the bright night. And, acknowledge you're terrified, every step of the way, beyond belief."

In the pitch darkness, Pipsqueak and the Navajo MPs, who as of yet had not uttered a single word, hurried. Peter, Campbell, and Sunny, despite their pain and weariness, slouched and shuffled as best they could from behind. It was cold, not quite frost-bitter cold, but far colder than the cells had been. Not one of the six-member team wore a sweater or jacket.

Time was getting on as the small party trudged and plodded on in silence. Surprisingly, Campbell revived, rallying to the point he could amble along by himself. Refreshed by the cold low wind, Sunny was able to maintain Pipsqueak's pace side by side with Peter, who muttered,

"No official confirmation from Hofmeister that we made it out. Apparently, no orders have been issued to mobilize, no alarms. But I bet every prisoner knows we're on the run. And, every one of them is rooting for us to succeed."

"The next few hours will be decisive, if we're to reach the utility hideout under the Highway 101 bridge I've staked out," reckoned Pipsqueak. "Even though the worst may be over, we can't be certain we're going to be clear and free all the way. We're still challenged. Listen, everyone. Huddle up to me for a moment. We're coming up to a ridge that leads to the tent camp at Linda Vista, eleven or twelve miles south of the main Elliott encampment. From there, we'll descend to a gully stream and follow that directly to the bridge underpass. Two things are critical. Watch your tracks. Follow me. Stay away from the water. Water means tracks which anyone can follow."

Then, he added, "We will have to hurry low-bent, shadow-silent on the ridge. We'll have to negotiate alongside near the top, not the skyline top. Just below the top. Crouching and as swift as we can. Don't forget. No matter how it looks black as ink. You may think it's plumb, utterly nighttime. That you can't see a thing. But remember this: No nighttime is so dark as people atop any elevation, any height with the black sky in the background can't be seen, distinguished. Meanwhile, we move fast. Enjoy the clean feel of the wind. I expect no trouble, but quickly let's…"

Just then, Sunny whispered loudly, "LOOK! To your right, due north! Small lights, like bugs floating around. No sounds, but dozens of lights!"

"Flashlights!" muttered Pipsqueak angrily. "But thank our stars, no dogs! They can't track us in the dark. This overwhelming blackness is our Savior. Let's go!"

Suddenly, a dozen scattered rifle shots from the vicinity of the bobbing specks of lights crushed the silence. As the six-man party whipped around in their tracks to stand like startled deer, heads erect, eyes disbelieving, ears taut, exerting to listen, a Browning Automatic Rifle crackled, its bullets snapping, popping, puncturing the top sands of the ridge, some ricocheting less than feet away from the escapees gripped in terror.

Amid the distant staccato of the BAR, and the resulting pinging sounds of bullets striking the earth, Pipsqueak cursed viciously,

"Down to the flats of the creek. Down! Down! The one thing I hadn't anticipated. That damn fox-minded Hofmeister outsmarted me!"

"Yeah, he figured this route," echoed Campbell, heavy-voiced. "Twice in the last year prisoners managed to get over the walls near the north stockade gate. It's not the shortest distance to 101, but probably the best since the fields are so rough and open."

The gruesome reality of their discovery gripped everyone in abject terror as they scrambled over the top, along the ridge that pitched down the bank to the creek.

"Quickly, into the creek waters. They'll cover our tracks. We've a distance to the overpass, but we'll make it."

Splashing into the cold shallows and forging up the narrow small stream, the men made their way briskly north, the shots still echoing. For more than an hour, no one said a word, although there was less confusion. The decline of the creek had diminished from thirty-degrees to less than fifteen, making the jaunt all the easier. No longer was anyone rattled, and all tumbling had ceased. The winds had increased their buffeting, but the near-freezing cold had warmed a trifle.

"Look," Peter pointed to the east, "There's the first dull streak of dawn above the eastern San Diego mountains. How much longer, Sergeant?"

"Not much. In fact, I see automobile and truck lights yonder to the right. We'll be approaching the overpass in mere moments."

Scanning the slopes' embankments from the gully bottom's creek flats, Pipsqueak, with a hint of excitement in his voice, pointed,

"There! There we are! The overpass. A few more minutes, then rest under the freeway most of the day. No more crouching, no more balancing, no more being shot at."

Looming on the dark grey-black distant horizon was what appeared to be a single light pole illuminating a horizontal line crossover or resting upon a pure black circle or hole. Streaks of light seemed to be continually flashing back and forth across it.

"That beautiful undivided four-lane highway bridge lit up for us to find!" exclaimed Pipsqueak. "Of the bridges over North and Southbound 101, I chose the smaller, least important one. To the north, is the large Santa Fe railroad underpass, part of the freight network in the Southern California area. Hofmeister is sure to look for us there. To the south is the massive interchange of connecting freeways and side roads serving all San Diego and the Miramar Naval bases and airfields. The MPs will scour the highway grade separation structures. Both are Army, Navy and Marine communication centers.

"Hofmeister's people are probably already in both places," agreed Peter.

"What I like about them all is that our Army and Marine Corps engineers made sure the wild animals of this part of the state, goats, deer, small harmless four-legged friends had a tunnel to go between the open fields," added Sunny.

"See the culvert and drainage conduit up there to the left? Both partially hidden where we are going to hide today.

Less than a minute later, with Pipsqueak leading the way, the six Marines started climbing up the embankment steps beneath the bridge to the 10-foot cyclone fence enclosure of the bridges' utility and drainage components. Here, behind a small pump station and free-standing panel-board of electrical powerline switches and water shut-off valves was a locked steel door with a "Storage--No Admittance!" sign.

Producing a key, Pipsqueak unlocked the steel door, and the six quickly entered. Pulling the door shut, he switched a dim light on and, although limited in space, each man was able to find space to sit or recline at will among tool boxes and equipment.

"Earlier in the week, I brought several stacks of sacks to sit or lie down on. Sorry, no blankets. Since the door is well-sealed, we can leave the light on. Get comfortable, because we'll begin our trek around 1600 this afternoon."

The men settled in for the day, the Navajo MPs sprawling themselves out on large road metal covering plates. Campbell, still in considerable pain, smiled at Peter,

"Who would believe it? We actually crashed out of that cell block guardhouse! I worked in a number of military detention structures, even studied some of the more classic examples, like the Navy's brigs, from inside out. Like a friend told me, 'A greased rat can't have get out of the Elliott Stockade unless he someone within giving it a stiff shove in the ass.' And, as of yet, we're not dead, burned to an easily crumbling, curled crisp, and tossed together into the dump. You, Sergeant, gave the shove. If we live through this, it's because of you."

Pipsqueak, on one knee peering through a crack at the door, turned, smiled, and nodded,

"Doing my duty, corpsman, doing my duty. But we're not 'home' and safe yet."

No sooner than Pipsqueak responded, when he whispered in a flat monotone of shock,

"Easy men, easy. I make out three figures climbing up our embankment. They have M-1s slung over their shoulders. Each has a large flashout despite the morning light. They're part of a patrol, coming our way. Get low behind the road plates, not a breath from anyone. If they open the door, I'll deal with them, one way or another, if they don't buy my lie that I'm AWOL. If they begin to come in to search, or threaten to take me back to Elliott, I'll kill them all."

As the steep climb became more demanding nearing the top of the ridge and its cyclone fenced-in utilities, the MPs stopped to rest. The leader of the three said,

"I'm calling a halt so we can eat the food we brought with us."

As they munched their provisions, they flashed their lights through the 10-foot-high fence all the way to the utility storeroom door, then on the ceiling of the overpass, finally agreeing nothing was out of order. Only one of the three had met the endurance test, the other two completely exhausted. For the following half hour, the three rested, then abruptly stood up and climbed their way to the top of the highway and marched alongside the edge, disappearing in the cold morning light.

With that, the six were reflective for a time. Although sleepless and Peter, Sunny, and Campbell exhausted from varying degrees of pain, they all knew other patrols were close.

"We'll make it!" Pipsqueak insisted. "Besides, they may not come this way at all. As late approaches, we'll leave, two at a time, maybe 20 yards apart so we're not observed as a group. But, all of us will be within sight of each other. Our route is simple. We'll have to cross Camp Elliott itself. Headquarters straddles the various camps. All their crossings are heavily guarded. Obviously, we'll need to avoid the main roads, bridges and rail lines crisscrossing the grounds. The units don't have the manpower to completely guard every stretch of the topography. We will hook up on the Headquarters step and spend the rest of the night sitting in the lobby until dawn. Our job now is to evaporate back into the military bases leading to the Miramar Administrative Center. Not for a single second can we forget that there are patrols out there scrutinizing every face of a man in uniform with explicit orders to shoot on sight if recognized."

With aching muscles finally consuming their remaining energies, all but Pipsqueak and Peter made themselves as comfortable as possible and closed their eyes. Pipsqueak, turning from his point of observation at the entrance, again smiled at Peter, gazing in wonderment at him. Peter responded, "If my life depended on it, I can't walk another step today."

"Rest, you won't have to. Try to take a long nap. I'll keep watch."

"Oh, Sergeant, I can't. I'm too excited to get back and give my oral account."

"Well, know this, Lieutenant. My year-long report is taped to my chest."

"Sunny and Campbell will have oral summaries like myself. Can you confide anything with me?" Peter asked searchingly.

"Sure. You'll hear it all anyway. The Elliott guardhouse; call it what you want, 'brig', 'stockade', was an unusual concentration of power and terror narrowly confined in one spot. Pure and simple. If you need to find murderers there, all you have to do is look behind desks. And, the desk of Captain Hofmeister is where terror was planned and started. And, he was the one who processed that terror in an orderly, systematic manner so that it appeared to be legal in the annals of military justice, that what he ordered done would pass muster in the minds of the inspectors."

"And," interjected Peter, "he had a special squad, a death unit, to carry out the punishments, some of which included murder, right?"

"Exactly. And, you were assigned to corroborate what we thought was factual. I was assigned to watch over Sunny who was planted early on to watch over you. The word, the noun 'almond' was selected as the identifying code, because it was the one name you knew well, having spent your summers on your grandparents' almond ranch in Galt, California. It is a term you wouldn't easily forget."

"They sure were right about that. unless it's my mother's maiden name, no word or name has more of an emotional meaning to me."

"So rumors of brutally tortured young Marines have been true. Most absorbed the torture, believing in the Corps concepts of discipline, the cowardice inherent in squealing and being 'a man' at all costs."

"And, the suicides?"

"Most accepted it as a by-product of war. Those who didn't, who questioned it, disappeared, presumably murdered."

"So, so sad. Unknown kid Marines, 18, 19, 20 years of age, willing to testify, refusing to bend, who did not take the easy route of closing their eyes, who opted for resistance and would not hesitate to risk their lives to prevent harm to fellow Marines--all gone, disappeared, murdered."

With that, Corpsman Campbell, who had awakened and was now listening, interrupted,

"Those were days one never forgets, days that tested a young Marine's character, integrity, resolve. I never knew so much physical and psychological torture without opening wounds, or even bruising men. I never know men to give themselves up to death so easily."

"Yes," added Sunny, "And the endless silence as shadows seemed to shoot from their wide, seriously wide eyes that were planted in pallid faces. When they were brought back from so-called 'interrogations' they looked as if brought back from the grave."

As the four gazed upon each other in what little light the cracked door had to offer, no one spoke. Each of them sat impassively, thinking his own thoughts, listening with his own ears to the first ever openly discussed eye-witness descriptions of the brutality.

"I remember how the first night I was pushed into a windowless cell on the lower floor," Sunny continued, "without even a blanket. On the wall, I saw a single five-word sentence, 'Welcome to murder basement'."

"In the infirmary," corpsman Campbell offered, "An interrogation was occasionally held when the basement was full. I saw for myself how questions came hard and fast, one after the other, question after question, from four MPs cross-examining, hitting the victim with their fists."

"No," Pipsqueak turned and commented, "detention meant, if not death itself, then a near-death event. And, the afflicted dared not say a word, yet alone complain. And, why, why, why? Not because of crimes, rule violations, or even juvenile infractions of less than less camp misdemeanors."

For a fraction of a moment, there was absolute silence. Then, Campbell said, quietly,

"The Camp Elliott Stockade has become a silent ghost-like death house. The solitary cells are hellholes of cruelty, perfidy, baseness. Supposedly those cells are for our young Marines to serve a little detention for minor violations of Article 51, Paragraph 3 of the Military Criminal Code. Now, there are dark, motionless men of pure evil who rule the stockade shadows, abetting murder."

Outside, the mild breeze, which had been refreshingly pleasing had, by mid-afternoon, turned into a crazily screaming wind. In the underpass utility storeroom, it felt more like a whimpering whisper. Soon, Pipsqueak knew, the party of six would be picking their way, cat-footed into its very howling, promising hours of treacherous journey throughout a second night.

"What I will never be able to erase from my mind," Sunny said softly, "are the screams lasing for hours, often throughout the night, finally turning to low whimpers, then loud screams again."

"Lieutenant," said Pipsqueak steadily in crystal clear language, "This is what you must know as fact. The MPs who were specially assigned to guard prisoners varied in both character and intellect. Some behaved correctly and even groused the system. Others were out and out sadists and tormentors of human beings. Harassment was vilest when it came to trifling matters. For example, tying hands and feed together for not saluting!"

"And," interjected Sunny, "never allowing us outside in the recreation yard for fresh air. One of their favorite tricks was to shut the cell door forcefully from the corridor so that the suddenly raised air pressure popping the poor fellow's eardrums. And, being manacled all the time, eating, sleeping, in the cells, relieving ourselves. And, for nothing. For having done nothing."

The final hours of that windy afternoon were the longest of Peter's life. All, including Pipsqueak and Peter were wide-awake, living the passing minutes in fear that a second search party would sound the alarm, having noticed a telltale sign pointing to the storage room. Their escape thus far, Peter felt, was successful because they had faithfully followed Pipsqueak's carefully directed guidance. He had been completely honest with the escapees, and, thus far, had saved their lives. He said,

"Our route is very simple. Follow me. Stand up and stretch. We walk in less than one minute…"

CHAPTER TWENTY

-

Flight to Headquarters

With the final vestiges of sunlight evaporating, Pipsqueak said softly with a wry smile to his assembled party outside the underpass storage,

"If you believe for a solid moment we've outrun, outsmarted Hofmeister's search parties, you could not be more sadly mistaken. With savvy MPs crisscrossing every known footpath trail, back alley, driveways, and roads, we're in greater danger than ever. We'll walk along in twos; the two Navajos in the lead, me and the Lieutenant second, and the boy with the corpsmen third. We'll remain behind each other's twosome by some 25 yards, enough to see the group ahead. My Navajo boys know the way, and, remember, stay behind enough to see the two heads ahead of you. We'll become lost in the myriad of the small tent camps, barracks, warehouses, storage facilities, and the terrain itself. Tonight's moonlight is both friend and enemy."

Pipsqueak paused a moment to collect his thoughts, then ordered everyone to drink several sips from the two canteens the Navajo MPs were carrying along with their personal kits. The Navajos and Pipsqueak were now officially AWOL and could be shot on sight.

As they walked behind the alert, ever-caution MPs, Pipsqueak hoped their silhouettes would suggest the highway traffic Mexican farm laborers on their way home to their huts and cottages. They crossed the fields, tiptoed past small hovels and through backyards.

Within an hour, the party, two at a time, reached the small railway branch line which ran southwest past the large water tanks. After crossing the railroad tracks, they approached a small stream, less than five feet wide, an easy jump for even the most wounded man. Although several dogs barked, there were no other responses as the six scrambled to the other side and continued to make their way. Pipsqueak whispered to Peter in a reassuring tone,

"We have no map. But the boys ahead remembered the way. Notice how they carefully listen for patrols, and when encountering unexpected sounds or shacks and other objects, they instinctively give them wide berths? Never forget, like all of Indian ancestry, they are Indian first, which makes them the best of the fighters. The Japs can't figure them out, let alone the mysterious language they try to decipher."

"Well," Peter returned," They appear to be doing a job leading us. How much longer would you say before we get there?"

"Maybe two, three hours…"

Meanwhile, with the Navajo MPs leading the way in the moonlight, all towers, structures, observation posts, warehouses, hangars and assorted repair and assembly shops 20 feet aboveground were given wide berths.

Within an hour or two, four of the six were pretty tired, walking for more than 7 hours the night before, followed by broken, uncomfortable sleep. Now, without adequate food, water, and with body muscles lacking proper conditioning, Pipsqueak, Peter, Campbell and Sunny were feeling drained and depleted.

Circling a newly-installed 12-foot deer fence required an additional hour Pipsqueak hadn't anticipated. Glancing at his watch, and seeing it was only a little past 10:00PM, he decided to rest the group for a half hour in a small clump of trees. Despite the stiff breeze, down from the powerful winds of only hours before, the men laid down. Hungry, thirsty, and a bit lightheaded, the fatigued men began dozing. A moment later, Pipsqueak instantly raised his head in apt attention when he heard cyclists approaching on a nearby rarely-used dirt road, hoping he hadn't settled the group too close to the road. Although the four motorcycles pulled up, and the cyclists scanned powerful heavy-duty flashlights over the terrain and along the deer fence, they soon remounted their vehicles and roared off. All was well, and as Pipsqueak glanced at the men, with the exception of one Navajo on guard across the area, he thought to himself, "We're right on schedule, and all is well."

What ensued in the final seven-hour moonlit hike was an event Lieutenant Peter Toscanini would remember for a lifetime. Pipsqueak's undercover assignment was to maneuver the escapees through what was referred to as the "California Desert Mecca for Marines". And, in late 1944, Camp Elliott was incredibly busy. Five separate commands were quartered there. They were the headquarters for the Fleet Marine Forces, San Diego Area, where the escape party was headed; the Fleet Marine Force Training Center; the Amphibious Training Command, Pacific Fleet; the Marine Barracks; and Base Depot. Each command was separate and distinct with specific responsibilities. Of these, the largest and most complex was the Fleet Marine Force Training Center with Pipsqueak must now lead his party of escapees. What made the journey so arduous was the fact the Training Center had approximately 30 schools that taught a wide variety of subjects, including individual combat and modern infantry. Following the Japanese attack on Pearl Harbor three years previously on December 7th, 1941, the USMS was flooded with new recruits, expanding the Center's facilities.

Pipsqueak whispered, "We are about to traipse through as many as 15,000 troops and officers as if we are a part of them. To get to General Clayton B. Vogel's Fleet Marine Force Training Center Headquarters, we have to simply negotiate our way past every necessary facility for quartering, feeding, equipping and training every single one of those 15,000 men."

And, so it was that two by two, all within eyesight distance of each other, the party walked briskly past mile-long rows of buff-colored double-deck barracks, educational Quonset huts, shops, sheds, storehouses, and maintenance facilities.

And even more.

Since the area was the home of the 32,000-acre Fleet Marine Force Training Center West Coast, it was entirely self-contained. Named after Major General George F. Elliott, a past Commander of the United States Marine Corps, the camp also contained several banks, post offices, grocery stores, cleaners, a clothing store, pharmacy, and several "personal services outlets".

Because Camp Elliott and its 30 plus programs specialized in the training of replacement organizations, that is, units of troops being sent to replace depleted units already engaged with the enemy in the Pacific.

Because virtually the entire base was illuminated and extraordinarily active with troop movements in maneuvers, and otherwise, well past midnight, the escape party walked nonchalantly down the sidewalks of the main streets and avenues toward the Fleet Marine Force Headquarters. Located at the end of Camino del Rio North at the Marine Corps Air Station in Miramar, the destination, the office of Base Commander General Clayton B. Vogel, Fleet Marine Force, was less than a few hours away. By his calculation, Pipsqueak figured the group would arrive by 5:00AM, an hour before sunup.

The only impediment to the final phase of the march was the two lead Navajos engaging in conversation with three fellow Navajo MPs at the busy intersection of Main Street at El Dorado Avenue in the small village of Miramar.

"Damn," Pipsqueak whispered angrily to Peter. "Look at that. Under the brightest streetlight in all of little, old Miramar, an Indian party of five Navajos. We'll have to signal Sunny and Corpsman Campbell to linger in an alley or doorway until our boys clear us to continue. And, we're so close."

Miramar, a small civilian village of less than 30 residents within the Fleet Marine Force Training Center, was located a few miles west of Linda Vista on the Mesa along the Penasquitos Road. The community center where Pipsqueak's party was temporarily halted was situated inside the current station boundary, and had a post office, elementary school, general store, blacksmith, and a cemetery. Historically, E.W. Scripps, the multimillionaire newspaperman and his family were the area's most notable residents and construction and maintenance of their mansion and estate were the foundation for the economy of the growing community.

As Pipsqueak and Peter waited in a dark alley, and Campbell and Sunny in a doorway, the five MPs were engaged in an animated discussion. Pipsqueak explained,

"Damn good Redskins, the Navajos. Especially those three talking to my boys."

"How so?" wondered Peter, aloud.

"Well, as the code was being developed, those three MPs, the just recruits, were brought into the program and trained, bringing the total number of trained Code-Talkers at the time to 32. By the end of August 1942, the first group, of which they were now a part, had been deemed sufficiently trained. Of the original 32, 13 were assigned to the 1st Marine Division and 16 were assigned to the 2nd Signal Company of the 2nd Marine Division. But those three remained at Camp Elliott where they served as trainers for the newly-recruited Navajos. The

Marine Corp was given the authorization to recruit up to 200 additional Navajo."

"On 'Canal'," Peter interjected, "I met and knew some by name. Invaluable, absolutely invaluable, service they provided. The Japanese were so perplexed they were all beside themselves!"

"Look!" exclaimed Pipsqueak, "Our boys are signaling for us to move forward. Those three MPs now know who we are, just as they know full well about the guardhouse murders. Navajo Six-Bits was as much a noble hero to them as to my two boys. I'm surprised they haven't killed Hofmeister, yet."

With that, Pipsqueak looked to his right down the street and gave a short save to Campbell and Sunny, who immediately returned the signal. Pipsqueak literally bounded forth, Peter following less than a few feet behind him.

"The little community of Miramar seems to thrive more at night than during the day!" Pipsqueak chuckled as they hurried past the three MPs hanging around the lamppost. As Peter nodded in respect, the three Navajos smiled slightly, and knowingly, as families, civilian, and military personnel crossed their paths.

Because the entire base had been activated as an "instant city", the streets were active. No one bothered to glance at the three sets of two military men pressing their way forward, past a mixed line of moviegoers waiting to purchase tickets in front of "Theater Marine Corps Air Station" featuring pinup star Betty Grable.

"They change the movies in there three times a week," Pipsqueak said, pointing. "Cinema celebrities, as well as westerns, especially with Roy Rogers and Gabby Hayes, are always popular fare with our troops. A lot of those guys just got back from two- and three-day maneuvers. As exhausted as they are, they showered and look spic and span, ready for an hour and a half of Betty's legs. They'll watch anything but morale films."

Even the older trade, utility and warehouse section of Miramar was active late that night. Past weedgrown lots, brick and weather-beaten wooden houses, gray with age, some abandoned long since by whites to a black populace of stevedores, warehouse workers, and military base laborers of varying sorts. Small, unpainted grocery stores were still open. Occasionally, and despite the lateness, a youngster darted toward them from his front porch and asked,

"Any gum, chum?"

Pipsqueak always smiled and answered,

"No. But will half a Hershey bar do?"

Turning to Peter, he chuckled, "That question is so incessant in England and France I hear it has become a standard form of greeting."

Leaving the old town of Miramar behind, the small party, still dispersed and always alert for movement, especially jeeps filled with MPs sneaking up on them, stumbled upon unmanned searchlights and camouflaged piles of large wooden boxes and crates stacked neatly 15 to 20 feet high.

"You know," Peter smiled. "That little town of Miramar seems to radiate a sense of exuberant hospitality. Wish we had time to explore its shops. That's the kind of community that lasting friendships are built upon. I like this entire area of Southern California. Someday I'll come back to really see and know it, the surrounding similar towns and countryside terrains."

As they hurried past a dirt road intersection entangled with vehicles from the supply services, Pipsqueak commented,

"Even this late at night, there's huge movement of supplies and munitions. Everywhere. Even out here. Supply dumps unlike I've ever seen. Bet this part of California is going to sink under the weight."

After the party entered and passed through an area where all the structures were essentially similarly built from the Quartermasters' 700 series plans drawn up in the 1930s, Pipsqueak said,

"All built from wood, the cheapest, fastest form of construction-- bare, sterile, and with an angular institutional look...only one of two stories high to reduce fire hazard, nothing decorative added, only the flagpole flying our stars and stripes the aesthetic point. All are painted the same drab green color. Notice the camp streets are not marked in case the enemy gets in here."

Peter added, "Is that a PX, post exchange, to your left?"

"Yes, and a huge one at that."

"And, the chapel up ahead?"

"Yes, and next to it a fair-sized mess hall. I supposed the wide building coming up is the base recreation facility. It's open 24 hours a day. At first, I thought we might bunk down there tonight. In the back room, there are cots and blankets. But six of up showing up at the same time might trigger a call to local MPs who are certainly aware of our escape. No, best we keep going to Headquarters. We may have to sleep on chairs, but it would be harder for them to extricate us from in front of the Fleet Commander's office."

"Yes."

"Yet, it's hard to pass the recreation center. Did you know the Marine Corps and Army has carefully screened hostesses on duty during weekends? Girls from throughout San Diego County are bussed in Friday and Saturday nights to dance with our boys."

"Really? I think that's just wonderful," Peter reacted.

"We're coming up to the YMCA. Across the way up to your right is the medical detachment, all units housed next to each other, and beyond that a winding hedge and tree-lined side road will take us right into Headquarters complex."

Walking rapidly past the base hospital collection of buildings, Pipsqueak explained,

"This hospital covers some 60 acres all by itself, alone. It rivals the best medical institutions in the country and accommodates more than 1,000 patients. We'll be moving through 50 buildings, dodging patrols and clusters of troops. We'll even have to widen our distances from each other. But this late at night, no one will be at work in the dietitian kitchens, laboratories, psychiatric clinics, barracks for minor patients, hospital staffs, workers in the supply outlets and their backroom warehouses. Let me tell you, what we're entering is so vast with so many streets and alleys, no one will find us.

As they continued their trek, Peter commented, "I expect we will be debriefed the moment we get in the lobby. I would like to hit a chair, throw a blanket over me, and go to sleep."

"Well," responded Pipsqueak, "Forget sleep. As soon as we present ourselves to whomever is on duty, we'll face obligatory confinement. Hopefully all the MPs will be arrested and confined at a different camp, brig, or stockade. Not one stray Elliott MP must be allowed free. If so, we risk assassination, all of us, either one at a time, or as a group. When a penitentiary, prison, jail, guardhouse is ruled by absolute authoritarian rule, deaths are inevitable. Military detention centers are especially subject to terrorist interrogation methods not human. Elliott has always had a scary reputation, undoubtedly because we are so far out on the edges of the base. No one wants to go out there to inspect, heal, or help. And, Captain Hofmeister is the chief horrormeister. And, it all takes places in a dehumanized, degraded jail bereft of reason and justice."

The Old Escondido Road the fugitives had carefully been making their way on yielded to a roundabout whose arteries spread in various directions.

"The one directly ahead will take us down Semper Fi Drive to the face of the Fleet Marine Force Headquarters. Camino del Rio Avenue runs directly into it, circulating the flagpole in front. We'll be there in less than an hour. Commander General Clayton Vogel won't be notified we've arrived until sunup when he awakens. Before the war, these roads were used by farmers and ranchers making their way to the San Diego markets. The last leg of the Butterfield Overland Stagecoach line from New York to Dan Diego wound its route along the Escondido Road in 1887. It was discontinued in 1912 when the postal service began transporting the north county mail from Escondido by automobile; some history, this place."

As the party neared the entrance to the Headquarters, they commingled with various officers and troops, some who acknowledged them with nods and waves, most simply ignoring them. In the crisp night air, Peter smiled when he read a large billboard sign which read,

"Led by Love of Country,"

and less than 25 yards behind it, a second sign in the same style of printing and colored background,

"So help us God to keep this faith."

Glancing up and down the increasingly active road emanating from the roundabout, Pipsqueak said,

"The 535th Anti-Aircraft Artillery…Battalion is assigned the responsibility of protecting the Fleet Marine Force Headquarters. The 535th was born in 1942, replacing the 65th Coast Artillery. The guns in use are 99mms, which can hit targets up to six miles away. Interspersed among those 99mms are 40mms, and .50-caliber machine guns capable of pouring out 500 shots a minute."

Suddenly, out of the darkness, a rough-sounding Sergeant emerged clutching a lower M-1.

"Where to, men?"

"Headquarters to drop onto cots. We're done-in."

"How so?"

"We're among the Mojave Anti-Aircraft Artillery from Camp 'Dusty'. One of the Battalion's trucks is parked behind Headquarters. In the morning we're off to the artillery range. We were allowed passes to enjoy Miramar for a few hours after a long day of 'dry runs', which included filling and hauling sandbags for furthering protecting Headquarters against shrapnel. Check with the gun unit No. 1 section of D Battery protecting the back of the Headquarters," challenged Pipsqueak.

"Did you enjoy yourselves tonight at Miramar?" he chuckled.

"You've got to be kidding," reacted Pipsqueak.

"Go ahead, men. We'll see you in the mess hall breakfast line."

So baffling was the flat one-story structure looming before them, the Pipsqueak entourage froze in disbelief.

"What the hell?" Sunny asked out loud. "Is that Headquarters? Looks like a lit-up Highway 99 honky-tonk."

"More like a whorehouse," chimed in Campbell.

"Well," chuckled Pipsqueak. "we're stateside now, so no fear of Jap bombers."

Peter, equally astonished, remained silent, relieved the party had arrived safely, equally puzzled by the facility before them.

Apparently, more than a dozen ordinary sleeping barracks had been bolted together in a huge square surrounding three interior gardens. Remodeled and reconditioned, administrative offices and officer quarters including a small kitchen had been fashioned. Now, Headquarters, accentuated by the variety of gun emplacements, and, behind it, a number of supplemental storehouses, two water tanks, and several troop barracks shined as a brightly-illuminated large diamond under trillions of sparkling stars.

"Makes you want to go in and play," mused Peter.

Hurrying past a large wood professionally painted signboard reading, the party noted:

TRAINING CENTER

ADMINISTRATION

USMC FLEET MARINE FORCE

A small sign attached to the bottom of it read:

COMMANDER

GENERAL CLAYTON B. VOGEL

Where for two days no one paid particular attention to any of the twosomes, all eyes were now on the six men. Two fully-armed sentries guarding the entrance left their post to quickly step forward quizzically riveted on each of them.

Almost simultaneously, a Lieutenant accompanied by five equally heavily-armed sentries stepped from the shadows of a covered walkway, surprising both the entrance guards and the Pipsqueak fugitives.

Holding up his hand as they stepped lively from the somewhat hidden area among the eucalyptus trees adjacent the lawns, "Stop, Marines! We've been expecting you. You are to follow me as a safety and security measure. After bedding down for the remainder of the night, then breakfast, showers, and change of clothing commencing at 0600, you're to be debriefed at 0900 in Commander Vogel's presence. Meanwhile, Sergeant, three of my five will join you at the entrance. Under no verbal or written orders are you to allow anyone into the facility. Headquarters will be completely surrounded and secured within minutes. Upon the highest orders which are being typed now from within, you are to fire upon and kill anyone or group who attempts to force his way forward. Now, gentlemen, follow me, under armed guard. Total closure and lockdown orders are in effect until 0600 when a Battalion of MPs from the Camp Irwin in the Mojave Deserve arrives for your protection."

Following the Lieutenant, Pipsqueak piped up, "We're anxious to get to our cots. The night is icy cold, and none of us had the proper clothing for our long jaunt.

After a long moment huddling with the entrance sergeant, the Lieutenant motioned for the party, with Pipsqueak and Peter joining him side by side.

"Who called us in? How did you know we were approaching Headquarters?"

"The sergeant of the Navajo MPs your boys conversed with on the street in Miramar. Of course, the military in all Southern California has been scouring cities and countrysides for you fellas."

Peter, sizing the Lieutenant up, instantly liked the officer. Deeply understanding, it appeared he knew all about the Camp Elliott stockade disappearances. He said as the party half-stumbled down the steps and across the small porch connecting long verandahs,

"I'm glad you are all safe and sound. But you're certainly nothing to admire, shoes heavily caked with mud, some of you stained with blood, filthy to the bone, hair matted with dirt, each of you a mess."

Peter, somewhat sarcastically, "Yes, compared to you, spruce, cleanly shaved, freshly out of bed at 0200. No, you, the epitome of sharp military, us the sad tragedy of murder."

"Yes, I'm sorry. All of us here were hoping to see you, none of us dreaming you were on your way here."

"Oh, for a hot shower, soap suds, and a cot of warm blankets," Sunny muttered.

"Well, come it," the Lieutenant, a good-looking man with obviously an extraordinary character, smiled as he led the way forth.

As the group tiresomely reached the top step of the lobby porch, Peter positioned himself near the rear of the group to reflect for a moment upon the overall aesthetics of the wood-framed Headquarters.

Designed and assembled to be low, slim, and virtually colorless, the bolted-together barracks provided a sufficient warm incandescence from the extra-clean skylighting and abundant wall windows that Headquarters' flexibility and nimbleness seemed to welcome rather than hinder or threaten the visitor.

The heavily-trafficked entry on the front porch consisted of standard double doors, encasing highly-reflective glazing. Peter whispered to Pipsqueak who had walked back to hasten the Lieutenant along,

"What a marvelous design from ordinary barracks. Even Frank Lloyd Wright would approve. Sleek, clean lines, obvious courtyards within, and all most certainly fire-resistant."

From a night that had been busy and noisy, the group was relieved that the open light-filled lobby was calm and quiet. Its layout hinted at a friendly, height-increased atmosphere. A table with a few dozen bottles of Sonoma, California mineral water, greeted them. Immediately indulging themselves as the Lieutenant and guards watched with a bit of amusement, the fugitives had a few moments to glance around as they gulped the mineral water, quenching their thirsts.

On the ground floor, they noted offices, conference rooms, lavatories, wash basins, and janitorial storage rooms. What mattered the most to Peter was the reception that Pipsqueak was receiving from the high number of officers and adjunct personnel sitting on lounge couches or standing and conversing in small groups. Peter was certain he glimpsed officers turn their heads and spit in contempt on the floor.

As the Lieutenant led the way down the main corridor toward the back of the Headquarters facility, with the three armed sentries bringing up the rear, Peter was delighted to see patio gardens with lush vegetation, including a number of rare, exotic Pacific Island flowers.

"Imagine that, horticulture during a time of death and destruction," he chuckled approvingly.

Along the lengthy rather sparse corridor, officers sitting on couches sipping hot coffee and munching freshly-baked pastries, eyed them unsmilingly.

"We're certainly out of place, looking more like tramps or hoose-gow bait," whispered Peter to Pipsqueak, "but maybe they know who we are and detest us for snitching. Look at those raised eyebrows!"

"Yeah," responded Pipsqueak rather defiantly. "I'm so weary of bastards like that, with no a single sing of war having touched them.

Fresh, crisp, and clean in smartly pressed uniforms, especially after what we've been through."

"Well, can't say that I blame them, us appearing like after-battle dregs."

Approaching a large double-door room, the Lieutenant announced,

"This is our small athletic room for staff daily workout sessions. Temporary cots are set up for your use until sunup. Strip and crawl under the blankets for at least a few hours of shuteye. Coffee and baked goods are on the way. Sleep, after, if you can. I'll get you at 0530 for a quick breakfast, shower, shave, and issuance of fresh uniforms right down the hall from here. You'll be then ushered into Commander Vogel's conference room at 0700. I understand a rather large gathering will be sitting in to hear wha you each has to say. Based upon that, arrests will begin immediately."

CHAPTER TWENTY-ONE

-

Captain Hofmeister, Again

To their surprise, the first thing everyone in the escape party saw as they entered the made-over gymnasium was MP Lawrence "Larry" Angelo, the only military police officer to show sympathy for not only Six-Bits and the other Code-Talkers, but also concern regarding the disappearances.

Sitting up wrapped in blankets on one of seven cots lined up next to each other, he was as surprised to see them as they were to see him.

"Well, I'll be damned," exclaimed Pipsqueak. "What foolishness brings you here?"

Angelo grinned sheepishly.

"Once I heard you all were on the run, I knew the Hofmeister Death Squad would immediately seek me. The hospital van was how I opted out."

"Good for you," one of the Navajo MPs said, walking up to him, rubbing his back. "You are a good people, one of us."

"Sure, so much so I couldn't save Six-Bits. I heard about when the squad returned and were laughing about it in the mess lounge," Angelo said softly, head bowed.

"Well, you saved our asses," Corpsman Campbell smiled, "I'll forever be indebted."

"Why? Don't you know we're at death's door? They're out there at this time doing their best to find you. They figured you'd be headed for the Camp Pendleton Commander. They've been swarming Hwy 99 and surrounding countrysides for almost three days now. I'm going back to sleep. I awakened with the commotion down the corridor. I knew it was you guys. As for me, I'm crawling under. I supposed we'll all be gathered in for the debriefing at the same time in the morning. Now, goodnight, men."

Everyone was too weary to further converse. And, it wouldn't have benefitted anyone anyway as the fugitives, uninterested in food or drink, began pulling off their filthy uniformed with their caked blood.

"Anyone want a hot shower?" the Lieutenant asked with a smile. For Peter, who leaped at the opportunity, it was the first hot water he had had on his backside since Camp Stoneman. The bulk military soap had a sweet, luxurious scent, its suds a relief for exhausted muscles. The fresh underwear that had thoughtfully been rushed forth as they all showered nearby. Refreshed, they were soldiers of the United States Marine Corps again. Respectable, clean and presentable. All they needed were shaves, but that would come soon enough. The cots with clean, crisp sheets and Navy blankets were surprisingly comfortable. And, for less than two and a half hours, all six men slept soundly side by side with Sergeant Lawrence "Larry" Angelo of the Camp Elliott Stockade Military Police.

Later, what seemed like only a few moments, everyone was up for yet a second hot shower, the welcomed shaves, and hearty breakfasts. It still wasn't daylight. The Lieutenant, who had remained with the party since their arrival on the Headquarters' step, said,

"The day may have surprises in store for everyone. This is Commander Vogel's show and he wants you outside his office door in less than 30 minutes. He says he wants to meet Lt. Toscanini, especially since he's the 'almond' spy extraordinaire."

Through the corridor skylights, Peter on the walk with the others to the commending general's office, noticed through the skylights that daylight had crept through the typical early morning overcast. Within, meanwhile, orderlies and staff were already going about their administrative paperwork. It would be interesting, Peter thought to himself, to tour the facility, inspecting office by office, the nitty-gritty management of war, day in and day out. Most of these would never hear a single gunshot, and certainly never know the fear of being shot at. Yet, these unsung heroes were absolutely vital for winning the war.

As the group silently approached the outer open desks in the foyer of the commanding General's Office, young staff officers in quiet efficiency typing, filing, and engaging in other secretarial duties looked up to see seven men descending upon them, six of them attired in varying military clothing. Peter smiled at the incongruity of pristine officers attempting to fathom the meaning of the seven-man party headed for the commander's office.

Flush with the wall at the end of the corridor was General Vogel's large office and conference room. Two armed MPs standing at ease, but eyes watchful and fully alert, guarded the entrance which was fashionable set back 18". Directly across at the end of the corridor, where 10 comfortable chairs facing the entrance to the Commanding General's office.

For more than an hour, the fugitives sat still and silent as death, each preoccupied with his own thoughts. Within the opposite office walls, there was considerable commotion, movements, voices, shouting, and other unusual notices and activities. As hard as Peter tried to hear what was going on, he could not determine the words and other sounds. He whispered to Campbell,

"Several different voices. Can't make out what's being said, but it sounds serious."

Finally, under the steady gazes of the two MP sentries, Peter stood up, walked a few steps, and sighed.

Just then, as a small chain scraped across metal, and the two MPs snapped to attention, the office door opened smoothly inward, and Commanding General Vogel stepped out. In a tired, almost angry voice, he motioned,

"Come in, men, we've been waiting for you. Sorry for the delay, but we had to clear up a few things. Go on in and take a chair."

Since Peter had already been standing for a moment or two when the general opened his office door and greeted the Pipsqueak party, the Lieutenant smiled, delighted to finally notch the face and figure of a man with the sterling reputation he had heard so much about during his entire enlistment. Just recently, both Pipsqueak and Campbell had spoken highly of the general's "soul of honor", referencing as well Vogel's geniality and sensibility. "Everyone who serves under him," commented Pipsqueak, "acknowledges the commander is a first-class soldier."

Now, despite being vapid and somber, the tall, thin, balding man with the barest hint of a smile stood at the threshold of his office door and shook the hand of each escapee who crossed it. The first thing Peter noticed as he entered the large office was a huge electric ceiling fan fully-functioning above the general's desk. Some 10 to 12 yards in front of Peter were more than a dozen ordinary US Army chairs arranged in a semicircle before a large reddish-brown and mahogany desk virtually devoid of all paperwork. Peter noted instantly as he ambled forward to the nearest chair the desktop was as pristine as the general's uniform, although he had rolled up his sleeves, his jacket stretched over the back of yet another common Army-issued chair.

"Clean, neat and certainly able and competent, without the slightest air of dilettantism or manners of a poseur. My kind of man, real, genuine, no nonsense, but kind and gentle."

Also catching his eye were the dozens of unarmed, other than long black batons, MPs, six evenly spaced on each side of the room standing at attention.

"Normal," thought Peter. "He must feel we're dangerous."

Suddenly, as he neared the semicircle, he noticed two vaguely familiar figures with their backs toward him facing the front of the desk. Momentarily stunned by simultaneously confusion and fear, Peter winced in pain. Grimacing in pure disgust, he recognized the two Marines handcuffed hands behind their back to their chairs. Just as the two turned their heads to see who was approaching, Commander-in-Chief General Clayton B. Vogel of the Fleet Marine Force, Training Center, dropped the bombshell,

"Gentlemen, I believe you know Captain Hofmeister and Dr. Simon Fisherly, the Chief Physician of the Camp Elliott Stockade. Both certainly know each of you."

Even before the full sentence could be completed, PFC Lawrence "Larry" Angelo, recognizing from the distance of the office entrance who they were, was so instantly enraged that he bounded past those in front of him, and literally leaped headlong, arms wide open, to grasp the two seated handcuffed men in a tumultuous whirlwind uproar. Pounding with his fist whomever the figure next to him sprawled on the polished wooded floor, it required the entire contingent of MPs, their batons beating all three of the prone man into submission. The noisy chaos and commotion lasted less than 60 seconds.

Pulled to his feet, badly bruised around his head and bleeding from his scalp near the left ear, Larry Angelo exclaimed,

"What the hell have I done?"

Struggling to stand with his hands still handcuffed to the back of his chair, Hofmeister, bleeding from a long deep cut above his eye, and

Dr. Fisherly, relatively unhurt, attempted feeble grins without comment.

As Vogel sat down in his chair behind his desk, he motioned for the aghast, eyes glazed over escapees to take whatever seats remained standing.

"Well, boys, we're used to hectic intent-to-kill moments, aren't we? But I understand the PFC's natural reaction," General Vogel commented, giving Angelo a sour grin.

Turning to the others now all seated, with the 12 MPs repositioning back against the wall, he said quietly, leaning slightly across his desk, "Gentlemen, there is business at hand we must confront. But before we begin, is anyone interested in a hot cup of Java?"

As inviting as the offer was, no one responded, each man paralyzed in thought.

After a brief stunned silence, Dr. Fisherly asked hesitantly, somewhat hoarsely,

"How can you think of coffee now? Man should not live by bread alone."

Peter glanced at him, wondering, 'What kind of daffy question and statement is that?' Then, he turned to study Hofmeister.

The square-jawed Germanic face of the Captain was dead-white. With long lines stretching downwards from his eye-sockets, he was no longer the "Hated Boche" that many of the Marine veteran inmates referred to him as. Instead, the cruel, sadistic Marine Corps Officer was wearing a simply combat sweater filthy between recognition, appeared weary to the point of collapse. Not a muscle moved. Whereas, the physician-administrator, who shook with emotion, seemed indignant, fiercely wrathful.

To Peter, the dumpy little man in charge of the stockade was pitiful as he appeared more a victim than anyone else. He was in a mighty distressful state and Peter felt sorry for him. He felt like rising, walking over to him and with his handkerchief, wiping the single tear that made its way down his tear-stained face. He hesitated, lest General Vogel, and the others, especially his fellow travelers, saw the gesture as a sign of collaboration. Because the sight of Hofmeister on the verge of slobbering all over himself turned his stomach, Peter turned away, gazing through the office's single window overlooking an open-skied garden. Midday had turned gray and a fine drizzle more like a thin mist had started falling, creating and deepening glistening hues on the vegetation.

As for Fisherly, his arrest and handcuffing, in addition to a sleepless night, seemed to strengthen him. His mouth was tightly closed in defiance as his eyes burned in a somber fire. Tightly cuffed and sitting side by side with Hofmeister, he turned sharply with a grimace, then sneered,

"You are the one responsible for the unspeakable things done to our boy by the inhuman goalers assigned to you in our brig. It is you by your cruelty who egged them on.

The commander raised his hand, and asked casually, "Am I to take it that no one wants a cup of coffee?"

Without so much as batting a single eyelash, the doctor continued, "You starved, interrogated, stripped naked, tortured to death, and burned to ashes many innocent kids."

Captain Hofmeister, who had been leaning forward, turned and yelled loudly,

"You piece of cow dung. You know damn well it was you! YOU! You kept the black list! You, the great doctor, kept the boys from medical help adding to the suffering. You made the Camp Elliott Stockade extremely dangerous. You, Doctor, are responsible for that sinister maze of murder. Yes, I admit I frequently saw nooks and niches of blood."

Hofmeister paused, then looked up at his commander, and, for a moment, reflected, 'He won't believe me that his chief physician, such a fair-haired, solidly-built, tall, gentle, good-natured, and distinctly dignified, was the head of the death squad'.

Suddenly, Hofmeister's face reddened as he turned back towards Dr. Fisherly. Pure rage now gripped him as he struggled to release himself from his handcuffed hands, as the physician nonchalantly looked at the Captain with a sneering grin.

"Why you dirty toe-sucker! You were in it every step of the way. On the selection of the Marines to be 'punished'. Oh yes, you knew what was happening all right. Your furtive expressing has become sickeningly habitual. It gave you away every day, from the very beginning," shouted the physician.

After a short pause, Captain Hofmeister retorted,

"Because of you, there was fear. In the air! Often, I had difficulty restraining from bursting into hysterical tears. Oh, how I hated what you and your Gestapo were doing!"

After yet another short pause, Hofmeister continued,

"It has been known ever since our bleak prison began that you ordered, organized, and coordinated the beatings and killings by all the special unit you organized. I repeat, you, it was you, who made the selections and punishments, including murders by 'special treatment'. The scene of all the crimes was the basement right under my office floor. Reports of these extreme punishment made their way back to the Headquarters and the commander."

"Yes! Yes!" screamed the physician. "True, all true and we should have killed you, too. Oh, how I wish we had!"

"You swine, you swineherd! At this very moment you had two more down there. Two so-called defendants awaiting your evil death-sentencing hand," Hofmeister snapped back.

"I was planning on commuting them, you stupid fat Kraupt."

"Yes," Hofmeister scoffed, curling his upper lip, "an American Kraut at that who will follow you to the stake before the firing squad. Best if high-explosive saturation bombing takes down that stockade with you in it."

Turing back to Commander Vogel, Hofmeister said in a low whisper, "I am so happy you liberated me from that horrible place. From all my guilt and sadness, I am free. Even my prayers couldn't help me. I, too, heard the screams. In that death squad, I was all alone. I, in my way, arranged for a number, more than you know of, boys to live by transferring them from our brig to the Pendleton Hospital with forged paperwork specifying the need for life-saving surgery. They are living proof I let them live and did not shoot them in the back of the head."

"You have their names?" interjected Commander Vogel.

"Absolutely," responded Hofmeister.

Angrily, the Doctor spit at the Captain, "You low-ranking official."

"Perhaps, but I am free to face the firing squad. I told the Commander upon their escape he had no further to look for the murderer of the guardhouse atrocities than behind the administrative desk of the infirmary."

Dr. Fisherly, snarling, did not respond.

Captain Hofmeister's final words before relapsing in a prolonged somber silence were,

"At last the horrible stench of death is lifted from my body."

As everyone in the office stared at the Captain in amazement, the physician, frowning sternly, began unleashing a spasm of pent-up emotion. In the calm and quiet, they seemed to rush up in horrific evilness. The somewhat hour-long tranquility of the proceedings was not shattered by noise, but by the words spoken in soft tones.

"Yes, I'm that physician who was relegated to that minor infirmary. My assignment was to ensure all measures were taken within the guard house to crush treasonable aggressions. My acts of defense of the homefront are legally justified. I was hard-hitting, unlike the patsy with the fat ass sitting there. Yes, I created a political police force from within. Yes, I coordinated its tasks from my office. And, it was me with unflinching perseverance who carried out the deeds. And, don't you try to wiggle out of it, you slop. You cannot ward off your execution by confessing. Our goal was the expulsion of the weaker Mariners. We meant to guarantee the purity of the USMC."

Commander Vogel suddenly put his hand up as if to stop Fisherly.

"So, you say you committed these heinous crimes to make the Corps more racially pure?"

"To paraphrase an old cowboy movie star, 'You're darn tooting!' And General, you know I'm right. Simply put, those unfit to fight were unworthy of life. Thus, the establishment of systematic punishment. If some couldn't endure it and survive, so be it. Murder isn't so bad once you get used to it. The Corps vital energies are what counts. Not mothering the weak and ineffective. Hitler has the right idea."

With everyone's jaws dropped, and all mouths agape in the deadly silence of the office, the open confession of outright systematic killing so smugly admitted was staggering.

After another pause during which Dr. Fisherly chuckled to himself, Commander Vogel said quietly,

"Well, Marines, we've heard enough. It seems we've had a Nazi sympathizer as our Chief Physician at Camp Elliott. We'll adjourn while these two are removed to their isolation cells. Lieutenant Toscanini, we have a PBY awaiting your arrival in the San Diego estuary harbor for immediate departure to Treasure Island. You brought nothing with you from Camp Stoneman, so there is nothing to forward. Apparently, Almond, a new assignment, more urgent than this one, is pending."

Motioning to two MPs standing with their hands behind their backs at the office wall, Vogel said,

"You'll go now, as you are. Commendations are in order for all of you. Mail from these men sitting next to you will be held until you return from your third official assignment. I can tell you only this, Lieutenant. It'll be far, far deep into the Pacific, almost all the way to Japan."

As Peter rose to salute the General and nod to his fellow travelers, then turn to make his way behind Hofmeister and Fisherly, the captain, in a fiercely desperate motion, jerked himself to his feet. With his powerful shoulders thrust forward in a frenzy, he slid forward partially across the desk, handcuffed hands in front of him struggling to grasp the bronze letter opener next to a small stack of sealed confidential letters and taped various memoranda and files.

The MPs leaning against the wall were so startled, they froze for a second, then, vividly alert, literally jumped across the 20 to 25 feet toward Hofmeister, letter opener clasped firmly in hands handcuffed together. Twisting around and turning off the desk back toward the physician, Fisherly jerked violently. He realized intuitively, and certainly instinctively; he was a dead man. "Unbelievable," was the last word he gasped, as the impact of the letter opener in a single backhand swipe slashed half his face and most of his upper throat open.

Strangling in the guttural sounds of blood pouring through his mouth and throat, his last glimpse of life was that of Hofmeister's sadistic snarl. Peter, with spattered blood on his face and clothes, stepped back weakly, trying to recover his strength. Less than a foot away, Fisherly's heavy body somehow continued to quiver tremulously in a rapidly expanding pool of dark red blood.

Despite the silence following the terrific crashing impact of the victim's body, Peter, eyes closed and his body wavering and swooning, believed he heard bones crunching, grinding, and grating although he knew that was impossible.

"You've paid, you evil, diabolical monster," Hofmeister bellowed loudly, dropping the bloody letter opener.

Peter, meanwhile, in half-suffocation for never having observed bestial cruelty up close, to his everlasting embarrassment, fainted dead away.

CHAPTER TWENTY-TWO

A Note from Naval Intelligence

Dressed in freshly-washed white skivvies and sitting comfortably in a single seat next to the navigation table behind the Engineer's Station aboard the Boeing B-314A flying boat, Lieutenant Peter Toscanini was the only passenger among a crew of eleven.

After circling the offshore Farallon Islands before approaching the Golden Gate Bridge and San Francisco Bay to avoid the remote possibility of being mistaken as an enemy aircraft and shot down, the huge water aircraft had begun a steady, laborious decent to the calm waters of Treasure Island's Clipper Cove and its moorings and newly constructed hangars. Bound for Noumea, New Caledonia, the California Clipper would deliver Peter, and, in turn, board a dozen or so Naval personnel for duty during a 20-minute stopover before resuming its nonstop journey.

Now, after napping off and on during the three-and-a-half-hour flight as the flying boat droned along at 135 miles per hour along the California Coast from San Diego in clear weather, Peter turned to gaze out his window. A late afternoon sun was bravely struggling to filter its fading light through a growing mist.

Skimming the surface toward the eastern portion of the San Francisco Bay Bridge and the adjacent cove, Peter enjoyed the splashing water pounding the heavy flying boat's hull and tin roof.

Upon landing, maneuvering and taxiing to the assigned berth next to the island's lagoon, Peter, upon deplaning, once again noted, and smiled, at how "Clipper Cove" became a popular gathering place where spectators and picnickers could observe the Clippers coming and going.

At the foot of the moveable ramp leading to the floating loading dock connected to the low wharf, two MPs stood in starched, carefully-pressed uniforms. Both were obvious high-ranking officers in the security unit assigned to Naval Intelligence.

"Lieutenant Toscanini," smiled the lead officer, walking toward him as he stepped onto the floating dock from the gangplank.

"Yes, sir," Peter replied. "You've come to fetch me, I presume?"

"Our staff car is waiting, as are your superiors. This way, please. Anything we can do for you before your conference?"

As a line of a dozen or more departing Navy personnel ambled down the wharf carrying suitcases past them to board the aircraft, Peter, without so much as batting an eyelash grinned, "How about an early supper with Nimitz and MacArthur ?"

When Japan attacked Pearl Harbor in 1941, the U.S. Navy took control of Treasure Island, making it a central part of its administration arm throughout the war. Under the Navy's jurisdiction, all arriving and departing flying boats, flight crews, and ground staff were supervised by the Treasure Island admiral.

Of the three permanent structures on Treasure Island, the prewar Pan American Air Ferries Terminal with its famed art-deco design and motifs served as the Navy's Pacific Fleet Headquarters and the island's control tower. Peter, of course, had been here before.

"Follow me," ordered the MP, as he led Peter down the corridor of the building's main wing housing the weather station offices to an unmarked door which led down steps to a vast well-lit basement with designated areas for mail delivery, freight, and customer services. Through an open door in the rear of the basement, Peter saw five loading ramps.

Finally, after what seemed hours of traipsing through hurrying officers and busy management staff, the MP stopped before what appeared to be an unmarked storage room. Although he had never been in this area of the station before, the door painted a dull gray appeared vaguely familiar.

"You're wanted in here," he said quietly as he knocked a few times on the door, then opened it and motioned Peter in, closing the door behind him.

Instantly, Peter felt he was in a room similar to the one he had entered in that basement weeks before when he returned from Pavuvu and met with the representative from Naval Intelligence. Long, narrow, dim-lighted, bare walls, windowless, and totally vacant but for a bare desk with only a lamp and telephone. Since there were only two chairs, one of occupier and, in front of the highly-polished desk, a chair for the visitor. The chamber certainly resembled an interrogation chamber, especially with a thick brown carpet muffling all noises and sounds.

With no one present, Peter suddenly felt lonely. He felt cold, near-freezing, as he walked forth and sat down. Earlier, even on the flying boat he had been warm, even hot. Certainly by then, the sun had descended beyond the coastal range to the west.

As Peter surveyed the room for the second time, the only door in the back of the room opened and an Army colonel entered with what appeared to be five white confidential envelopes in hand. Freshly-shaven and dressed in an immaculately clean and pressed uniform, the balding, tall, thin officer was a complete stranger.

After stepping into the room, he chuckled, "Come, Lieutenant. This will be brief. A staff car is nearby waiting to drive you over to the Alameda Naval Air Station near the foot of the bridge, yonder there. The sun's setting over San Francisco and we can watch its last rays bounce off the skyscrapers with nightfall in this basement, tensions increase. You get so busy down here you no longer see anyone, but feel like a million eyes are watching your every move. Only around 0200 do things quiet down then, at down everything gets back to normal. Right now, this room, one of five just like it, is too coffin-like. So, let's go in the garden, watch the sun go down, and talk."

Startled by the liveliness of the Colonel, Peter, finding no words to respond, smiled, stood up, walked around the desk, and followed the officer out the door. Through low-hanging clouds hung over San Francisco across the waters of the Bay to the west from Treasure Island, wan, pale shafts of early evening light tipped the spires across the Bay.

"No matter how many times you watch sundown from Treasure Island, it's a mystic glow to experience regardless of mist, fog, wind or rain," the Colonel said. "The garden is across the avenue there. We'll sit on the bench overlooking the beach. The usual sharp gusty wind blast that blows in from the Golden Gate in the late afternoon diminishes by now. Anyway, Lieutenant, heroes are always welcome."

What was there for Peter to say? Strangely, his once-fiancée Joan Ikeda was more present in his mind than any other time during his now-completed assignment. His last kiss, her hands that refused to let him go, her beloved hair, her sweet face. For a long moment he said nothing as the two Marines walked toward the bench, watching San Francisco come alive with lights, colorful neon lights in the increasing darkness.

"The bench is only a few yards away. We'll then sit down, Lieutenant," the unidentified office explained. "There goes a twin-engine Martin Mariner, a PBM-3. It taxied downwind from the eastside of the island toward Berkeley, after making the 180-degree turn for takeoff into the wind. Power had to be added only to the downwind engines to avoid dragging the wingtip into the water. Just before Pearl

Harbor, I was inducted into the Naval Intelligence Unit from the Naval Reserve on inactive duty. On December 8th, as an aging, white-haired, balding Captain, I was commissioned as a Lieutenant Commander. That's all you have to know about me and my identity. The small garden off the main avenue is a leftover from the 1939 Golden Gate International Exposition, built by the San Francisco Public Works Commission and groomed and cared for by our own naval people including Headquarters, the former Pan Am's stunning Art-Deco Terminal. From this bench, people still flock to Treasure Island's unrestricted park areas to watch Clipper flying boats take off and land and observe sharply uniformed flight crews marching to and from, as well as observe ground staff remain operational 24 hours a day. What do you think of our prized little garden nook?"

From the sidewalk of the busy thoroughfare, the Naval Intelligence officer led the way on a short curving path through mingled together acacia and olive trees to a small cluster of jacaranda trees and, in the adjacent nook, a vine-covered column overlooking Bay bench. Surrounding the niche's bench were three and four-foot-high clipped Japanese boxwood hedges left over from the Exposition five years before. Lone, delicate racemes of wisterias softened the entire scene.

As the two settled down, the senior officer said, "We'll get down to business as we watch that magnificent city over there come alive. You'll note my security team all about closely observing our every move."

"I certainly do. Counted eight so far."

"There are ten, one in the headquarter tower across the avenue, and one off to our left on the beach."

"I see him now."

"Well, your job is just to listen. No comments or questions until the end. Then ask, or say your piece, and immediately after that hightail you over to the Navy's HE-Is Piper Cub revving up just about now. It's used to transport casualties and is clearly marked with a Red Cross on the fuselage as well as the U.S. star insignia on its wings."

"Care to guess where the Gooney Bird is going to fly you?"

"Can't imagine. Certainly not far. Easier to drive me there."

"Well, how about Stockton, California? Care to be flown there for a 10-day, much-earned furlough? And, by the way, I've been carrying around your mail that's been accumulating, including your next assignment."

As the unidentified officer handed the confidential, sealed envelopes to Peter, he read the names out loud, one by one,

"...Private First-Class William Lundigan...Adele and Aldo Toscanini, Joan Ikeda. The fourth letter is official and as I hand it to you, I will explain cursorily what it's all about."

Peter's face was frozen in stone, his thoughts uncalculatable. He was so astounded he could no longer speak. He no longer was present, listening to what was obviously genial and sensible talk from a first-class officer. Dazed, the apparition was totally unexpected, so marvelous that for a moment, Peter felt a sense of unreality, of being in a dreamland, a realm of pure fantasy. Then, regaining a semblance of reality, he simply stared incredulously as the words sank in. "Stockton and his parents, Bill Lundigan, and...Joan, all in one breath?" he reflected lightly. "How could this be? Best I hear about my new assignment, then get on home. Their letters will be on hold until I'm airborne." Turning to focus on the officer, Peter, weak yet buoyant, asked quietly,

"Can you tell me about my third assignment?"

"Only this," the unnamed officer grinned, amused, trying not to sound jocular. "Within three hours, you'll be knocking on your parents' door, unannounced. In less than 30 days, including your 10-day furlough, you'll be behind Jap lines."

Peter blinked. Then asked,

"How so? Where?"

"You're needed for the upcoming assaults on Iwo Jima, Chichi Jima, Volcano and Bonin Islands, and most important of all, apparently, Okinawa. We've just taken Peleliu. the last element of the 1st Marine Division on that atoll was relieved by troops of the 81st Infantry Division. It's the 4th Marine Base Defense Aircraft Wing redesignated 4th Marine Aircraft Wing that needs you, urgently. Believe it or not, it was none other than MacArthur himself who said all operations will stop until you return from your 10-day furlough. Some compliment to you, huh, hero?"

In the crisp night air, Peter was suddenly sullen, even as his heart throbbed with anxiety.

MacArthur? Involved in the planning and ordering his long overdue furlough? Where are all those islands this dignified man with the sad eyes knew by heart?

"Now, you listen," the suddenly quiet, constrained officer said in a resolute tone, his normal facial expression as grim as an post-mortem.

"What you've shown in daring, imagination, ingenuity, and courage has earned you the admiration, respect, and trust of Naval Intelligence, all the way to the top, and frankly, beyond. What lies ahead, and the true reason for you being chosen for the special assignment, is laid out for you in that confidential memo you're holding."

"Your assignment is top-secret. It is a bizarre plan proposed by the supreme command, the Joint Chiefs of Staff in Washington, D.C. and personally approved by the President. The Strategic Services Operations Office of the Pacific Fleet in Honolulu will supervise your journey by submarine to the beach of an unspecified island where you will be met and led inward to meet, welcome, then guide a high Japanese officer who wants to change sides. The operation has not been given a code name, being so secret. Your effort, and success in facilitating his extraction is being considered one of the biggest items in the Pacific War. I can tell you nothing of the men you'll be working with, timeframe, or the Japanese officer you're retrieving."

Peter waited for the officer to continue.

After a pause, the officer asked,

"Do you think you can sneak onto a Jap-occupied island and bring the turncoat out?"

"Of course, I can, or I'll die trying. tell me more about the man."

"I will, but let me tell you, by God, your answer is the most refreshing thing I've heard thus far in this ocean war. No one in Naval Intelligence has said it was possible. Now, let me share with you what I know as the Chief, Liaison Office, US Naval Intelligence, attached to both the Army and Marines, for your information, sir," he said with a mitigating look.

"Now, for the Japanese officer you're to get out and bring back, Second Lieutenant Minoru Wada, an 100th Division Staff Intelligence Officer in the Imperial Army. He's only 26, but a man of absolute peace. Such men are always welcomed by the U.S. because they are the most dangerous adversaries of established military orders."

"Well, it seems throughout the Pacific, the Japanese Army is fighting to the bitter end. The 100th Division is commanded by General

Jiro Harada. Wada is on his staff and is willing to bring to our side valuable information on entrenched positions, fortifications, and troop movements. He stands apart from fellow Japanese officers. He speaks very little English."

"How so?" Peter asked.

"Wada is a Kibei, born in the San Joaquin Valley of California, went to Japan for education, then was trapped in Japan by Pearl Harbor. Because he really is a U.S. Citizen, he wants to desert and get back to this country, even though his family is interned."

"So," Peter continued, "he was pressed into the Imperial Japanese Army, disillusioned with the Pacific War, and is in touch by a secret transmitter with our intelligence people."

"Yup, that's it. Your final instructions and route by submarine will be revealed at Nimitz's headquarters at Hickam Field in Honolulu."

Peter thought a moment, then commented, "Intelligence personnel of the enemy is critical to winning the ware. Not only could he help interrogate captured high-ranking Japanese officers, but also, he could prevent Japanese soldiers who, because of the Bushido Code, would rather die by their own hand than surrender. Wada is a traitor and wants to help our boys live rather than kill them. I have to go get him, no question about it."

"Yes. Now you skedaddle to Stockton and surprise the living daylights out of Mom and Dad. And, if you leave this moment, you'll just catch them before bedtime. Once airborne, by the time you finish reading your letters, you'll be landing at the municipal airport south of the city. A staff car will be waiting to drive you home. Now, go, Lieutenant. We'll be in contact with you as your furlough ends and you return here at Treasure to board a PBY for the nonstop to Hickam. Good luck, boy," the officer said with a quick, disarming smile as he patted Peter's shoulder.

"My Elliott stockade fellow escapees? How will I know how to reach them? Where they are? I want them as my lifelong friends."

"We're taking care of it as we speak. Peter, if I can address you by your first name. When you return with Wada, they'll be waiting for you. I'm seeing to it personally."

"How do I possibly thank you? In less than an hour you jarred me so much I'm floating so high I don't need one of your medical Piper Cubs to fly me to South Stockton."

"Go, son, go. Your instinct of self-preservation will get you through, then back to our lines with Wada. God only knows how many lives of our boys you two will save."

The night was no cold as the staff car sped Peter to the Alameda Naval Air Station airfield and waiting Piper Cub Navy HE-1's. Without fanfare of any sort, he boarded and sat beside the pilot. Reaching behind him, he pulled up a blanket, settled himself as much as he could. Myriads of stars glittered at him as the aircraft taxied for takeoff. Although everything in Peter's life had become topsy-turvy, he was overjoyed. For 10 days, his responsibilities in eradicating reptilian cruelty and absolute ruthlessness would fade. He would momentarily be free.

Although he was exceptionally weary and yearned to close his eyes for a short catnap, he fondly fingered the envelopes he had shoved into his front pants pocket. He would save and favor them, upon awakening. Suddenly, Peter, fondling the letters almost lovingly, fingered a folded one-page piece of paper. Opening it, the strange hither to unobserved note read as follows:

To: Lieutenant Toscanini, USN
From: Men of Naval Intelligence
Subject: An Unofficial Statement of Support

Despite the War in the Pacific, nearing completion with unconditional surrender, death and destruction, commotion and chaos, it is impossible to predict the future. You and the other warrior-intellects in the shadows of today's atrocities are destined to shine in tomorrow's future. The Ghoul's evil iniquities and stockade murders could have crushed your soul, leaving you suffocating and impotent. Yet your unselfish acceptance of infiltrating a dangerous enemy area to liberate a former enemy bolsters our hope of shortening the conflict, saving undetermined numbers of lives. Such true heroism is born of valorous spirit of your patriotism and therefore carry you with confidence on our shoulders.

(Signed by 26 officers, USN Naval Intelligence Six Fleet)

The worlds of the Chief Liaison Office of the U.S. Naval Intelligence, and many others were so meaningful they seemed to lightly vacillate in his head. He was so tired, so terribly tired, that with a sign, and a fading glimpse of a trillion bright twinkling starts, he closed his eyes, and amid the drone of the aircraft, fell asleep.

THE END

MEET THE AUTHOR
Don DeNevi

Don DeNevi was born in Stockton, California, where his father ran a hardware store. Seeing the Stanley Kramer film "My Six Convicts" at the age of 14 incited a life-long fascination with the psychology of imprisonment and the viability of rehabilitation. In the late 1950s, he interned as a teacher at a prison near Stockton before graduating from College of the Pacific with a B.A. in History. He continued his education at U.C. Berkeley, from which he received his Ed. D in the early 1970s, and has since taught classes such as Criminal Profiling, Organized Crime in America, Classic Crime Cinema and Understanding the Criminal Mind at multiple colleges throughout the Bay Area. In addition, Don was Recreation Director at San Quentin State Prison for 15 years, where he introduced a comprehensive recreation program and built the prison's first tennis court. The author of dozens of books, Don is a prolific writer and a fan favorite for many readers.

THANK YOU FOR READING!

If you enjoyed this book, we would appreciate your customer review on your book seller's website or on Goodreads.

Also, we would like for you to know that you can find more great books like this one at www.CreativeTexts.com

www.ingramcontent.com/pod-product-compliance
Lightning Source LLC
Chambersburg PA
CBHW050245110726
47898CB00007B/2291